Atlantis Riptide

by

Allie Burton

Atlantis RIPTIDE

LOST DAUGHTERS OF ATLANTIS
BOOK 1

ALLIE BURTON

"I loved ATLANTIS RIPTIDE. A fast-paced story, a wounded heroine who tugged at my heart and a swoon-worthy hero who kept at it until he uncovered all her secrets. What a wonderful launch to the Lost Daughters of Atlantis series." – Author Addison Fox

Chapter One

Nix Normal

I ran away *from* the circus.

What a joke. Most teens want to run away *to* the circus, but not me. No, I could never do anything normal. Not with a name like Pearl of the sea Poseidon.

And yes, that is my real name. It's on my birth certificate. Even though the certificate is fake.

My heart hardened with past pain. I clenched my hands around the broom handle. I continued to sweep the walkway around the fake lagoon at the Kingdom of Atlantis Miniature Golf Course. Instead of focusing on my past, I watched a teen balancing on a two-inch-wide black rail like a tightrope walker, his arms out for balance.

Trapeze artist or boneheaded boy? Only with hours and hours of training could a trick like that be pulled off.

I knew. It takes a lot of practice not to die.

Even though I didn't want to be noticed, I had to say something. "That's a twelve foot drop into a shallow pool. You want to crack your head open?"

The guy, wearing a black hoodie, narrowed his dark eyes. He wavered on the peeling black iron rail that guarded the fake lagoon. "Who are you? The janitor?"

His group of friends laughed.

Heat flooded my face and I found it difficult to keep my head up. I remembered all the times kids had made fun of what I did or what I wore. These teens didn't realize the khaki shorts and T-shirt weren't the real me. Just a uniform—another costume.

I ignored their cruel jibes. "Get down."

My gaze searched for one of the workers dressed in mermaid costumes. Based on the designer's idea of the lost island of Atlantis, the course boasted running rivers and a huge waterfall cascading into a murky pool. A cheap plastic statue of the sea god watched over the kingdom.

Funny, how my name related.

"Ah." The hoodie guy glanced at a girl with purple streaks in her hair. "The janitor cares more about me than you do, babe." He tossed a phone in the air and caught it.

"My cell." The girl's high pitched squeal hurt my ears.

An obviously-harassed mother squeezed by the little scene, pushing a stroller and dragging a small toddler behind her. The toddler scuffed his feet on the ground and smiled in my direction.

I smiled back but I didn't want to seem soft, so I changed my expression to a scowl and glared at hoodie guy. "Get down or I'll call a security guard. They'll kick all of you out of the entire Boardwalk park."

"Come on, Joe. Get down." The busty girl held out her hand to him. "We're supposed to have fun today."

Must be nice to have a fun day where you didn't have

to worry about your next meal, your sleeping arrangements, or if you'd ever be discovered. If only ...

The steel inside me wavered for a second. But just a second.

"Only cause you asked nicely, babe." Joe shook his dyed-black bangs before jumping off the rail and back onto the path. He wrapped his arm around his *babe* and then cocked his bushy eyebrows at me. "Janitor-Girl better watch her mouth. I'm not going to be bossed around by a wage slave."

The put down should've hurt, but I'd been called worse things. Telling a customer where to shove his attitude wouldn't be smart. I needed this job and didn't need any extra attention.

Or questions.

Joe tossed me a superior smirk before moving on to the next hole. Disaster diverted. I blew out a large breath and returned to sweeping the walkways.

"Mommy. Look. I'm a big boy." A bit further up, the sandy-haired toddler stood on a railing of the bridge that arched over the water. Balancing like Joe.

The mother, holding a dirty diaper, turned toward her older child's voice. "Brandon, no!"

The toddler teetered, waving his arms in a lopsided-windmill fashion. His body leaned over the bridge railing toward the water. His sandaled foot slipped and his extra-large eyes widened. He lost his balance, tumbling into a free-fall. He plummeted into the pool below, landing on his back as he hit the water.

My heart plunged like the boy.

Water splashed. The mom screamed. The teens, the other families, the entire crowd in Kingdom of Atlantis went silent. People froze like they were watching an action scene in a movie. But this was no movie. No staged accident or stunt.

I dropped the broom, hopped over the railing, and peered into the dark waters of the fake lagoon. The murky water appeared about six feet deep. My mind trembled with varying scenarios. Diving in could expose my special abilities. *Not* diving in could lead to the boy's death.

No other thought required. I couldn't risk the child for my selfish reasons. I dove.

Submerging under the dirty water it should've been difficult to see, but I saw clearly in any depth. The icy water would make most people shiver, but the circus owners had loved that they didn't have to spend money heating the pools because cold water didn't bother me.

The boy, on the other hand, would become hypothermic. My talent could save him. If I hurried.

The narrow pool was for decoration and it wouldn't take long to cover every inch. My gaze scoured the water as I swam. Clumps of mud gathered at the bottom. Stains lined the walls like a disgusting bath tub. I bet the lagoon had never been cleaned. Sludge dragged my speed, but I still swam faster than the average swimmer.

Or, *not* so average.

I flicked around and spotted Brandon at the bottom. I swam deeper and grabbed hold of him, but his tiny body wouldn't budge. His stark expression broadcasted his fear and begged for help. His cherubic cheeks puffed with the water already inside. His arms and legs kicked and flayed. He understood the danger.

So did I. My body shuddered. I ran my finger down his soft cheek. *Calm down. I'm here to help.*

He stopped kicking and I pulled harder. His yellow

jacket stuck to the bottom of the pool. I pushed the windbreaker aside revealing the filter cover at the bottom.

The six inch by four inch metal cover was slimy and old and Brandon's body stuck like glue. Suction pulled at him as the drain sucked water to be recycled in the waterfall flowing at the top of the lagoon. The strong force held the boy in place.

I reached for the zipper and pulled the tab. Jammed. The zipper was broken and the jacket was too tight to pull over his head.

The boy reached out and touched my arm. His eyes gleamed with hope. He totally trusted me.

But time ticked away. I gritted my teeth trying to smile, to show reassurance and confidence. Inside my tummy twisted and my muscles tightened. I needed to hurry.

His eyelids flickered and rolled backwards. His lids closed. He reached out again and then went limp. His skin was cold to the touch. Way too cold.

Panic prickled through my veins at the possibility of loss. My chest burned and I found it hard to breathe. Like hyperventilating, but only with water instead of air.

The concern wasn't for me. I could stay underwater for indeterminate lengths of time. But the boy, if he didn't get oxygen soon he'd die.

My nerves rattled. Indecision wavered like the surface above. No one could see this deep in the dirty pool. No one had jumped in to help. No one would know. I placed my fingers in between the lines of the cover and tugged on the metal. The thick grate bent.

Another one of my weird powers that had been taken advantage of—super strength underwater.

"See the strongest girl in the world. See how long she can hold her breath. See her break diving and swimming records." The master of ceremonies hawked night after night after night. I'd never forget his exploitive voice.

Shivering at the memory, I jerked myself out of the past and into the present. No time for day-nightmaring.

I yanked on the metal grate again. The six screws holding the cover in place popped out and sucked into the hole temporarily breaking the suction. I yanked the toddler away, tucking him under my arm like a football. I fought against the current to a position a few feet away but stayed under the water to conceal my next move.

The kid had been under water too long. If he wasn't already dead, he'd have substantial brain injuries. I needed to take pro-active action. And fast.

I settled my mouth over his and breathed into him. His lungs inflated and his heart calmed. Another trick I'd learned in my other life—performing CPR worked better in the water, at least for me.

He opened his mouth. The boy didn't choke on the water but inhaled it like air. His eyelids reopened with a new brightness. He didn't look scared anymore. He was going to be okay, like he'd just fallen in, instead of being underwater for minutes.

A loud splash sounded a few feet away. A guy with longish-brown hair swam underwater toward us. His shirt and shorts dragged. Panic jolted my core. Had he witnessed my life-saving breath?

The guy held out his strong hand. He wanted to help pull me up. With Brandon tucked under my arm, I put my hand in his. Together, we kicked to the surface.

People clapped when we broke through the water. A crowd surrounded the lagoon. I gasped for air, not because I'd been underwater but because the people and the clapping circled me, closed me in.

My body flushed and grew clammy at the same time. Claustrophobia knotted my stomach. I hated applause directed at me. I'd left that life behind.

I searched the audience. Fear cascaded down my back like the waterfall behind me. No one here could discover my talents.

"You okay?" The guy wrapped an arm around the metal ladder built into the side of the lagoon. His wavy brown hair almost covered the concern in his blue eyes.

"Yeah."

"Hand him to me." His striped manager's polo shirt was covered in mud and his khaki shorts were half hidden by the dirty water.

I'd never seen him around Mermaid Beach Boardwalk before. But I'd only worked here a couple of days and it was a big place with hundreds of part-time seasonal employees.

I handed him my valuable cargo. "Where's his mother?"

"Up top. Ambulance is on the way." His blue gaze pierced me. "Sure you're okay? You were under for awhile." His caring attitude threatened my anonymity.

I nodded and glanced away, avoiding his penetrating stare.

The guy climbed the ladder and laid the boy on the Astroturf grass near the fake palm trees. He rolled the toddler on his side and cleared his airway of debris. "He's breathing."

Of course he is. The guy didn't even need to take any precautions. My breath was a life saving guarantee.

The mom rushed over to her son's side.

I went up the ladder and climbed over the railing. Searching out the mother, I mouthed, "He's going to be okay." There was no doubt in my mind. I'd seen it all before.

Her eyes, bright from tears, sparkled. "Thank you."

A gaggle of girls dressed in worker mermaid costumes rushed forward toward the Astroturf where the gorge-guy kneeled by Brandon. The show of concern on their faces appeared genuine, but focused on the guy. Not the small boy.

"Are you okay?" a red-headed girl who worked the snack shack cooed.

"You're a hero," a bleached blonde mermaid gushed.

"Save me next time." A brunette shot him a flirty smile. "I'll definitely need mouth-to-mouth."

A disgusted snort shot out from between my lips. Sure, now the other workers showed up. Female workers.

Compared to the mermaids, I probably looked like a drowned Floridian rat. My clothes dripped like I'd been caught in a storm. I smelled like sewer. My long blonde hair in its once-neat ponytail shed water like a dog's tail.

And because of the rescue my newest home might be my last.

***

Air wheezed in and out of my lungs as I rushed past the arcade and rides on the Boardwalk. I needed to get far away from the miniature golf course. Shaking, I tried to control my constant fear of being found, of being discovered.

All the memories I'd been trying to keep down rose in my mind, like a big top rising to the sky. The pop, pop, pop of the shots from the rifle game didn't make me jump running past because my mind was somewhere

8

else. I had to get away. Escape.

Like I always did.

I rubbed my burning eyes. Burning not from tears but because I wasn't used to the salt-scented air of the Pacific Ocean.

Yeah, keep telling yourself that.

Tinny music scraped against my ear drums reminding me of the life I ran from. Only, today reinforced I'd traded one bad deal for another. A hysterical laugh bubbled out of my chest. From star of the show to custodian of the carnival. And I couldn't catch a break.

I reached the edge of the Boardwalk and clomped down the wooden steps. Sand stuck to my damp feet and ankles. The tiny particles were like a massage on my skin as I continued toward the wide creek that flowed into the ocean. At times the creek ran fast and furious, at other times, like now, the flow was a trickle.

My natural instincts tugged west, toward the ocean, but my instincts weren't so hot lately so I turned toward the rugged cliff walls instead. An ancient trestle bridge crossed the chasm between the cliffs and a new housing subdivision with the creek flowing beneath. It was there I headed.

I dropped down onto a large boulder shaded by the bridge and grabbed my head between my hands. My chest heaved in and out fighting a display of emotions.

"Stupid. Stupid. Stupid." I banged the back of my head against the rock wall. "I never should've exposed myself to all those people."

But I couldn't let the boy drown. Not for my own selfish purposes.

My move to southern California was to get away from the circus. To be a regular person. To find myself.

It was not to show everyone on the west coast what I could do. To show them I was a freak.

"A super freak." My voice cracked.

Saving the boy was simple compared to some of the things I'd done in the past. "I'll pretend I was nowhere near the golf course lagoon when it happened. Maybe no one will figure it out."

"Figure what out?"

"Ack!" I jumped and my eyes popped open.

The manager guy from the lagoon stood a couple of feet away. His blue and orange striped shirt still dripped with the lagoon's dirty water. "Didn't mean to scare you but I heard you talking…"

My muscles stiffened. I calculated why he was here. "What do you want?"

He took a few menacing steps forward. "I had to track you down. Followed your footsteps through the sand."

I swiped my cheeks hoping tear stains didn't show. Showing weakness never helped the situation. "Why?"

"I'm Chase." He stuck out his hand.

I considered his tanned skin on long, lean fingers. I'd learned to trust no one, no matter how kind they pretended to be or how good looking. "I appreciate your help at the lagoon but the boy is going to be fine and that's all that matters."

"I can find out your name, you know. I have ways." Chase imitated a bad foreign accent and his lips turned into an I'm-a-smart-guy smile.

My heart pulsed in a sharp rhythm and little pains shot through my ribs. Might as well tell him my name, it would appear less suspicious. Standing out, being different, only caused trouble.

"Pearl." I stuck my hand in his.

Our fingers intertwined and tiny tremors ran up my arm, down my spine, and to my toes. Like holding a live wire under water, which I'd done in my previous life, little zaps shocked me. I yanked my hand away.

He held his hand in mid-air for a bit as if he'd felt the tremors, too. "Why'd you run away?"

"R-run away? What do you mean?" The vulnerability I'd lived with since leaving the circus coalesced in the rapid beats of my heart. How could he have found out about the circus?

"Why'd you take off from the lagoon?"

My shoulders loosened a bit and I let out my first easy breath. He hadn't meant run away-run away, he'd meant run away from the accident. Whew.

"Break time." I added a touch of bravado to my voice. Forced since birth to act, I decided to put the skill to good use. "I needed to change clothes." Before too many other people noticed their condition.

"So do I." He tugged his wet shirt away from his body, before peeling it off. Then, he tossed the shirt onto the rocks.

I sucked in a breath. His bronzed and sculpted abs made him look like a young Greek god. He didn't just ride around on a manager's golf cart all day telling others what to do, he must really work. Or workout.

"Are you going to change down here?" I'd never seen a naked guy before and didn't want to start now. The warmth in my belly contradicted me.

"Are *you*?" His lips crinkled and his blue eyes widened, reflecting the Pacific Ocean nearby.

I wanted to dive into them.

Whoa. I didn't even know this guy.

"No. I just...I just..." My glance swiveled around searching for an explanation from the rocks. A gasping, hissing sound caught my ear. "Do you hear that?"

His gaze narrowed and he tilted his head. "Sounds like an injured cat."

I was already scrambling up the rocks toward the sound. "Oh my."

In the cliff, a sea otter lay inside a small hole about the size of the over-inflated basketballs in the games section. A large rock sat on its belly and he was trapped. Green gook clung to his whiskers and covered a shiny, black nose. The otter hissed again.

"He's stuck." My heart ached for the little guy. All alone like me. Possibly injured. No one to help him or hear him cry. "We have to help."

"I'll call the lifeguard station. They'll know what to do." Chase had climbed behind me.

"That will take too long. We have to free him now. Who knows how long he's been there." I couldn't let the animal die while we watched. And since the otter wasn't in water, I couldn't use my special abilities.

"Okay. Let me find a long stick or something to get the rock off." He maneuvered around the rocks that had tumbled from the cliff, searching between all the crevices.

I moved higher, trying to get a better view. "What's that green stuff?"

"Looks like paint." He tugged on a piece of driftwood. "I wonder if the paint threw off his sense of smell and he headed in the wrong direction and got stuck."

"But how'd he get paint on him? The spot is in a circle."

"Don't know. They're usually pretty clean animals." Chase got the stick free and moved to the side of the sea otter. Balancing above the place where the otter was stuck, he inched the stick down. "Okay boy, I'm not going to hurt you."

Sweet how Chase talked to the otter.

"How's the little guy going to get back to the ocean?" My gaze traveled the distance of the creek. "He won't let us carry him."

"Sea otters can walk on land, just not well." He sounded so smart, like he knew lots of facts about ocean creatures.

Chase moved the stick closer to the otter. The otter hissed. His tiny front paws tried to whack the stick away.

"He's trying to help you." I made my voice soft and smooth, calming.

The otter's beady black eyes sized me up. His paws stopped moving. His whiskers twitched.

Chase inched the stick under the rock. He shoved. The rock tumbled forward off the otter.

"You did it." I sagged against the rocks.

The otter flipped to its feet. With one last long stare at me, he shuffled toward the trickle of water, and then started to follow it toward the ocean. The little guy appeared fine.

I almost reached out to hug Chase. "Thank you for saving him."

"It was nothing." His wavy brown hair touched his shoulders and I itched to run my fingers through it. "You saved a boy's life."

"You helped." Again. There'd been a lot of people playing miniature golf and none of them jumped in. Except Chase.

"I didn't do much. You probably didn't even need my help."

True.

"You're the real hero."

"No, I'm not." Just like last time. A bitter taste filled my mouth and my head spun like the Tilt-A-Whirl on the Boardwalk. Being a hero, being different, could get you burned.

I wasn't a hero. I was a freak. A circus freak.

"I gotta go. I'm already past my break time and I still have to change my uniform."

"I'll talk to your boss if you're late."

I needed this new job, but I needed it without additional attention. Free uniforms. Lunch at a discount, that I could always afford to eat. No proof of age required. And I was paid in cash, which met my chief goal—anonymity—just fine.

Pushing my shoulders back, I placed a defiant expression on my face. Chin up, mouth firm. At least I hoped it was defiant. "Thanks, but no. I don't make excuses."

His smile widened. "Good to know. For when I ask you out."

Chapter Two
Duh Duh Duh Date

After changing into my second uniform, the rest of the day I kept my head low and my hat on. Rumors of the water rescue by an employee spread, but because I wasn't on friendly terms with any of the other workers I didn't get the full scoop.

Which was okay with me. I knew the full scoop. Every single detail.

Gossip I could do without. Especially gossip about me. The circus workers' whispers still scratched down my spine like the yelp of a lion being whipped.

After punching out, I shoved my wet uniform in a bag, picked up my backpack and headed out.

"Pearl." Chase strolled next to me.

I jumped. The guy snuck up on me like he'd been waiting.

Quit being so suspicious. He was punching out. Nothing more.

His perfectly white teeth gleamed when he smiled. He wore an untucked, button-down plaid shirt rolled up

15

at the sleeves and pressed Docker pants. No guy who looked like that ever waited for me. Not unless they wanted my autograph or the secret to my tricks.

"What?" Not friendly of me, but I didn't want to be friends. I couldn't afford to be friends.

"How was the rest of your day?" His smexy smile made my knees weak.

"Okay." I walked faster, forcing my knees to hold.

He was following me again. "Anything else interesting happen to you today?"

I halted and stared. "Why?" I remembered his threat from earlier in the day and a thrill shot through me that I doused. I couldn't get excited about being asked out because I couldn't say yes. I had to stay strong. Independent. Alone.

"Can't a guy make conversation, be nice? What kind of people do you hang—"

"Don't make snap judgments." I held up a hand. "Who I do," *or don't,* "hang out with is none of your business."

"What if I wanted to make it my business?" He flashed another of those knee-melting smiles.

"Why? I've been nothing but harsh to you." Which wasn't like me, but I had my reasons.

"Which intrigues me all the more." He took hold of my hand and a hot current pulsed up my arm. "You saved a boy and a sea otter."

"You saved the sea otter."

"You insisted." He shrugged. "How about hanging out tomorrow?"

My jaw dropped like a fish on a hook. "Like a real date?" I'd never had one of those. No time before. No chance now. And even though he'd threatened to ask earlier, I hadn't expected him to follow up. Most guys didn't.

"Yeah. Like a real date." His smile deepened and a slight dimple appeared by the side of his mouth.

I shook my head, but it moved slower than it should have, like I wanted to say yes. Which I didn't. "Can't. I have to work."

My boss Karl had ordered me to clean the lagoon because it had to be drained after the boy's near drowning. It sucked having my free day taken away, but I needed the money so I hadn't complained.

"I thought you never made excuses." He laughed at me as if knowing something I didn't.

"It's not an excuse." I wasn't a liar. Well, only when I had to be.

"I checked the schedule. You're off tomorrow."

"Check again." I yanked my hand out of his, immediately feeling the loss of warmth.

"How about dinner tonight, then?"

"No." I clutched the plastic bag holding my damp uniform to my chest. In the face of his persistence my resolve weakened. "Things to do."

"You gotta eat."

I didn't. I'd skipped many meals in the past few weeks, like lunch today. Unfortunately, my tummy picked that moment to growl in protest.

"You might say no, but your stomach says yes." His easy laugh made me feel less threatened. "Come on. I know a great burger place right near the beach."

Being alone was a form of protection. No one could discover my many secrets. But it was also lonely.

Chase was cute and interested in me. Not because I could teach him a trick, or because I was the star of the show. The idea was tempting. Going on a, gulp, date would be so normal. Plus, I'd been so mean to him and he'd been nothing but nice.

"Well." What could a burger hurt? I was hungry. He was paying. My lips stiffened flashing him a genuine smile. Obviously those muscles didn't get much of a work out. "Your treat, right?"

***

We walked a few blocks to Barney's, an old burger joint. Grease scented the air making my stomach rumble. Chase picked a booth in the corner with a scarred wooden table and ripped plastic benches. "The place doesn't look like much but the hamburgers are the best. I promise."

After the waitress took our orders and delivered sodas, Chase went into twenty Q's mode. "Where'd you work before the Boardwalk?"

I should've known dinner wouldn't be that easy, but my suspicious nature had been over-ruled by my tummy. "A campground in the Midwest."

Needing money and a place to stay, I'd accepted a lifeguard job at a tiny campground. An unexpected thunderstorm blew in and I'd saved a pontoon boat full of campers. The story made the news so I had to move on.

"What brought you to southern California?"

I slouched back on the bench acting casual. "The beach. What else?" It was every mid-westerner's dream to move to California and live on the beach, or at least that's what one of the other campground worker's had said.

For me, it had been more of a pull or a yearning. I could've picked New York or Oregon or even Alaska, but my heart told me to travel to the Pacific Ocean, to Southern California. Sneaking away after my last show at the Poseidon Family Circus in Florida, I'd hopped the first bus north. Then, changed to another bus heading west. After a couple of short stops to earn money, I got off the bus in Mermaid Beach and fell in love.

Studying me over the rim of his cup, Chase sipped on his soda. "You a big swimmer?"

"Me?" I choked and grabbed my drink, taking a big swallow. How do I get myself into these situations? The reason I didn't apply for a lifeguard job in Mermaid Beach was because I didn't want anyone to find out about my special skills. A janitor job is practically invisible. "Not much. How about you?" I tried to steer the conversation toward him.

"You dove into the small Kingdom of Atlantis lagoon like an Olympic champion."

I held my breath. He'd jumped in to help with the boy, but I hadn't seen Chase while confronting Joe. I hadn't seen any other employees. And I hadn't realized he'd seen me dive in the lagoon.

"You stayed underwater for like fifteen minutes."

Shaking my head, I denied the truth. If the kid had been under that long he should've been brain dead. He probably *had* been brain dead, but I...well, I didn't know how it worked but I could resuscitate people who'd drowned.

My single breath was more than CPR.

"Fifteen minutes is impossible. No one can stay underwater that long. In an emergency situation time seems to go slower than it actually is," I babbled, trying to find a way to rescue myself. I couldn't be discovered yet. I'd only been in Mermaid Beach a few days and already the place felt like home. "You know, like during earthquakes, you think the ground shook for minutes when actually it was only seconds."

"Mermaid Beach has never had an earthquake." His brows dipped. "I checked the time after I called nine-one-one. Definitely over five minutes, probably closer to ten."

The waitress set our plates in front of us. A huge, juicy burger and fries. My mouth salivated and I picked up the burger and took a big bite to avoid his question and because my stomach demanded food now. The burger tasted like a five-star meal. The best thing I'd eaten in months, maybe years. In heaven, I savored every bite.

About half-way through the burger I noticed Chase staring. I finished chewing. "What?"

"Nothing." He glanced at his own burger where only a couple of bites were missing. "You must be hungry."

My ego deflated and my shoulders slumped. Did he like his girls to be anorexic? Not that I was his girl or anything. And I used too much energy not to eat. I straightened my shoulders. "Did you expect me to order salad?"

He picked up a fry and took a bite. "I like a girl who enjoys her food. No dieting for you."

Except the starvation diet. No money equaled no food. It was that simple.

"I, um, missed lunch." And breakfast. And dinner the night before. I took another big bite and swallowed. "What do you do at the Boardwalk?"

My job encompassed the entire park, so I cleaned the rides and games area, changed trash bags in the food court, and swept the lines at the various rides, and the mini golf course.

He surveyed the restaurant avoiding my gaze. "This and that."

"You're a manager." I knew that because of the type of polo shirt he wore.

"Temporary. For the summer."

"Do you live close by?"

"Not far."

Odd, he didn't want to talk about himself either. Something we had in common.

"How about you? Where do you live?"

Wiggling in my seat, I felt the redness climbing my cheeks. I couldn't confess my current living arrangements. Drumming my fingers on the table, I tried to think of a new topic. If neither of us wanted to talk about ourselves, then what did we have to discuss?

Nothing. I couldn't tell him my deepest secrets or my darkest fears. I couldn't tell him my hopes and dreams for the future. I couldn't even tell him my address.

Why would he care when no one else ever did? Brutal hurt mixed with my well-learned cynicism. It made me mad that I could still feel pain. But what I needed to remember was that he would betray me. Like everyone else did.

My hands tightened in my lap. My heart closed against him. Even if I had a home to go to, I would never let him in. Into my home or my heart.

I smushed my lips together to stop the slight tremble. "I should get going." I folded my napkin on the diagonal and set it on the table.

"But it's early." He signaled for the check, so obviously he wasn't protesting too hard. "How about a walk on the beach?"

Then again, he still wanted to spend time with me. I froze. I could admit to myself I was enticed. Lured like a fish grabbing a worm on a hook.

But I couldn't risk it. Living a lie wasn't conducive to making friends. Hiding wasn't easy. I stood and grabbed my bag and backpack. "No. I should get...home."

Before he had a chance to pay, I walked out of the restaurant and ran down the street, my bruised heart bumping in my hollow chest. I never should've agreed to dinner. Friendship only caused pain. Catching my breath, I walked to the beach and followed the path to the campground wishing we could've gotten to know each other better, wishing I could've stayed longer.

But wishes were for fantasies and I lived in the real world.

Stiffening my spine, I trudged over the slight hill to the camp sites located inland from the beach in a canyon lined with giant sycamores. I passed the small, general store and manager's office and continued to my green and much repaired tent. The damp air lingered between the four canvas walls. I brushed off the sand and lay down on the green salvaged sleeping bag.

The bag was better than the first time I'd camped out. When I was eight, I couldn't eat the burnt crisp of hardness Carlita had put on my dinner plate.

"You don't like the food I provide?" Her wide body had bumped against the kitchen table. "Kids under the ocean wish they could have a cooked meal."

I remembered thinking most parents would have said kids in Africa or China, but Carlita always had been different.

I'd murmured, "Overcooked." Way over cooked.

"You ingrate." She'd grabbed me by my tank top and

yanked me from the chair. "If you don't like my food, go find your own." She'd shoved me out of our trailer and locked the door.

I'd stumbled down the stairs, hot tears running down my face. After knocking on several other trailers, with no response, I knew I was on my own for the night.

Thunder rumbled and rain poured out of the sky. With my stomach growling, I'd curled under the tarp covering the wood pile and used a log for a pillow.

Owls hooted. Coyotes screeched. Once I heard a snake hiss. I'd lain awake all night not thinking about finding food but thinking about *being* food.

After groveling to Carlita the next morning, I'd learned to cook and had become her chef from that point forward. At least tonight, after the burger from Barney's, I wasn't hungry.

Staring at the stained canvas ceiling, my eyes burned remembering my conversation with Chase about why I'd moved to California.

Yeah, I was living the dream.

I might not have a home, but I felt like I belonged here. I might need to stay away from people, but I was in control of what I did. I might not know what drew me to Mermaid Beach, but I planned to find out.

***

After tossing and turning for what seemed like hours, I got up and headed to the campground's small beach. I couldn't sleep and my mind raced.

I'd fought the tug of the water since arriving in Mermaid Beach. I'd never swam in salt water before and I needed to know what would happen to my skills in the ocean. I couldn't stay out of the water forever. I loved to swim, loved my skills. I hated being on display.

The moonlight cut into the darkness of the night. A few stars twinkled and the fog seemed to be in a holding pattern off shore. The ocean called. Each wave seemed to, well, wave at me, welcoming me to southern California and Mermaid Beach.

The beach was deserted. Now was the perfect time.

I jumped up and yanked off my sweatshirt and sweats revealing my star-studded bikini. Sand squished between my toes marching to the end of the beach where the waves met the shore. Tangy salt tickled my nose.

No more wimping out. I dipped my toe in, not too warm or too cold, but much warmer than the fog-misted air. Using my whole foot, I splashed water around and then, took a step in deeper.

The salt water came to my knees. A tiny silver fish darted between my legs. A wave rolled to mid-thigh.

I ventured further, the ocean waves rising to my waist and then slipped into the silky softness of the water. My body melded into the sea like my skin and the liquid were one. The water's buoyancy lifted me and my spirits.

Dunking my head under, I opened my eyes. The salt didn't sting and I could see for a long distance, better than in any dirty pool.

Now for the big test—I opened my mouth and—breathed.

My entire body loosened and un-tensed. I could breathe and see in the Pacific Ocean. My abilities might make me a freak, but I still enjoyed them.

Stroking deep, I swam underwater. Faster than in any pool. I dove further down, twirling and twisting and having fun. I let my body glide through the ocean, floating and swirling.

Since running away I'd never felt this sense of

liberation, of exhilaration, of happiness. There was no one here to gasp or applaud or question my talents. Finally, I was free to enjoy myself.

Skimming the bottom, I noted where the sand changed from beige to darker brown, where the rocks started building up toward the cliffs. Placing my hand on a super-large boulder, a rock I could never lift on land, nerves scratched at my spine. I bent my knees and lifted the boulder up and over my head. Then, I tossed it. The rock hit the ground and the disturbed sand rose and settled back down.

A powerful charge surged through me. Yes. I still had super strength. All my skills seemed better, sharper, stronger in the ocean.

Saving Brandon today had felt great. If only I could find a way to put my talent to good use without attention or questions or fuss.

I swam around the rocks in a wild dance, raising my arms up and down, twisting at the waist. Green and brown tangled seaweed floated by and schools of small fish swam past. I waved and smiled. It was a world different than any I'd known before and I loved every drop.

A blur of black darted past and spun around in front of me. I stilled until I recognized the furry shape. A sea otter swam to the surface and then dove down again. Its thick fur skimmed my legs, tickling me, and then he swam back up top.

He dove down again, spun around in front of my face, and went back up again.

Curious, I kicked my feet and rose to the surface.

The little guy lay on his back, his white face sticking out above the waves. He looked like a stuffed animal from the carnival games, only much cuter with his little black nose and small, dark eyes. A streak of fluorescent green tinged the side of his nose.

"Were you the little guy caught on the rocks today?"

He nodded and used his paw to point to the beach.

Point? "Sea otters don't point."

The otter's head nodded again. He stared with an intensity that sent a chill through my body. On second thought, not at all like a stuffed animal.

"Do you, um, communicate with people?" My words slowed. I tried to take everything in.

This time his paw pointed at me.

I gasped, sucked in air and water, and started coughing. Guess my lungs couldn't handle air and water at the same time.

The sea otter twirled around behind me. His cold snout bumped me on the back.

"Are you trying to tell me something?" The question sounded so stupid leaving my tongue. I'm mean, come on, talking to an animal?

He swam back in front and nodded his head up and down. Yes.

I reeled back and caught my breath. I was talking to a sea otter.

The otter ducked under and swam around me in a circle. Then, he lay on his back and used his paw in a "come here" motion.

I ducked under and swam in a circle around him. He circled again, and so did I. We were swimming in a constant figure-eight pattern under the water.

Unbelievable. I was playing with a sea otter. My spirits soared. My smile widened. Like being a five-year-old at a playground, I'd made my first real friend.

Not that the otter was a human friend, but it counted. Didn't it?

Following for a bit, I stopped when I realized he headed to shore. "I don't want to go back yet." I wasn't ready to leave the comfort of the water and return to my lonely tent.

The sea otter shook his head fast in an agitated motion. Even his furry face appeared upset.

"Can't we play longer?" I remembered reading about sea otters and how they played. Slipping and sliding and diving. Turning and twisting underwater, kind of like I'd done earlier.

He did the "follow me" motion again. Then his eyes grew wide and his whiskers twitched.

I twisted around, but saw nothing. The fog had rolled closer to shore, but the stars and the moon still gave off a little light. A small motor boat sounded in the distance.

I faced him again. "What's wrong?"

The sea otter was gone. My furry friend had left me.

Alone, again.

An ache tore through my chest and I sniffed. "That's okay. I'm used to being by myself."

The water around me swirled. Waves gathered in a big circle, expanding out in further and further concentric loops. The pattern repeated with more strength and velocity. Like a toilet being flushed, the water pooled into a vortex.

My body caught in the current. I couldn't move out of the circle, surrounded by a ring of water. My tummy churned with the motion. My gaze glazed over watching the water go round and round like a hypnotist's trick.

A strange sensation sucked at my toes. The feeling continued up my legs to my hips. I kicked and clawed but the water tugged like a ginormous vacuum at the bottom of the ocean.

Panic spurted through me, exploding in my flaying arms and legs. I kicked. I stroked. I screamed. Nothing helped. My super strength wasn't helping at all. I couldn't fight this weird force.

I knew about the dangers of swimming alone. Knew about dangerous ocean currents. Knew the rules.

But they didn't apply to me. I was different.

And so was this force that had me in its grip.

My heart began a pointless race against disaster. None of my other limbs could move. I couldn't get free.

As I went down, I remembered dreams of being dragged under the ocean. The people in my dreams looked normal, nice. Not a faceless, evil suction. Terror froze every one of my muscles. I couldn't struggle, couldn't swim, couldn't even think.

Could this be a deadly riptide, or something even more ominous? Irony struck. How could I drown when I could breathe underwater?

Chapter Three
Fabulously Flushed

The underwater tornado swirled around me. Faster and faster, the water storm whirled and sucked. I twisted and turned like flotsam caught in an upside down waterspout. I felt like Dorothy from the *Wizard of Oz*. Dizzy, confused, and terrified.

My mind kaleidoscoped. I couldn't drown. Instead, I'd twist and turn forever like a constant merry-go-round—minus the merry.

The water couldn't hurt me. But a shark could devour me. Bacteria could infect me. Crabs could pinch me to bits.

"Ahhhhhh!" Panic swirled and scraped and spit. My brain blurred. "You need to focus."

Focusing on the problem helped my brain clear. Options presented themselves in bullet points.

At the age of ten, a determined reporter had cornered me alone after the show and started asking questions about "how I stayed under water for so long?" and "what was the trick?" It was the first time I realized my abilities were different from most people. I spent a lot of time online researching oceanography, lifesaving and survival techniques, and yes, even mermaids. I learned if caught in a riptide, the victim should swim parallel to the coast, not fight the strength of the current.

This soaked twister wasn't a riptide, but I could try the same philosophy. Now I had plan.

I quit fighting the tide and forced my body to relax. I went with the flow. Spinning with the circular motion, I lay on my back and reached my arms out. The force of the vortex pushed my body toward the outer limits of the whirlpool.

Finally, progress.

Flipping to my stomach, I stroked with my super strength toward the edge and fought the tendrils of the storm trying to grab and bring me back into the swirling motion. Stroke. Stroke. Stroke. My arms ached with the effort.

My muscles trembled and sharp pains shot up my legs with each kick. Two inches forward and one inch back. Even with my strength, I stroked a losing battle. This thing was way too powerful.

I'd die and no one would realize I was gone. My life meant nothing to anyone above the sea. The depressing thoughts slapped me with exhaustion. No one would care. Why bother? My body sagged and I stopped for a second. Why go on?

Because I had to.

I needed to warn people about the dangerous whirlpool, needed to protect the sea life, needed to fight. Struggling, I reached the surface. The whirlpool still clutched me in its grasp but I saw the night sky.

"Pearl." My name whispered across the dark ocean.

I couldn't see anything. Thick fog had rolled in blanketing the surface. Besides no one knew I was out here. No one knew me. Period.

Tiredness seeped into my bones at the thought of my aloneness.

"Pearl!"

Was I delusional? Or in this case, hear-lusional? I giggled at my brain's pathetic attempt at humor. I must be dying.

"Pearl. I'm almost there." An angel leading the way.

Instead of heading toward the light, I was swimming toward the voice. Nothing could be normal for me. Not even dying.

"You can do it. I'm only a few feet away."

Using my precious reserve, I lifted my head out of the water. A brown head bobbed in the surf only ten feet away, holding a red rescue tube.

An inner light glowed warming me inside. "Chase." His name squeaked past my cracked lips.

About fifteen yards behind him, a small boat rocked in the waves. Another guy manned the boat and held the rope that attached to the tube and Chase.

"I can't get any closer or I'll be sucked in. You have to swim to me." The sound of his voice lifted me, made me try harder. "Kick."

Someone would notice my absence. Maybe even care.

My heart swirled around in my chest. Chase cared. Maybe not about me specifically, but about me as a person, as another human being. I wasn't all alone. There were other people out there. People I could meet, get to know, maybe even become friends.

I reached out and plunged my right arm into the surf, then left. Right. Left. Right. Left. I told my feet what to do. Used the rhythm of my inner voice to motivate.

A few more feet. My hand hit the plastic tube and I grabbed for it. My fingers slipped but Chase took hold of my wrist. Relief passed through me and my body shook like a massive earthquake. Aftershock after aftershock, I couldn't stop the shaking. I was going to be okay.

Chase grabbed my waist and held on with long, strong fingers. "I got ya."

I raised my head and stared into his blue, blue eyes. The lines of stress seemed to lighten around his firm lips and square jaw. Water dripped down his drawn-out face.

"Thanks." Totally inadequate but that's all my numbed brain came up with. I'd never needed help in the water before. This was a new experience and I didn't know how to act.

Which made me question everything about myself. If I couldn't handle the Pacific Ocean, how could normal people?

He signaled to the guy in the boat and the rope tightened. We were tugged toward the rescue boat with Mermaid Beach printed on the side.

Drained of all energy, I relaxed against Chase, loving how his sinewy muscle protected me. Shivers of something other than cold took over my body but because I felt like an over-cooked noodle, I couldn't appreciate the sensations.

When we reached the boat, Chase lifted me, while his friend helped pull me on board.

"I'm Cuda." The curly-haired, blonde guy shoved a couple of white towels at me. "What were you doing swimming alone? At night?" His hard voice cut through all the shivery sensations.

I wrapped a towel around me and then ducked to twist my hair in a second towel avoiding Cuda's glare. I didn't plan to tell this guy anything. He meant nothing to me and I didn't have to answer his questions.

Chase climbed on board. "Leave her be. You're not on duty tonight." He took a towel and rubbed his wet and goose-bumpy skin. The cold water affected him and yet, he'd dived in to save me.

My hero. Saving me from the turbulent ocean and Cuda's questions. The shaking on the outside turned to quivering on the inside. Chase had helped this morning with the boy and the otter. And now, he'd risked his life to save me.

I slumped onto the bench built into the back of the small motor boat. With time, I probably could've gotten out of the whirlpool on my own. I had been making progress. Though it was nice, different, to have someone looking out for me. Warmth pooled in my belly and a smile landed on my face. No one had ever done that before.

Not the circus owners. Not the circus workers who I'd known forever. No one. Until now.

I tugged the towel tighter wanting to keep all this new-found warmth inside.

"We're in the lifeguard squad's rescue boat." Cuda studied me as he started the motor. The breeze whipped the red windbreaker he wore. "I've got every right to ask questions."

"Don't mind Cuda. He takes lifeguarding seriously, like he's protector of the ocean or something." Chase plopped next to me with a lopsided smile on his face. He must be used to Cuda's questions.

"I want to know why a girl is swimming in the ocean at night, by herself," Cuda's tone accused me like I'd done something illegal, instead of stupid.

Maybe I was stupid. Even with my powers, I'd almost been history.

I bit my lip thinking of an explanation. "It wasn't dark when I went in." A small lie.

The fog now blanketed any source of light. There was no moon, no stars. Just emptiness.

"You're nosy." Chase threw a towel at him.

Cuda caught it, keeping one hand on the wheel. "And you're not?"

"If I could find an interesting story, I'd be all over it." Chase trembled and put his arm around my shoulders. "I'm freezing. How about you?"

I nodded, unsure if I was answering yes or no. Heat flashed down my spine from the skin-to-skin contact. Being so close to Chase, I found it difficult to concentrate. "Story about what?"

"Nothing." He glared at Cuda as if daring him to keep his mouth shut.

I wasn't interested in stories. I didn't believe in fairy tales because my life had always been more of a nightmare.

My mind returned to my near catastrophe. "Are whirlpools common in this area?"

"Not that I know of." Chase bent over and picked up a big camera wrapped in plastic. "Got a few photos of the whirlpool before spotting you."

"How did you find me?" Must've been a miracle. I shivered again.

He scooted even closer. "Cuda wanted to follow this little sea otter that kept swimming around the boat."

"The otter wanted to play." Cuda sounded defiant like he didn't want anyone questioning his reasons. "He kept circling and waving with his paw."

"Like wild sea otters play with people." Chase's sarcastic tone made fun of his friend.

I held my breath. Could Cuda's sea otter be the same one who had played with me in the waves? Who wanted me to get out of the ocean? I gulped. The animal friend I'd thought had deserted me. The otter had known about the danger in advance and tried to warn me.

Staring at the black sky, I thanked my lucky stars I was alive. I praised Chase, too. And if the sea otter had helped? Well, I'd thank it, too.

***

Chase held a flashlight pinpointing the wooden dock as we got closer to shore. Cuda must've had a ton of practice because even with the waves the boat barely bumped against the supports. The boat cruised into place. Still holding the light, Chase climbed out. He tied up the boat and then held out his hand to me. "Drive you home?"

Placing my hand in his, I tried to stop the good-shiver that ran up my arm from his touch. Without success. I climbed onto the dock.

"Are you sure you don't need a doctor?" Cuda jumped onto the dock beside us. He double checked Chase's knots.

Doctors meant forms and questions. "I'm okay." Wet, tired, hungry, and still a bit scared, but nothing a doctor could fix. "I just need sleep."

Chase still had hold of my hand. "I'll take you home." He didn't ask this time.

His take-charge attitude made me feel safe and

protected but worried, too. I couldn't allow myself to get too close. To become too dependent. What if I had to leave?

But after my near death experience I didn't want to be alone right now. A few more minutes wouldn't matter.

"I left my sweats on the beach." I didn't own that many clothes and couldn't afford to lose the warm ones. "It'll be gone if I wait until morning."

"I'll bring the flashlight and walk over to the beach with you, find your clothes, and then I'll take you home." His concern warmed my heart, even though I didn't want these feelings.

"Okay." I'd let him walk me to the beach and help find the sweats. Then, I'd think of a way to leave.

"Don't go back in the ocean tonight," Cuda warned as we walked down the dock.

"Quit worrying, Fish-man." Chase waved the flashlight at him.

"Why do you call him that?" Pretending to need to take the towel off my head, I slipped my hand out of his. The first step to regaining my independence, to staying strong on my own.

My wet hair chilled my body in the cold night air. Or maybe it was because I no longer had direct contact with Chase.

"Cuda's last name is Fisher and he's totally into his job and the ocean." Chase took the towel and tossed it on a lifeguard station. "They'll put it away in the morning. Did you want to hold onto the other towel?"

"Until I find my sweats." I clutched the white towel tighter. The frigid night air seemed colder than the frigid water. Plus, my swim suit was a little too flashy for my taste. The circus owners had picked out all of my swim suit costumes for the show. I didn't have a choice. "What were you guys doing on the boat tonight?"

"Cuda wanted to patrol. I told you he took his job seriously." Chase swung the arm holding the flashlight and the beam tossed light back and forth in the sand. "I invited myself along after you walked out on our date."

"Sorry about that." I did feel bad. I was so confused about Chase.

Liking his company. Fearing his questions. Wanting him near. Terrified of getting too close.

"Why were you swimming alone tonight? It's dangerous."

I thought I'd dodged his curiosity earlier. Guess insistence and persistence paired inside Chase. "I wanted to take a dip and stayed in a little too long."

A lot too long.

"You probably haven't met a lot of people in Mermaid Beach yet." He bumped his shoulder into mine. "Anytime you need a swimming buddy, call me."

Warmth shot across my skin. A slight touch or a long look from Chase had me reacting in strange and wonderful ways. I liked it, but I was afraid of the feeling, too. Maybe it was because he'd helped me tonight, and with the boy and the otter. Maybe it was because he paid attention to me. Maybe it was because he made me feel less alone.

More confusion. Common sense told me to stay away, to not make friends. But my heart, my emotions, struggled to stay separate. I enjoyed being with Chase.

We walked in silence for a bit. The waves crashed on the shore. In the darkness all you could see were the whitecaps rolling in. Kinda like my thoughts—crashing and rolling.

"So, how uncommon are whirlpools in this area?" Why had one happened where I happened to be swimming for the first time ever in the Pacific Ocean?

This may sound paranoid, but I wondered it if had anything to do with me. The circus owners had refused to let me swim in any natural body of water. I was only allowed in the circus tanks or the bathtub.

And I liked Mermaid Beach. Wanted to stay, even if I didn't become friends with Chase.

He put his arm around my shoulders. "You must've been terrified." His concern lightened a dark place in my heart and the little sparks that flared at contact burst into a bright flame.

"Whirlpools can happen anywhere, but they're mega uncommon off the Southern Cali coast." He adjusted his pace to match mine. "Good question to ask at the local university. I could contact a few professors."

"I'd like that." I might get a few of my questions answered.

Chase stopped and faced me. His eyes held a curious light. He was interested in the questions, and possibly me. "Cuda mentioned weird occurrences happening near Mermaid Beach lately. Maybe global warming is contributing to ocean chaos."

I smiled at the calming effects of his words. If Cuda had noted earlier disturbances, I didn't cause the whirlpool. "What kind of disturbances?"

"He wasn't specific. I'll talk to him first, and then talk to the professors."

"Let me know what they say." I needed to learn about my new environment, both in and out of the ocean.

"I will." Chase's gaze glowed as if he'd spill his soul. "I'll tell you everything."

My body warmed from their light. For some reason, I didn't think he was talking about research. I regarded the view beyond his shoulder. Even though nothing had happened between us, things were moving way too fast. In one day he'd become involved in my life. Too involved. I wasn't ready for a relationship of any kind. I had to think this through, make a plan, decide if I could have a friend in my current situation.

"It's getting late."

"Yeah." He took my hand and we continued walking toward the campground.

Our fingers intertwined like we had a special connection. Like maybe, just maybe, this meant something.

I'd never had a special connection with anyone. Not Bill and Carlita, the circus owners. Not any of the other circus workers. No friends, and certainly no boyfriend.

Tightness pulled low in my stomach like a stretched trapeze wire. I kicked at the sand. I might have never been to the beach before moving here, but I lived in the water. I spent most of my waking hours in the dunk tank at the circus.

The only time I'd been kicked out was the summer I turned twelve. It was the hottest summer on record and the circus workers had demanded their kids be allowed to cool off in my swim tank for a couple of hours in the afternoon. Bill and Carlita refused to let me join them.

So, I'd hidden behind one of the tent's support poles and watched as about a dozen kids jumped and splashed water at each other. Two boys hit a blow up ball back and forth. A couple of girls pretended to be mermaids. Laughing and shouting, they'd been having so much fun.

Their playfulness called to me. I wanted to be part of

that, part of them. I inched out from behind the pole.

One of the girls waved at me. "We're playing mermaid. Come join us."

My heart thudded in my chest. She was including me. Finally, I had a friend.

I rushed over to the edge and dove into the water. Undulating my belly, I swam like a real mermaid. I guess I stayed underwater for a bit too long to be considered normal because when I surfaced all the kids were staring.

"You're the girl who does all those tricks in the show." The girl who'd invited me stuck out a stubby finger as if pointing out a big flaw. "You never come out to play with us."

I'd seen them through the window playing four square or hopscotch. Carlita wouldn't let me play with them, or anyone. I was too busy practicing my show, cleaning the trailer, or cooking. Not a lot of time for anything else.

"My mom says you're...different." The second girl examined me like I should be under a microscope.

"You swim weird," a boy said.

"You are weird." A second boy threw the plastic ball at my face.

The ball bounced off my nose and hit the water. My eyes burned. My cheeks heated. I wanted to sink to the bottom of the tank and never come up again.

I still felt that way around kids my own age like Joe and the other teens at the miniature golf course. But not Chase. He made me feel special, even when he didn't realize that I wasn't special, just different.

Chase and I reached the beach in front of the campground. "The whirlpool happened right out there. You swam from around this spot, right?" Chase shined the flashlight up and down the beach in front of the campground. "What color are your sweats?"

"Red." I glanced at the path that led to the tent area and took a few paces forward. "I don't see the sweatshirt or pants."

"Let's look around." He moved away and ran the spotlight up and down the empty beach. We searched for a bit. "I don't see anything."

"Do you think the waves took it?"

"Possibly. We can search again in the morning." He strolled back over to me and took both my hands.

Sparks shot from my fingertips to my toes. I didn't want to break our connection, didn't want to leave, didn't want to be alone again. But I also didn't want to be made fun of or abandoned. Didn't want to get close only to be burned. "I should get going. It's been an exciting day."

Exciting, terrifying, tempting.

His gaze gleamed with fascination and he leaned in a bit. "I'm glad you came to Mermaid Beach."

I swallowed. "Me, too."

"You've made life interesting."

Weird, how his thoughts aligned with mine. "Interesting good or interesting bad?"

He reached up and took my chin in his hand. "Interesting good." His fingers stroked the sensitive skin underneath. "I've wanted to do this since we first met."

My eyes stretched like the canvas over a trampoline. His lips moved closer. My heart pounded. "Since I climbed out of the dirty lagoon?" Ugh. I shouldn't have reminded him.

"Pretty much." He gave me a lazy, lingering smile. "You were so brave."

He thought I was brave. Thought I was interesting.

41

My backbone folded upon itself and I wanted to slip to the ground. If he kept talking like that, I'd be like wet sand clinging to him.

He must've realized my need for support because he wrapped his other arm around my waist and held me against him. The warmth of our bodies mingled and heat flared between us. His scent of ocean and spice tickled my nose.

Closing my eyes, I sensed his lips move within a millimeter of mine, felt his warm breath, heard his beating heart at the same fast pace.

His mouth touched my lips and moved slowly, carefully, as if testing my reaction. I sighed at his sweetness. My body melted against his. Like a whisper-soft caress, his lips kissed me.

My first kiss. Ever.

Chapter Four
Phenomenally Fumed

My. First. Kiss.

My heart tripped. Warmth flooded through my veins. My insides went soft and mushy. I wanted to lean against him. Forever.

Forever?

Suddenly, my body froze. What was I doing? My eyes opened wide like the circus arena in the big tent. Being friends was one thing, but this—whatever this was—was not right. I barely knew Chase. He knew nothing about me.

I placed my hands on his chest and pushed him away. "I can't do this."

What I protested I wasn't sure. The kiss? The friendship? Any kind of bond with another human being?

I twisted around and ran toward the path leading to the campground. I had to get away. To think. My breath came out in shallow pants. I tripped on the sand and fell to my knees.

I stood and scrambled up the small hill where the

43

grove of trees broke the strong breeze off the ocean, and stared back.

Chase still stood in the same place, a thoughtful expression on his face. His hair blew in the wind and his arms dangled at his side. The flashlight beam focused on one spot of sand.

Shame flooded my veins, heating my body. I'd run away not like the sixteen-year-old I was, or the eighteen-year-old I pretended to be. I'd run away like a baby.

Not inconspicuous at all.

***

Swish. Swish. Swish. The scrub brush scraped against the blue concrete lagoon walls. Yellow caution tape circled the area saying "Keep Out," but my boss had left instructions to go around and get inside. I'd clocked in before seven this morning to clean the lagoon before the inspection later in the day. While not big, the pool had a lot of wall space to clean. I was still fried about my boss nixing my day off, but I needed the money.

Even wearing a mask, the chlorine-like scent burned my nostrils and my throat had that raw, scratchy feeling you get right before a cold starts. My hands hurt from gripping the giant brush and my sandaled feet squished in the small amount of dirty water left at the bottom of the pool.

"Hello. You down there." Sarah Fowler, owner of the Mermaid Beach Boardwalk, called from the other side of the railing. "Are you from the custodial team?"

No, I wanted to inhale a few fumes. "Yeah."

"I've got something for you to install." She glanced around and then held up a box. "We need to get it done before the inspection."

We? I arched a brow. I couldn't imagine Mrs. Fowler

climbing into the empty lagoon and doing the dirty work. Not in her flowered dress and high heels. With her hair pinned up in an old-fashioned bun, she looked like a mom from a classic fifties sitcom.

"What is it?" I set down the brush, walked over to the ladder and climbed up.

"New safety cover for the up-flow filter." She handed me the box and I caught a whiff of her heavily floral scented perfume. "Instructions are inside."

"But I'm not a gadget gearhead." The Boardwalk had a fleet of guys who ran around and fixed the rides when they broke down, which happened often from what I'd observed.

"Should be easy. Just tighten a few screws."

"But—"

"I wouldn't normally ask, but all the mechanics are busy and this needs to get done. We want this lagoon to sparkle during inspection. Wouldn't want The Mermaid Beach Boardwalk to get a bad reputation." She sounded like a cheerleader at a prep rally. "Thank you for helping out."

Back at the bottom of the lagoon, I opened the box and took out the cover, except it didn't appear so new. The dented, white plastic had black markings like it had been hit by a blunt object. Made sense to replace the cover since I'd bent the old one, but you'd think the Boardwalk owner would've paid for a brand new one.

Not my business. I needed to get the job done before my blonde hair turned green with all the chlorine in the air.

With a kink on one side of the *new* filter cover, I struggled to make it fit over the hole. Holding the cover down with my forearm, I worked each corner into place.

Then, I tightened the screws. The filter cover looked, well not like new, but good enough. I returned to my scrubbing.

"Pearl." Chase's voice echoed around the empty pool.

I stiffened and my heart picked up its pace. His voice alone interrupted my normal rhythm. Now I understood why his kiss had thrown me like the Loop-to-Loop ride.

The kiss should never have happened. I'd been weak and foolish. Even more foolish-looking the way I'd run off.

"Where'd you go last night?" His angry voice bounced announcing my foolishness to everyone.

Maybe I could ignore him and he'd go away. I didn't want to analyze what had happened between us. I'd done enough of that last night.

Maybe, just maybe, I could be friends with Chase. After nearly dying I deserved some type of relationship. But it could never be more than that.

"I was worried you wouldn't get home."

My heart raced at the thought of his concern, but I couldn't show my emotions. He couldn't learn how he affected me. I dropped my arm holding the brush and turned around, firming my mouth. "You offered to help me find my sweats. They were gone so I left."

End of story. There couldn't be more hand holding or kissing. My life was way too complicated. Running from the circus owners, staying below the radar of the law, hiding my secrets.

Chase's lanky body leapt over the railing with the yellow caution tape. He climbed down the ladder. "You ran like a frightened rabbit. Again."

I stuck my chin out. "I don't run."

Okay I do run, but not from guys like Chase. I run from overbearing circus owners who'd taken advantage of me for way too long. I'd been on the run for over six months now. The wariness had lightened but I didn't think it would ever go away.

"You don't run, and you don't make excuses." He counted the points on his fingers. "I'll have to start keeping a list." He stopped right in front of me, a serious expression on his face.

"Why would you want to keep a list about me?"

He reached up and tugged the blue mask from around my mouth and nose exposing my lips. "I thought I'd communicated that last night."

My heart ba-bumped in my chest. "I'm nothing special." Nope, just your average-runaway-from-the-circus-because-I'm-tired-of-my-freak-abilities-being-taken-advantage-of-type-of-girl.

"I think you are," very-kissable lips only inches from my own said. "Special that is."

The ba-bump in my heart squeezed tight. Special? My breath hitched. No one had ever called me special before. Weird. Strange. Different. Maybe a uniquely-strange now and again. But never special in a sweet way.

Our bodies were so close. Only within inches of each other. If I leaned toward him I could thank him for the compliment. Instead, I tilted back to remove my mouth from temptation.

Guess I leaned too far because I lost my balance and stumbled.

He grabbed my arm to stop me from tumbling. His strong fingers wrapped around my arm. "You okay?"

"Must be the fumes." I waved a hand in front of my nose, hoping it appeared I was trying to clear the air but really I cooled my flushed face. "Toxic stuff."

I couldn't let him see how much he affected me. Affected me because he acts like he's interested in me as a person, not a freakish performer. Tells me I'm special and makes me feel special.

Or does he suspect something? My skin tingled in a suspicious way. He'd been around when all of my weird incidents had happened. Was he being nice to learn my secrets?

"I'll help." He bent over to dig in the cleaning bucket for a brush offering a nice view of his backside in clean khaki shorts.

If my suspicions are correct, I didn't want his help. Or his nearness. The temptation was too great. I'd get to know him and like him more and then when he disappointed me, like everyone else, I'd be hurt. "Don't you have other work to do?"

Rejection flashed in his aqua-blue eyes before they sparked with anger. "Yes. I do." He dropped the scrubbing brush and it hit the brackish inch of water with a splat. "I won't bother you anymore."

The blackness of loss hit me first. Then, a twinge of surprise that I felt such loss. "Chase. Wait."

He halted but didn't turn around. His shoulders were stiff, unbending. He was waiting.

Waiting for me to make the next move. The next overture. "I'd love help." I swallowed the fear in my throat. I didn't want to hurt him and I didn't want to be hurt. But I'd decided we could be friends, and friends help each other out. "From you."

Turning to face me, his feet squished. Pain still shown in his soft gaze, coupled with an uncertainty. "You're sure?"

"Yeah. Sorry I—"

"No need to apologize." He picked the scrub brush up. "Besides, you need help. The police are coming to inspect the lagoon later today and this needs—"

"Police?" All the air whooshed out of my lungs. I stayed well clear of the cops. They tended to ask way too many questions. "Why?"

He took a mask and slipped it over his face making it more difficult to read his expression. "Routine. A kid almost drowned, so they need to write a report."

"Oh." I slipped my own mask back on wanting to hide any fear displayed. "What time is the, um, inspection?" Cause I planned to be miles away.

"Around four."

The sooner I got this done the sooner I could get out of here. Now, I was glad for Chase's help.

He grabbed a brush. "Tell me what to do?"

I liked how he asked, didn't act like he was a know-it-all manager. The circus owners had been dictators. Their way or the highway. I chose the highway, although it had taken me sixteen years to gather the courage.

After giving him a quick run-down of what still needed to be done, we got to work. We worked in silence for a bit and even though we didn't talk, it was nice not to be alone. Since running away, I'd been alone a lot.

Who was I kidding? Even before running away I was alone. I'd lived with the circus owners, Bill and Carlita, and no one else under their employment came near me. Only a few brave souls approached and then the need was dire. It was like I carried an infectious disease.

Like the kids at the dunk tank. Once they'd realized what I was they panicked.

"Get out of the water! Get out of the water!" They

swam and ran and scrambled to get out of the pool. One girl in her haste slipped off the ladder and fell back into the tank. Her panic-filled screams sounded like she'd been murdered.

I'd never forget the fear on her face when I swam over to help. "Don't touch me." As if she could catch my weirdness.

Seconds later, the twelve of them stood around the edge of the dunk tank while I floated in the middle. Alone. Like a leper island.

Their expressions accused me of ruining their fun. Of possibly infecting them.

My lower lip trembled. I couldn't show them how much they'd hurt me. I gave my show biz signature salute, an undulating hand like an ocean wave, and sunk to the bottom, staying there until they left.

"Have you been to Mermaid Beach yet?" Chase had moved to a spot near where I scrubbed.

My eyes burned from the chlorine not from the memories. "I thought this *was* Mermaid Beach."

"Well, there's the Mermaid Beach Boardwalk, the town of Mermaid Beach, and then the actual beach. It's got a great campground…"

That, I knew about.

"…where you were last night, more wonderful sandy beaches and some real neat coves and tide pools."

"Sounds cool. I'll have to explore on my next day off."

"How about after shift today? You clocked in pretty early. We could have a late lunch and go swimming."

Having Chase help me clean the lagoon was one thing, spending time with him, especially at the beach, was too risky. I couldn't chance the exposure of my skills. "I don't swim."

"You've said that before, yet," His eyebrows rose higher above the mask. "I saw you dive like a champion and you survived last night's whirlpool."

My brush stopped scrubbing. "With your help."

"You seemed to know what you were doing."

I jerked the hair away from my face. My stomach turned over. Did he suspect I was different? "Can we forget about the whole thing? It's over."

"Sure thing. Didn't realize how touchy you were." His own touchy tone sent a warning to my natural protective instincts.

"I'm not touchy." But I was. I needed to blow both incidents off by acting less jumpy and sensitive. If he was curious, I needed to deflect that curiosity. "Sorry."

He raised his hands in mock surrender. "I wanted to get to know you better." His gaze lost their humor, seeming almost disappointed. "If you're not interested ..." He shrugged and turned back to scrubbing.

I bit my lip. He seemed sincere. And I was coming off like world-class cow. Doubt warred with wistfulness in my chest. "I'm not using you to help me clean the lagoon."

"Could've fooled me." The hurt in his tone cut across me.

Hanging out was normal. Dating was normal. Kissing was normal.

I wasn't normal, but I wanted to be. Wanted to pretend if only for an afternoon that I could hang out and not worry.

But I had so many secrets to hide.

***

So this is what it was like to have a *fun* day. Sitting

on a blanket on the beach, watching the waves roll in, my body relaxed like it never had before. Soaking up the sun, listening to the surf, and smelling the salty air.

Maybe it was Chase and his laid-back attitude. Maybe it was being near the ocean. Maybe it was because Mermaid Beach seemed like home, or as close to a home as I'd ever get.

"This is great after the cleaning we did this morning." Chase lay next to me in longish blue swim trunks, his arms crossed behind his head, his eyelids closed against the brightness of the sun.

He'd been a trooper, helping me finish scrubbing the lagoon. He'd been sweet and nice and entertaining and... The list went on, even though I tried to erase it from my mind.

"I still stink like chlorine." I'd taken a quick shower at the campground bathrooms, and then met Chase back at the Boardwalk an hour later. I'd thought about backing out, not showing up, but then I remembered how he'd called me special.

And I so wanted to feel that way.

I didn't know where he'd cleaned up, but he'd definitely showered because I smelled the fresh spicy scent of his shampoo. He'd changed into long board shorts and a white T-shirt that hugged his buff chest, and he'd brought a blanket and cooler filled with sandwiches and sodas.

He rolled to his side and his face moved in next to my neck. His breath whispered against my skin causing tingles of delight.

"Let me check." He sniffed obnoxiously. "You smell ocean fresh, with maybe a bit of chlorine on the side."

I slapped his chest and hot sparks singed through my

veins. Whoa, was that the cleaning solution from this morning or did we have some type of personal chemical reaction? It's like we were combustible. Or toxic.

I was attracted to Chase, but one of us was bound to get hurt.

He sat up and tugged my hand. "Come into the water and we can get rid of that chlorine scent."

I shook my head, even though I longed to dive into the ocean. If possible I'd spend every waking minute in the water. I loved it that much. But the water could betray me. I'd get excited, forget people were watching, and do something stupid.

"No, I'll watch." I took a sip of orange soda and observed a lifeguard blowing a whistle at some kids jumping on top of each other in the waves.

"How about tossing a Frisbee?" He fidgeted something fierce and then glanced at his watch.

Bored? My stomach flattened like air being let out of a ball. "If you don't want to hang out with me, it's cool." A touch of hurt sounded in my voice no matter how hard I tried to disguise it.

"I can only lie around for so long. Let's walk over by the tide pools." He stood and held out his hand and then put them together begging. "Please."

Laughter bounced out of my chest and I couldn't stop the smile from slipping onto my face. He wasn't bored with me. He didn't like lying around. Guess he wasn't a completely laidback type of guy.

"Since you said please." I stood and brushed off my red, white and blue bikini bathing suit. The swimsuit featured a large, gem-studded star design. A bit flashy for my new stay-out-of-the-limelight role but it had worked theatrically in the circus and he'd seen it the other night.

We walked through the sand toward the cliffs surrounding the beach area. The cliffs stood tall protecting the beach. The waves crashed over the larger rocks. A love-hate relationship, similar to mine with the water.

I loved swimming and loved what I could do in the water, but because I could do those freaky things I was picked on, spotlighted, forced to perform. The circus owners had taken away my ability to feel completely free in the water, and with other people.

"How do you like working at *The Boardwalk*?" He pronounced the last two words with an echo effect.

"It's a job. How about you?"

"It sucks, but it's...a job." His laugh sounded forced. "I've been working there every summer since I was eight."

"Is that legal?" Maybe he was getting paid in cash, too.

"Who knows." He shrugged. "While I love summer, I'm looking forward to going to college this fall."

He was a college freshman, while I should've been in high school. He was smart, while I'd been taught to read by Carlita and done most of the homeschooling myself. He had plans, while I didn't even know if I had a future.

He was two years older than me. Not that I gave my real age on the Boardwalk application. They thought I was eighteen. And I would be soon, in less than two years.

I'd love to go to a real school. "Do you know what you want to study?"

Nodding, he bent over and picked up a small, smooth stone. "Business and journalism."

"Two majors? I'm impressed." Now I felt real dumb.

I didn't have a clue what interested me. Up until this point, I'd only known the circus. Thought it would be my life. That I didn't have a choice.

But once I learned the truth, I couldn't stay at the Poseidon Family Circus. I didn't have to anymore.

He threw the stone side-armed and skipped it across the water. "My aunt insists on the business major, but I like journalism. I've got a job working for the school paper."

I missed a step. "Doing what?" Please, let it be advertising, or public relations, or a paperboy.

"Investigative journalism."

My stomach vaulted up my throat. Curiosity was part of his personality. He'd been asking questions since the moment we met. I swallowed past the sudden lump and tried to respond. "In-interesting."

"I need to break a big story wide open to prove to my aunt reporting is the right career for me. Got any leads?"

"L-l-leads?" My lips tripped over themselves. My heart plopped like the stone he'd thrown earlier. So, that's what he'd meant by stories last night. Journalism stories.

I hated reporters. One reporter, specifically. Ben Collins, a reporter in the local town where the circus was based, wanted to break out nationally with a big story. Just like Chase. My breath caught in my chest.

Ben had decided I was that story. He'd hounded me, peppered me with questions, and dogged my every move. One time I found myself alone in the big tent. After glancing around to be sure no one watched, I strutted onto the music stage where bands would perform during intermission.

I bowed to my imaginary audience. Then, I started

singing and dancing like I was a famous pop star and not a circus freak. Flipping my hair and shimmying, I danced around the stage pretending like all thirteen-year-old girls do.

My voice screeched the lyrics. My body jerked the dance moves. But at that moment, in my mind, I was marvelous and free.

Clap. Clap. Clap. The sound interrupted my impromptu performance. I froze. My heart pounded like the bass of live music.

Ben stepped out from behind the dunk tank. With a video camera in his hand. "I guess musicality isn't one of your talents."

My face flamed. My entire body heated like a volcano. I wanted to die on the spot. "What are you doing? You're not supposed to be in here." My voice whispered no real challenge in it at all.

"I'd planned to secretly videotape you practicing your show but this performance was so much better."

I knew I was a terrible singer. My voice sounded like a whale's mating call. I was klutzy out of water, so I couldn't dance.

"W-what do you mean?" I hadn't heard his sarcasm at first.

He tapped the camcorder. "This will make a laughable internet video. I bet you get a ton of hits."

I scrambled off the stage. "No." I'd be laughed at by millions. Carlita would kill me.

"I tell you what." He strolled oh-so-casually over. "I'll give you this disc in exchange for information. Tell me how you do your underwater tricks."

I didn't know the answer to that myself. Breathing, super strength, and seeing clearly underwater came naturally. No one taught me how to do it, just like no one had ever taught me how to swim.

This mega-embarrassing internet video would haunt me for the rest of my life. I couldn't give him an answer and I couldn't let him blackmail me. "I'll show you."

My legs shook climbing onto the edge of the tank. He followed. The red light of the camera blinked on.

"Get closer to the edge." I beckoned him forward and then leaned over the water. "Do you see that?"

"See what?" He leaned a bit further.

"That." I swung my arm around and shoved him hard on the back.

He tumbled. His arms flayed. He and his camera landed with a big splash in the water. Ben was all wet and his camera ruined. He could never show that video to anyone.

I contemplated Chase leaning over a tide pool. His muscular thighs bunched for balance. His white T-shirt came up at the waist revealing toned muscles. His wavy hair blew in the slight breeze. Hair any girl would love to run her fingers through. So why was he here with me?

The reaction from the mermaid girls at the miniature golf course proved he was popular. I didn't act like them and I hadn't gone out of my way to be nice. Were his attention and compliments part of a plot to discover my secrets?

Should I push him in the water like that other reporter? Or push him away?

Chase climbed onto a rock near the cliffs and held out his hand to help me. "What about you? Any plans to go to college?"

I spluttered trying to refocus on the conversation, still unsure how to handle him. Too late to push him in the water. Plus, if I had he'd only have more questions.

With hesitancy, I put my hand in his and climbed on top of the rock next to him. Of course, he didn't mean high school. He thought I was old enough to go to college. "I don't think so."

I'd never attended a real school. I was home-schooled and I'd learned from the school of life, from the school of hard knocks, from the school of the circus which had its share of cliques and drama.

"What do you want to do in the future?" He bent down to study another small pool of water. Purplish anemone stuck to the sides and tiny plankton swam around.

"I usually take one day at a time." Sometimes, one hour at a time. At the moment, surviving was my only goal.

"But you have to do something." His defiant tone went soft. "Don't you have a dream?"

I'd had plenty of dreams, most of them downright weird with hands reaching out to grab me under the sea, taking me so far down I'd never reach the surface again. The people doing the grabbing didn't seem scary. They looked normal, except for the whole breathing-under-the-water thing.

"Pearl?" Chase waved his hands in front of my face. "Where'd you go?"

I couldn't tell him the truth. My chest echoed with emptiness. "Off to one of those dreams you're talking about."

My deep, down in my heart dream. My impossible dream. The dream that I wasn't alone, that there were others like me.

***

Chase pointed out the miniature environment living in the tide pools. He explained about high tide and how the ecosystem survived. It was like attending a mini-marine biology course. He was a smart guy.

And fun.

He told me about his childhood antics living in Mermaid Beach that made me laugh, told me interesting stories about some of the local people, and ideas for local story angles.

Entertaining, knowledgeable, intelligent. Except for the whole reporter thing, how could I not like the guy?

My suspicious nature fought with my loneliness. I didn't trust Chase, but I was having fun. We weren't in the water. Unless I said something stupid, he'd learn nothing.

"Have any plans for your next day off?"

Add persistent.

I laughed in spite of the fact I had an idea what he might ask—to spend more time together. Which I sooo wanted to do, but shouldn't. I stalled. "Why do you want to know?"

"You're new to the area. Thought I'd show you around. We could drive up the coast."

My stomach rolled like the waves. "How do you know we'll both have the same day off?"

"We will." Instead of irritating me, his confident tone only charmed. He was so sure of himself, so sure of the world and his place in it.

While I didn't belong anywhere, didn't know where I should go, and didn't know what I wanted to do tomorrow.

I tiptoed around a small tide pool like I tiptoed around my answer. "Do you play tour guide to all the new girls in town?"

"Only the pretty ones."

"There must be a lot of those." After all, he lived in southern California.

"No. Just you."

My limbs weakened. The compliment zinged up my spine and sparked a smile. Since running away, I hadn't bothered with make-up. I didn't want to be noticed. Still, Chase had singled me out, sought me out, asked me out. Again.

Why, why, why? The question thumped in my brain.

In Mermaid Beach I wasn't newsworthy or a star. At least not yet. He happened to think I was interesting. If I kept my guard up even more than usual, maybe I'd learn what he was after. If anything. And learn more about him and my new surroundings. Call it research.

Chase's cell phone rang and he slipped it out of his pocket. He glanced at the screen and frowned. "Sorry. I've got to take this."

"No, problem." Straying away to give him privacy, I climbed a large rock that jutted out into the ocean.

Large waves hit the cliff and sprayed water high. The droplets refreshed. I took a seat on the edge and stared across the ocean toward the horizon.

My shoulders relaxed. I took in deep breaths of the salty air. I was at home in Mermaid Beach. Loved the proximity to the ocean, loved the weather, loved the atmosphere of the small beach town. If possible, I'd love to settle here, maybe find a small apartment to splash with my personality, fill with the things I loved.

I took another deep breath. Thinking, hoping, wishing.

A squeak caught my attention. A furry sea otter

swam by the rocks. Lying on his back with his head lifted, his dark eyes studied me.

"Are you the one from last night?"

"How many guys were you with last night?" Chase's joking tone lightened my mood. He sat down beside me.

"I meant the sea otter."

The little guy dove back under the waves hiding from Chase.

"Oh." Chase made an exaggerated sad face. He fiddled with his cell phone. "That was uh, Mrs. Fowler on the phone. She owns the Boardwalk."

"So, I've heard." It would be a drag if Mrs. Fowler called her managers while they were off work.

"The police have questions." Chase took hold of my hand. "Pearl, they want to talk to you."

Chapter Five
Cop Clash

My ribs pierced my heart with sharp pain. The cops had found me. The pounding of the surf sounded like boom after boom after boom of explosions sounding my doom. The Poseidon Family Circus must've spent a ton of money to get cops across the country to search for me. They wouldn't let their *little gold mine* disappear.

"Wh-when?"

"Now." Chase stood. The lines of his forehead bunched together in fear and concern. For me or the Boardwalk? He held out his hand, understanding I might need the help. "They want to hear your version of the rescue."

The pain in my chest eased but didn't go away. "You mean about rescuing the boy?"

"Yeah."

Ignoring his helping hand, I stood on my own. Relaxing had been a mistake. Letting down my guard had been the wrong decision. Getting close to someone and then being ripped apart would be too painful. At least being alone, not connecting with anyone, was safer for me and my heart.

The cops might be questioning me about the rescue, but if they dug a bit under the surface they'd discover my false identity, my runaway status, my lies.

I yanked down the frayed edges of the large T-shirt I wore over my suit. Chase grabbed hold of my hand and wouldn't let go. We crossed onto the Boardwalk property. He must've sensed my turmoil. I should've snatched my hand back, ran to my tent, grabbed my things, and caught the first bus out of town. But I didn't.

Because maybe, just maybe, the questions would be about the rescue and that was all. Maybe the cop wouldn't ask my age or realize the name I used to work at the Boardwalk was false. Maybe I could stay in Mermaid Beach.

That's why I let Chase hold my hand. I needed all the comfort I could get, needed to build my strength before the interrogation, and in case I had to run again breaking our connection permanently.

The tinny music from the midway caressed my ears like a familiar friend. The scent of corn dogs and taffy wafted in the air. The winking lights on the rides promised happiness. I wasn't ready to leave this place yet.

"You look pale. Are you feeling all right?"

I probably looked guilty. Or terrified. "I, um, must've drunk too much soda. Maybe I should talk to the cops another time." *Like never.*

"Mrs. Fowler said they were waiting for you." Chase led the way behind a few kiddie rides toward the back of the administration building. "I'll take you in the back way. Mrs. Fowler wants to talk to you first."

Was the boss mad about something? Was I going to be fired? Chase, the manager, dutifully bringing me in like a deputy sheriff in a western town.

Yanking my hand out of his, I struck out at him in a nasty tone. "Do you always do everything she says?"

Like the Drop Tower ride, my emotions went up and down. I wanted the comfort and strength he provided, but I didn't want him pulling me in to see the boss. Nerves made me jumpy and cruel. I'd run all the way across the country, and now because I'd had to rescue someone, I could get caught.

Chase's face tightened and he opened his mouth, but then snapped it shut. He rolled his shoulders and stared at the ground. "Pretty much."

My entire body drooped. He wouldn't help me out of this jam, but he didn't understand the problem so he didn't deserve my attack. "I know she's your boss."

"Yep. That's right. Gotta listen to your boss," Terse, he rapped on a door with peeling paint. Before anyone answered, he shoved the door open.

The hinges creaked like they didn't have enough grease, sending a chill of warning down my spine. Mrs. Fowler paced on a frayed carpet in front of faded curtains behind a desk piled high with papers. Bookshelves lined one side of the wall filled with books, trophies and family photos.

Intense longing snapped my scared streak. I didn't own a single family photo. Because I didn't have a family.

She turned toward us and halted, her mouth dropping open. "This is her?"

"Yes." Chase nodded.

She studied me. "Thanks, um, for doing that job for

me this morning." Her glance went from my flip-flopped feet to the top of my head. "I tried to reach you on the phone number you left on your application." Her intensity charged the room and made her appear older. "It was a pay phone."

When you didn't have a home, you didn't have a phone. And I couldn't afford a cell. "Yes, um, well, I just moved here when I applied for the job. I didn't have a phone yet." I swallowed the phlegm in my throat. I took a step back toward the door.

"Make sure you give my secretary the new information." She nodded and then looked at Chase. Her eyes softened. "Thanks for bringing her here, hon." Calling one of her managers *hon* seemed odd to me. "Why don't you get a snack while I talk to Miss Seidon."

Miss Seidon. Right. That's the false last name I gave on the application along with the fake phone number. I figured Poseidon stood out a little too much.

"I'll stay with Pearl." He acted like my protector.

Which was sweet. But I didn't want him to hear whatever ugly details might come out. "It's okay. Go."

Chase paused searching my face. I could tell he wanted to object by the tight lines around his lips. Instead, he shot a glance at Mrs. Fowler before leaving by the back door.

Mrs. Fowler pointed to a chair. "Why don't you have a seat?"

With trembling limbs, I walked to the upholstered chair with the worn patches on the arms in front of the desk. Perching on the edge, I jiggled my legs, waiting for the yelling to start.

She leaned against the edge of the desk, too close for comfort, and continued to examine, sizing me up. "Did you know the Kingdom of Atlantis miniature golf course lagoon isn't for swimming?"

I crossed my arms and frowned. "I wasn't swimming."

"I understand, dear." She reached over and patted my arm with a dry, papery hand. "You were heroic. But you'd understand why a person might overlook, or forget, to make an expensive adjustment."

I squinted, telegraphing my bewilderment.

"I didn't realize you were both the rescuer and the person who installed the filter cover this morning." She pinched the bridge of her nose. "Just my luck."

Large bags weighed down her sharp, blue eyes and deep worry lines formed around her mouth. Running the Boardwalk wasn't all fun and games.

Compassion replaced my fear. This woman had a tough job and by the dilapidated condition of the rides, not doing it very well.

She blew out a large sigh. "When the police interview you, I'd like you to *not* mention anything about the up-flow filter cover replacement."

"Why?"

"Because that law should only apply to swimming pools, not decorative lagoons." She squeezed her hands together and closed her eyelids. "A lawsuit would be expensive and the Boardwalk has gotten off to a slow start this season."

A lawsuit would only increase the amount of questions and all I wanted was to not be discovered. "Okay."

Her smile brightened her face making her appear much younger and more carefree. "Besides, why should it matter now? Thanks to you, the little boy is fine.

We've cleaned the lagoon. And if we need to," she sighed again, "we'll find the money to build new, higher railings."

A knock sounded at the door and the secretary entered. "Officer Clayton is waiting."

"Send him in." Mrs. Fowler stood and rubbed her hands on her thighs.

The cop entered.

"Officer Clayton, I hope you found everything you needed at the lagoon. This is Pearl Seidon, our hero." She squeezed my shoulder.

I licked my lips and stood to face my nemesis. My heart thrummed in my chest blocking my lungs from processing any air. One of my most humongous fears stood before me—interrogation by a cop.

Officer Clayton stood at least six feet tall, towering over the diminutive Mrs. Fowler and me. His uniform was starched to perfection, but a small red stain marred his blue tie. He took out a small notebook and clicked his pen. "How do I spell your last name?"

Gripping my slippery hands together. I spelled out my lie.

He turned to Mrs. Fowler and escorted her toward the door. "I'd like to speak with Miss Seidon in private."

"But..." Her expression panicked with raised brows and dropped chin.

I gripped my hands tighter. All feeling fled my fingertips. Police officers were trained to observe people and recognize lies. By standing here, I was living a lie.

He closed the door and silence filled the small, cramped office. "Congratulations on your rescue. From what I've been told it was a pretty amazing feat."

A single bead of perspiration slipped down my back.

"Thanks."

"Why don't you sit down?"

Another command to sit. I felt like a dog, but obeyed the direction. If it would get him to leave, I'd bark, too. The scenario reminded me of listening to Carlita's commands. Dive higher, stay under water longer, scrub harder.

He took the chair next to mine. Guess he wasn't going to play the authority figure game.

"Why don't you tell me in your own words what happened yesterday at the lagoon?" His tone was soft, coaxing, a you-can-tell-me-anything-confidence-sharing type of voice.

I licked my lips again, my mouth sand dry. "I was sweeping the sidewalk when these teens started goofing around by the railing-"

"Joe. I already interviewed him."

"So you know that the little boy copied what Joe did, balancing on the railing. It was his fault." Blaming someone else sounded juvenile, but I had to give it a try.

"Unfortunately, we can't arrest people for stupidity."

For a second, I relaxed with a small smile. The cop didn't seem so bad.

Then he said, "Go on."

My tummy turned because the man wanted details. Details I didn't want to tell. "The boy fell. His mother screamed. And I just reacted by diving in after him."

"I measured the height. That was an incredible dive into such a small amount of water. It's amazing you weren't hurt." Officer Clayton's face showed concern before his expression changed to impressed. "You must be quite a diver."

Wanting to downplay my role, I shrugged. "Lucky, I

guess."

Or not. If I hadn't dived in, I wouldn't be being questioned by the cops, I wouldn't have to lie again.

He laughed and then seemed to school his features. "Go on with your story."

"I searched the entire length of the lagoon." *Oops, I need to make the time sound shorter.* I bit my lip before more words rushed out. "Not that it's big. And found the boy at the bottom."

Officer Clayton leaned forward. "Where exactly on the bottom?"

"I was a bit disoriented." Another lie, but it would make sense.

"And then what?"

"I picked him up," I did not mention how he'd been stuck to the filter cover because that would've added time, "and brought him to the surface where I handed him off to Chase, who gave him first aid before the paramedics arrived."

Never would I tell about the breath I breathed into him. I'd never even told the circus owners about that special skill.

"How long would you say the boy was under water?"

"Gosh, I don't know." I forced sincerity into my tone, hoping he believed me. "You know how emergency situations are, it seems so much longer than it really is." I delivered my rehearsed line precisely the way I wanted.

"Did you notice anything about the kid? Any injuries or strange markings?"

Alarm rang and I sat up straighter. "No one pushed him. I saw him fall off the railing."

"You didn't see any markings or lines on his back?"

"It was hard to see in the water." Well, it would be

for most people.

He nodded slowly as if in thought. "When I was down at the lagoon today it smelled like cleaning solution. Do you know why?"

Mrs. Fowler didn't say anything about not mentioning cleaning the lagoon. "I think the lagoon was scrubbed after draining it."

"The initial report from the scene said the lagoon was filthy. The water so dark, no one could see into it."

A trick question. He wonders how I found the kid in the murky water. I lifted my shoulders in a slight shrug but stayed silent. The less I said the less that could be used against me.

Officer Clayton stood. He reached into his shirt pocket and handed me a business card. "If you think of anything else, give me a call." His expression appeared warm, not menacing or threatening.

Even so, I couldn't trust the cop. Not with my illegal status.

"Yeah, I will." *Not.*

I sagged in my chair. The questioning was over and I'd gotten through it without too many lies. He didn't suspect a thing.

He opened the door, but before leaving he turned back. "The boy Brandon is doing fine but he's got red welts on his back, stripes, almost like he was sucked against something."

The muscles in my stomach tightened. So, there was evidence of the struggle to get him out. That's why Mrs. Fowler asked me not to mention changing the up-flow filter cover. It must have something to do with the law she'd mentioned. That's why the cops were investigating.

Unknowingly, I'd been involved in a filter cover

cover-up. Another secret I'd have to hide.

***

After work that day, I hustled into the camp store and waited while Mr. Plankson finished helping a customer. His stiff smile appeared rarely used, which was too bad because he was good-looking for an older dude. He didn't talk to the woman ringing up her order of milk and marshmallows, even as she fluttered her hands and batted her eyelashes.

The cramped store had shelves filled with the essential items for camping like bread, cereal and batteries, and a few unessential items like candy bars and magazines. The scent of coffee filled the air.

When the woman left, he turned to me. "Checking out?"

Tomorrow I'd have been at the campsite for exactly two weeks, the legal limit. "Um, I wanted to talk to you about that." I shoved my hand in my pocket and rubbed the two twenties folded neatly inside. "I hoped to stay a bit longer."

His brows arched like a sideways dollar sign—one going up, the other going down—or maybe that was my current state of mind.

"State Park rules state two weeks maximum." He turned away and sat down on a creaky chair in front of an old metal desk.

"You're not full." I'd spotted several empty camp sites.

He swiveled the chair back around to face me. His gaze bore into mine. He angled his head. "Odd. Young girl camping alone."

My legs wobbled at his unstated question, but I held myself together. "I'm a nature-girl."

"No camp stove. No car. No friends." He spelled out my inadequacies with a flat voice.

Each shortcoming was like a slash to my heart, but I refused to be cowed. I pulled out the bribe and slapped forty dollars on top of the desk. "Will this cover any inconvenience?" I held my breath, waiting for him to laugh at my puny offering or yell at my boldness.

He opened the top drawer of the desk and dust flew in the air. Then, he took out a stack of registration forms and thumbed through them.

He squinted, reading from a page. "Seidon, Pearl."

"Th-that's me."

His glower tried to puncture through my lies. "You left most of the spaces blank. Where are you from?"

"Nebraska."

"What're you doing in California?" He sounded like a cop. Not like Officer Clayton, but a more hard-nosed detective who I hoped accepted bribes.

The bells over the door jangled when someone walked in. "Excuse me, I'm looking for a missing...Pearl?" Chase stood on the threshold.

Mr. Plankson pursed his lips and scrunched up his nose. "We don't sell pearls."

I licked my lips and peered between the two of them. "Chase, what're you doing here?"

"So, you do have friends," Mr. Plankson mumbled.

I wanted to kick him for belittling me, but I held back. I hadn't gotten an answer to my bribe yet.

Chase's glance darted between me and the camp manager. "Since we didn't find your sweats last night, I decided to search again after work, thought the store might have a lost and found..." He clamped his mouth shut and then opened it again. "What're you doing here,

Pearl?"

"She's a camper." Mr. Plankson took the money and shoved it in the pocket of his dirty jeans. His grouchy face scowled. "If you're not going to buy anything, then why don't you two scoot."

I rushed out of the store before he changed his mind. By taking the money, I assumed he took my bribe. Assumed I had a place to live at least for a while longer. Which was good. I couldn't afford anything else.

"You're a camper?" Confusion laced Chase's deep voice. He jogged to catch up to me.

I'd escaped one sticky situation and landed right in another. Chase was going to have more questions than Mr. Plankson.

"Got a problem with camping?" Putting a bucket-load of sarcasm into my tone, I slowed my steps but instead of heading to my tent I went toward the beach. No need to humiliate myself further by showing him my actual living conditions.

"Why would you camp so close to home?"

My tummy churned like the waves. I put on a fake smile and lightened my voice. "I enjoy camping, especially by the beach."

He grabbed my hand and jerked me to a stop. His fingers wrapped around mine, but not in a caring way. In a way that demanded I listen. "By yourself?"

The fog hung low on the coast with the sun barely visible. Seagulls squawked. My pulse pounded at the base of my throat. If I told Chase the truth, would his opinion of me lower?

I stared into his eyes searching for an answer. The depths of those indigo orbs changed colors with his mood. Right now, they looked inquisitive, like my unusual situation brought out the reporter in him.

Which I so didn't need. I had to answer the question and deflect him from digging deeper.

"I'm..." I dug my toes in the sand. "I'm... temporarily living in the campground." Heat flared in my cheeks. He probably lived in a normal home with normal parents.

"Why?"

The churning in my stomach reversed directions. I shouldn't be embarrassed by my situation, I should be angry he asked. I huffed out my answer. "It's a free country."

I'd never felt free until arriving in Mermaid Beach. Bill and Carlita were like prison guards, not parents. My circus act penance for having my skills. Here, I could enjoy my freedom, enjoy my skills, enjoy my life.

"Whoa." He dropped my hand and held both of his up in surrender. His surprised expression cut through my anger. "I'm just asking questions. It's what I do."

"You sound like an interrogator." I crossed my arms in front of me giving him the big back-off sign. We might be sort-of-friends, but he didn't need to know all about me. No one did. "You won't tell Mrs. Fowler, will you? You won't tell anyone."

His eyebrows rose as if the thought hadn't crossed his mind. "Why would you think that?"

"You're so deferential to her."

His lips flat lined and he turned away to gaze at the horizon. "No. I won't tell her." He gentled his voice. "What's wrong with an apartment? Or a hotel?"

"Those things take money, a deposit." *Forms and a legal signature.*

"Your parents won't help?" He touched my shoulder with a gentle hand.

I wanted to turn into the caress, but instead I jerked away. Because for me it wasn't a casual touch. Every touch, every glance, every word meant something.

Bill and Carlita weren't demonstrative. At all. I wasn't used to anyone touching me. And with Chase, his touches meant more. More of what I didn't know. I didn't want to find out.

And yet, I did.

He placed his hand on my shoulder again, not put off by my rejection. His light touch turned into a massaging caress, like he wanted to take away the burden I carried. It would be so easy to lean into him, tell him everything, let him help me figure out what to do with my life.

I straightened, knowing I couldn't drag him into my nightmare, and hoping he didn't want to sell my story. "My parents and I parted ways."

That last night we'd argued. Again.

I'd been sick all week. Didn't want to get on stage or dive in the water. Didn't want to act like everything was okay when it wasn't.

"I'm tired of performing every night." My muscles ached with fatigue. My heart hurt from the lies I'd uncovered like the fake birth certificate they wouldn't explain.

"Take a chill pill." Carlita's pudgy hands had thrown my bedazzled bathing suit costume in my face.

I shouldn't have expected any sympathy. "I'm a kid. I shouldn't be working this much."

"Did you expect the life of a princess?" Carlita's cruel tone cut like a serrated knife. "Servants waiting on you hand and fin."

"Wwwwhat?"

"Nothing." Bill glared at his wife. Then, he angled

his greying head at me. "There are people waiting to see you. You can't disappoint them."

"Why not? Everyone always disappoints me." Like the time I'd sprained my arm and they'd forced me to perform. Or when I'd wanted to go to school so I could be a normal kid and they'd refused. Or when I'd tried to make friends with the other circus kids and been rejected.

"The show must go on." Bill's scraggly voice scratched the mantra I'd heard from the time I was a toddler.

I couldn't take it anymore. So I'd left. Packed up the few things that were mine and slipped out after the show at the Poseidon Family Circus. My final show.

No one would make me perform like a trained seal again.

No one would shove me on stage when I was tired or ill or injured.

No one would make me fake a smile when I wanted to cry.

Ever.

Chase put his arm around my shoulders bringing me back to the present. "I'm sorry."

"I'm not." Best thing I'd done in my entire life. My only regret is that I hadn't done it sooner. If only I'd known.

"Do they know you're living in a tent?"

"They wouldn't care." I'd lived in a tent with them. Under the "Big Top" or in a trailer right beside it.

I barked a harsh laugh at the insanity of my circumstances. From star of the show to custodian of the carnival. From the big top to a tiny tent. Not only had I demoted myself in jobs but in living conditions.

My harsh laughter changed to real laughter. I didn't

care about the job or the tent. All I cared about was living my life the way I wanted. Living free.

"Why is that funny?" Chase gave me a curious half-smile, where one side of his mouth tilted up.

I shrugged and shook my head, not ready to give him an answer. And never would be. Some things I'd never share.

He took off his blue sweatshirt and held it out. "Keep mine until we find yours."

I started to shake my head. "I can't."

"Please. I want you to have it."

My muscles stiffened. "I'm not a charity case." My voice sounded hard. I didn't want him feeling sorry for me.

He grabbed hold of my chin and held it still. "I want you to have it." He lowered his mouth.

His soft, full lips caressed mine. Tingles of electricity spread through me and my insides heated. Fireworks flared behind my closed eyelids. I didn't feel like a charity case now.

He wanted to kiss me. And I wanted to kiss him back. My mouth molded to his and I leaned against his solid frame.

I should be running fast and far. What Chase wanted, I couldn't give. But his lips were persuasive. So I responded.

Responded by showing him how I felt deep inside. Even though I could never tell him. Knowing this couldn't last.

He lifted his head and stared. "Now I can always keep you warm, even when I'm not by your side."

Chapter Six
Bird Bombardment

The next day, while my body handled menial chores like emptying garbage canisters, my emotions raced like the rollercoaster screaming past. One minute I was angry, then defensive, then hysterical, then awed-out by Chase. Not only by the gift of his sweatshirt but by his words.

Staying away from him would be so much easier if he was mean or arrogant or a complete jerk.

"Hey." Chase stopped his golf cart by the garbage can I emptied.

Or if we didn't work together.

"Hi." I shoved the new garbage bag in and put the lid back on, trying to control the awful stench. And the feeling that I might stink, too.

"I talked to Cuda this morning about the other disturbances he's seen lately. Rogue waves, a shift in currents, sea lions gathering in large groups, even a couple of other whirlpools."

"Like what happened the other night?" I tied the full bag of garbage.

"Not nearly as large." Chase took the bag from my hand and set it on the back of his cart. "Hop in and I'll give you a ride to the dumpster so we can talk."

"Okay." I wanted to talk with Chase, but I didn't want to be seen getting help from a manager. A few of the other employees already gave me funny looks. The last thing I needed was for them to think I was kissing up to one of the managers.

I grimaced. I guess technically I had kissed Chase. But none of the employees knew that.

Chase slowed the golf cart in front of the shooting arcade. A big guy dressed all in black, turned around with the rifle in his hand. Joe.

He lifted the rifle and aimed at me, exaggerating his trigger finger motion.

My body stiffened expecting to be shot. Which was silly because those guns shot lasers, not real bullets. Plus, why would Joe want to hurt me? I might've embarrassed him in front of his friends, but he was acting like an idiot.

I shook off my thoughts on Joe, and switched back to the topic with Chase. "What else did your friend Cuda say?"

"Not much. He sort of clammed up." Chase laughed. "The guy takes caring for the ocean to an extreme. Like the ocean has its secrets and he knows them all."

"Nothing wrong with caring about the environment."

"I agree, but he's ultra-serious." Chase braked in front of the large dumpster beside the main office. "Anyhow, I've emailed a couple of biology and environmental science professors at the local university about the situation."

The office doors opened. Mrs. Fowler and Officer Clayton walked out. I didn't want to be seen by either of them, so I scrunched down in the golf cart.

"Miss Seidon." Officer Clayton gave me a half-wave, half-come-here motion. "I wanted to talk to you. Is now a good time?" Nice, courteous. Was it all a façade?

Licking my lips, I considered Mrs. Fowler and Clayton. "I'm working right now."

He tossed Mrs. Fowler a sharp look.

"We should be helpful to the police." Mrs. Fowler put a hand to her throat and played with the pearls hanging there. "You may speak with him now."

"I'll take care of the garbage," Chase volunteered.

So not helping Chase. I needed work for an excuse not to talk to the cop.

"O-okay." I got out and walked toward the office.

"Why don't we talk out here." Clayton dismissed Mrs. Fowler, who after one uncertain glance headed back inside.

Chase drove a few feet to the dumpster and killed the engine. He fiddled with the ignition.

"Can I call you Pearl?" Officer Clayton asked.

"Sure." I was much more comfortable with the name I'd answered to my entire life.

"Call me Frank," he said in an I-want-to-be-your-friend tone.

I jiggled back and forth on my feet. I didn't want to be on a first name basis with him. "Uh, okay."

"You haven't worked at the Boardwalk long, have you, Pearl?"

"No." Glancing anywhere but at Officer Clayton, I watched Chase lift the bag ever-so-slowly out of the cart and set it on the ground.

"Where'd you work before?"

"A campground."

"Do you like camping?" Officer Clayton's gentle tone sounded conversational.

"Sure." *Not as a necessity though.*

"How long have you lived in California?" Each question seemed innocent but added together, he sounded like he was building a case. Against me.

The bluck in my brain pounded as if the mallet from the Ring the Bell game hit me upside the head. If this was a friendly chat, I shouldn't answer. I wasn't under oath. "Why?"

"I couldn't find any records of your existence." The blank expression on his face meant he had an ulterior motive.

Bill had used this expression a lot. He pretended not to know about Carlita's demands and shouting.

Scrambling for the possible reason he was asking the questions, I had to think on my feet. "That's a good thing." I forced a stiff smile. "It means I don't have a record."

"No driver's license."

"I don't drive."

"No social security number."

"My parents never applied."

"No current or last address."

A loud rushing sound filled my ears. My tummy twisted and plunged. "What's this really about?"

I had to control myself, not show my fear. Fear that he'd figured out my history. Cocking my hip, I placed a hand on it and stared at the cop. "I've done nothing illegal."

Unless, of course, you count lying to a cop.

"It's like you don't exist."

"I'm standing right here. Talking to you." I wished I

wasn't. Wished the circus magician could make me disappear.

"Your Boardwalk application says you're eighteen."

"Yes." That's what the application says.

"Where do your parents live?"

"Why does it matter, *Frank*?" I used his name, adult to adult, but the sass at the end was all teen angst.

His friendly expression morphed into one of authority. His lips firmed. His gaze drilled into mine. "It's unusual for an eighteen-year-old to be completely off the grid."

***

"You okay?" Chase put his arm around me.

I stood in silence as Officer Clayton got in his car and drove away. I normally would've had a reaction to Chase's touch, but my entire body stiffened like a surfboard totally water logged. I'd distracted the cop for now, but how long before he figured me out? Figured my situation out?

"Yeah." Too shocked, I couldn't decide whether I loved or hated that Chase cared.

My first thought was to pack up and run. That's what I did best. When Clayton realized I'd lied on my Boardwalk application, he'd be back. He'd have more questions. He might even contact Bill and Carlita.

"Why were you so antagonistic?" Chase *had* been eavesdropping.

Chase was getting too close. If, no *when*, I had to run, I'd leave him behind. Not tell him when I was leaving or where I was going. Our whatever-type-of-relationship would be over.

I pulled my shoulders back and let my mask fall into place. The façade didn't seem to fit. "Because that's who

I am."

"No, you're not." He dropped his arm and stepped in front of me blocking the light from the sun, blocking the warmth. "It's who you pretend to be. You pretend to act so hard, but not only did you care enough to save Brandon but the sea otter, too. You're so independent, and there's nothing wrong with that, but I can see you're lonely."

I jerked my head up trying to decipher how much of that speech he believed. His glare pierced into my soul. Insecurities fumbled in my chest. Defensiveness was my shield. It kept people from seeing the real me. I couldn't let people guess. I couldn't let Chase guess right.

"I am pretending." Pausing, I let the silence add weight to my words. I steeled my nerves. I didn't have a choice. My decision was best for both of us. "I'm pretending to actually like you."

Chase staggered back. His lips narrowed so thin they looked like cracks on the sidewalk. His blue eyes became slits of frozen ice. "Then you're an excellent actress. Because I believed you were vulnerable and caring."

"You're wrong on all counts." If Chase saw the real me, he'd discover all my lies and half-truths. I hid my trembling lips behind a smile. The rasping from my chest I used to put force in my voice. "Except for the actress part."

Because I was putting on the show of my life.

Although I hoped he believed the acting had been when I'd been with him, when I'd shared the information at the campground, when he kissed me.

I didn't need to worry about that happening again. The coldness in his glance told me how angry he was. He believed I'd used him.

"Then, I guess I don't need to worry about you anymore." His tone tried to convey nonchalance.

I wasn't sure I believed it. But his next sentence slashed through my heart.

"Cold-blooded actors do well in Southern California."

* * *

After my long and lonely shift was over, I headed back to the campground, where I found Mr. Plankson prowling around my tent. I didn't like his questions from the other day, and I hated his inquisitiveness. "Why are you snooping around?"

He stood in front of the tent opening with an air of innocence that I didn't believe. "Looking for you."

The zipper pull swung back and forth. There was no breeze.

"Inside my tent?"

"Just knocked on the canvas." He held up a fist like that was evidence. "You've been gone since this morning."

"I was working."

"Where?" Plankson didn't even fake concern like Officer Clayton. Who did Plankson think he was? My father?

"Boardwalk." I answered to end the conversation.. "How do you think I paid for your bribe."

"About that." Plankson grabbed a strand of his longish, distinctive-grey hair and twisted it around his middle finger. He looked like a well-aged rock star. "Since I'm breaking the rules for you, you're going to have to do a few things for me."

I didn't like the way that sounded. "I paid you."

"Forty bucks?" His laugh warbled. "That's not

enough to cover my cigarettes."

I'd never seen the man smoke.

I placed my hands on my hips and tried to sound tough even though my knees shook. He was a creepy old man and I was alone. Maybe I should've kept Chase around a little longer. As a friend. "What do you want?"

"Help around the camp." His smile showed even white teeth but there was nothing friendly on his face. In fact, the grin seemed sinister. "I need you to pick up litter by the rocks at the edge of the cove this evening."

"But—"

"You want to stay?" He picked up a metal stick with a sharp end and pointed it at me. "Pick up garbage."

I yanked the stick out of his hand. He had me. If I wanted to stay at the campground for a little while longer, I'd have to do what he wants. "This is dirty blackmail."

Dirty in several ways.

***

I'm going to be known as garbage-girl. Stabbing a yellow hamburger wrapper, I shoved the paper in the plastic bag I carried. Grit clung to me like a second skin. Beer bottles and dirty diapers littered the rocks near the cliffs, either carried by the current or partying people.

The phenomenal view would definitely be a draw. The rocks jutted out at the end of the small cove surrounded by water on all three sides. You could see for miles.

But it was a dangerous spot for stupid people doing stupid things. I'd slipped several times on my climb to this point.

The waves crashed close to where I stood. Spray showered me. I licked the sea water off my lips tasting its saltiness. While I'd love to jump in the ocean, diving at this spot would be idiotic.

Stabbing a plastic water bottle, my feet slipped on the slick rocks again. I almost lost my balance. Now I understood why Plankson didn't want to do this job—it's dirty and dangerous.

The sun rode low in the sky. A group of seagulls gathered on a nearby ledge. There must be hundreds. The birds cawed arguing with each other. Their beady eyes watched me tread from rock to rock, careful where I put my feet. The birds should be happy, not suspicious of my actions.

Balancing on a rock near the edge, I poked my stick at a crushed Styrofoam container. Waves washed over the garbage and pushed it around the small pool formed by the rocks. I jabbed again.

A thunderous sound, louder than the waves, caught my attention. I jerked my head up. The blue sky had turned white and grey from the seagulls taking flight at the exact same time. Their wings flapped and flapped, covering my view of the sky. They flew toward me.

No, correct that. They flew at me.

I ducked covering my head, fearing their sharp claws. Hunching my shoulders, I tried to become tiny. My exposed skin seemed to screech waiting for the bird attack. Dropping the stick and garbage bag, I hunkered down.

The crazy birds swooped. They were like a bird battalion attacking their target.

And their target was me.

My heart pounded faster than their flapping wings. Wings and webbed feet fluttered hard at my head, my face, my shoulders. Bright orange beaks pecked at my arms.

"Get away." I swatted with my hands at the birds, trying to scare them. My futile attempts did nothing.

The sharp points of their beaks tore at my skin. Sharp pain pulsed from the open wounds. The birds attacked in tandem as if they'd planned the entire thing.

I shifted my feet to get lower. My foot slipped and I tumbled. My stomach tumbled, too. Reaching out, I tried to grab hold of a rock but a seagull nipped at my fingers. Pain pulsed in my hand. I released the rock...

And fell.

Off the jagged edge.

Into the churning water.

Chapter Seven
Intended Interference

A wave crashed and shoved me against the jagged rocks beneath the surface. I covered my face with my arms. My body scratched on the sharp rock edges. Pain stung my arms and legs. I uncovered my face and took note of deep gouges on my skin. Blood—my blood—trailed into the water.

A second wave crashed into me. Before being sliced again, I dove deep. The waves were less strong further down. The force wouldn't be as powerful. Soft algae clung to the rocks and cliff bottoms cushioning the blow against my body. Kelp wiggled with the waves creating a natural break, and an underwater forest.

Using my strength, I swam away from the rocks toward the sandy bottom staying far down from the surface, and the birds.

Spiky anemone jutted out between crevices. A school of silver fish darted past. A group of mussels clustered together on the bottom.

The view below fascinated. It was like another world.

A world where I belonged, even though the fish probably didn't think so. The current caressed my skin. The warmth enveloped me.

All my fears about the fall and my injuries floated away. I spun around and the water circled with me. I made my own mini-friendly whirlpool. Nothing like the other night. Fish and bubbles floated around. Sand twirled from the bottom. Strands of grey mixed with the green and brown seaweed. Rocks swung by my kaleidoscope of underwater colors. My gaze caught on something in the blurry kelp forest. An oval-shaped, pale something.

A face.

A human face.

I stopped spinning and turned in the direction of the kelp and stared. Nothing was there. I thought I saw someone. Something.

I shivered.

Probably nothing. Just my spun-out imagination.

Still, I needed to inspect the area. A bit dizzy, I kicked my feet and headed to where the seaweed grew from the bottom like upside down streamers at a birthday party. I parted the strands and peaked inside to satisfy my curiosity.

It was darker under the seaweed where the sun doesn't penetrate the growth of kelp. The green and brown fronds crisscrossed and tangled with the current. It was like entering a jungle. Good thing I knew there were no lions, or tigers, or bears.

Of course, there could be sharks.

Or whatever else I'd seen.

But I found nothing. Exiting the kelp forest, I gave up my search and swam closer to the surface. The face had probably been a rock cut and worn over the years. Or a large fish. Not a person at all.

A plunging sound disturbed the peacefulness of the water. The shadow of a small boat and an anchor sinking to the bottom of the ocean nearby. A guy dove from the boat and into the water.

Chase.

I recognized him by his muscular legs, his taut abs, his wavy hair, and his expression of fear and determination on his face.

Letting the seaweed float back in place, I swam to him. Better for me to find him then for him to find me.

He took hold of my arm and pulled me into a loose hug. My chest tightened from the contact and my heart stirred. With the way we'd left things he shouldn't want to come near me.

Together we surfaced, Chase believing he'd rescued me.

Breathing heavily, he grabbed hold of the edge of the rowboat. "I can't believe you're all right." His other arm tightened around me. "I saw you fall."

"You did?" *Uh oh.*

He huffed out another breath. "I saw you on the rocks and the birds attacked and then you went off. You never resurfaced. I thought you were dead."

I glanced around racking my brain for a way to explain. For a normal person, I'd been under the water way too long. Plus, the fall had been nasty, possibly not survivable. "Let's get out of the water."

"I'm an idiot." He shook his head and drips fell from his hair. He rolled his eyes. "You're probably hurt, exhausted, and cold. And here I am having a conversation."

I wasn't any of those things, but I couldn't tell him.

"Hold onto the boat. I'll get on board first and then pull you up." He let go of me making sure I held on tight. Then, using his arms, he lifted himself and swung his legs over the edge of the row boat. "Now you."

He leaned over and put his arms out. I lifted myself, and he seized my waist and carried me up and into the boat like I was precious. A feeling I'd never had before. I'd been used, abused and ignored for as long as I remembered. I wanted to act helpless so he'd continue to care, and then I wanted to kick myself for pretending to be needy.

"Did you hurt yourself?" He scanned my body lighting a small fire inside. "A few of those scratches seem deep." He probed my head with a light touch. "Did you bump your head? Lose consciousness?"

I was tempted to say yes so he'd continue touching me. "No."

"Does anything hurt?"

The cuts might burn later, but right now they felt fine. "No."

"You're probably dazed. Lack of oxygen, possibly hypothermia. Relax and I'll row to shore." He sat down on the center bench, took hold of the oars and rowed. "I don't even have a towel to give you."

I wasn't cold or in shock. Unless you count my shock at Chase's rescue. I'd been so mean before. "I-I didn't mean what I said this morning. About acting."

He stroked with determination and speed, the muscles in his forearms bulging with the effort. His mouth gritted together focusing on his task of making sure I didn't faint or die. "I realize that now."

I wasn't good at apologizing but Chase understood.

91

No need to actually say sorry. My shoulders relaxed at the idea of not having to say the words.

Searching the rocks where I fell, I spotted the garbage bag stuck between two sharp points. The seagulls were gone.

What had set the birds off? Maybe I'd encroached on their territory. Maybe they were nesting. Maybe they just didn't like me. Another abnormality I'd need to ponder.

When we reached the surf, Chase jumped out and pulled the boat to shore. He acted like my champion and guard. The wall around my heart, the one I'd tried to rebuild, crumbled at his thoughtfulness. Not even my circus parents cared like this. They hadn't cared at all.

Never a gentle touch. Never a hug. Never an encouraging word.

Instead I heard, "Practice again." "Make it perfect." "Stay underwater longer or you won't get dinner tonight."

They'd never showed love. I bit my quivering bottom lip. Maybe because my circus parents weren't my real parents at all. They kept a million secrets from me, controlled me, and lied to me.

Mr. Plankson entered the surf and helped Chase pull in the dinghy. The binoculars he wore around his neck got caught on the oar. "What the heck were you doing stealing my boat?"

"If I stole it, I wouldn't be returning it." Chase yanked on the rope. "It was an emergency. Pearl was drowning."

I sat straighter and glared at Plankson. "I fell off the rocks." The rocks he'd sent me to clean.

"Should've asked permission." Plankson's gruff voice sawed on my nerves.

"No time. She was underwater forever. I thought she'd drowned."

Plankson examined me. "How long?"

I waved my trembling hand in a fake careless move. The last thing I wanted was Plankson getting suspicious. "Not long at all. Just seemed like forever."

"It took me at least five minutes to row out—"

"Chase." I grabbed my arm in pretend pain. "My arm hurts."

"We need to get you to emergency." Concern immediately lit his face. He splashed over and held out his hand. "Can you walk?"

I wanted to shut him up, not create a new problem. I didn't like the way Plankson watched me, or the way he'd been snooping around my tent. "I don't need a doctor. The scratches only sting."

"I've got antiseptic in my office." Plankson's offer to help raised my suspicion higher. Did he feel an ounce of concern for my accident?

Chase took my arm and helped me walk up the path from the beach, following Plankson. "Are you sure about the doctor? You almost drowned."

"Shh." My gaze drifted to Plankson's back. I swung my head back and forth. "Not now. We'll talk when we're alone." My terse toned tried to convey the urgency.

"But?"

"Please, Chase." I gave him a pleading look. "Later."

When we reached the office, Chase settled me on a lawn chair on the porch while Plankson went inside. He came out with antiseptic and bandages and handed them to Chase. Then Plankson locked the door, and mumbled something about breathing and bleeding, before walking away.

The man's actions contradicted. One minute angry for stealing his boat, the next helpful. He'd sent me out on those rocks. Unease shivered across my mind. Something didn't add up.

Chase kneeled beside me, his dark head bent over my left leg. I wanted to run my fingers through his wet hair. Wanted to wipe away the worry he'd had. About me. Wanted to tell him that there'd been no need to risk himself to save me. I wasn't going to drown.

"This is going to sting." He poured antiseptic on one of the larger cuts.

I winced.

"Did that hurt?" His eyes were the deepest blue I'd ever seen, out-coloring the sky and the ocean.

Honest eyes. Chase had no hidden secrets or agenda.

Unlike me. I swallowed the knot in my throat, almost choking on my frequent lies. "No, but it should hurt more. I deserve it after what I said about pretending to like you."

He continued to clean my wounds, one cut at a time. Every spot he touched, my skin tingled. "No one deserves to get smashed against the rocks."

I skimmed his shoulder with my fingers, unsure of his reaction. Sure, he thought he'd saved me, but any decent guy would do that even to a girl they hated. "I shouldn't have been so mean. Especially to you."

The one person in my life who'd been nice with no ulterior motive. Who liked me for who I am, not what I could give him. Who cared about my well being.

His hands stilled and he shot me a confident-and-a-bit-cocky smile. "Spend tomorrow with me. There's a cool beach called Shell Cove where a lot of the locals hang out. I'd love to show you."

My shoulders sagged wanting to go, knowing I shouldn't. At least I had a real excuse. "I've got to work."

"Only in the morning." He finished with the first leg and started on my left arm. "We can leave after your shift," he paused. "Then again, with the way water disasters follow you..."

"They don't follow me." Well, they had but he didn't know about the incident in Nebraska or the time I saved a man from the circus.

"First you rescue that boy. Then, you almost drown. Twice." Chase held up two fingers. "Water emergencies stalk you."

"I love water, especially the ocean." Although, since moving to Mermaid Beach the scary incidents had multiplied.

Was it me or coincidence? Cuda had said strange things were happening even before I arrived on Mermaid Beach. Still, I had to consider the danger.

"The water sure doesn't love you."

Chase was wrong. The ocean and I had an affinity in a way I couldn't explain. The waves welcomed me. The salty water felt like silk against my skin. The underwater scenery was like a familiar tapestry.

Similar to the feeling I have with Chase. Holding my breath, I beheld his familiar features. His strong and serious face. His sparkling eyes. His tug-at-my-heart smile.

Chase got me, or at least the part I shared with him. Somehow he understood when I put on a fake and angry face for the world. He just doesn't know how much I have to hide.

"I'm drawn to the water." Like I'm drawn to Chase.

"And there's a good reason."

Was I about to reveal to Chase my biggest secret of all?

Chapter Eight
Tricky Truth

"**A**nd what reason is that?" Chase finished cleaning my arm and scooted over to the other side. "You have a death wish?"

Like standing on the edge of the circus tank waiting for the spotlight to find me, I debated. "I wouldn't have drowned." I sucked in a breath.

Indecision swayed back and forth in my tummy like seaweed in a wave. He wanted to be a reporter. He was looking for a big story. I could become that story.

"I wouldn't have drowned because..."

Chase understood me, the real me, not the façade I put on for everyone else. He'd shown kindness and humor and strength of character. He cared about me, as a person.

"Because?" He angled his head. One of his eyebrows rose in a question mark. A slight smirk lifted his lips.

My shoulders sagged. My weary bones wanted to collapse. I was so tired of keeping secrets, tired of hiding the real me, tired of being alone. Taking a deep breath, I lifted my shoulders.

"I wouldn't have drowned because I can breathe underwater," I blurted out the words fast and then held my breath waiting for a response.

I expected incredulity, or laughter but I was greeted with silence.

My mind swirled. "Did you hear me?"

"Yeah, I heard you." He patted the cut on my leg harder. "I'm trying to figure out why you think you need to lie."

"I'm not lying." I crossed my arms and pain tore through my skin, not from the scratches. I'd worried about him exposing my secret and instead I should've worried about him believing. "Even you said I was under water for a long time."

"And you said it wasn't that long." He screwed the antiseptic cap back on and set the bottle on the ground with a thud.

"I didn't want Plankson to hear. I don't want anyone to know." My voice rose higher. I'd been so worried about Chase writing a story, I hadn't even thought that I'd have to convince him I spoke the truth.

"Why tell me then?"

I swallowed again, all my thoughts and feelings balling up in my throat. I wasn't even sure I knew how I felt about Chase and I'd already taken a huge risk. My heart thundered like waves at high tide pounding the shore. "Because..."

"Because?" His lips tilted up at our replay of words.

"Because I feel like we have a connection." A compromise, not the full truth. I liked Chase and our connection was strong. Stronger than anything I'd experienced before. "Was I wrong?"

Chase tugged on my hand, unfolding my arms, making a physical connection. "There's definitely something." His voice rasped. "But I don't like lies."

Then, he probably wouldn't like the real me. I've lied from the first time we met. Lied about my age, where I'd lived, my previous life.

"I'm not lying." *This time.*

"What you're saying is impossible." His gaze dulled by disbelief. "Maybe you hit your head harder than you think." His concern was an insult.

I dropped his hand and gripped the arms of the chair, ready to get up. Each accusation shot through me like a sharp arrow. I'd finally trusted someone enough to tell the truth and he didn't believe me. Didn't trust me enough to believe me. He must think I was totally insane.

"I'll prove it."

"No." He pushed me back down into the chair with a gentle touch. "You're hurt." He thought I was nuts or hit my head hard.

I couldn't get angry because he cared. That's why I'd confessed in the first place. But I couldn't let him believe I was lying or crazy. "I'll prove it tomorrow at Shell Cove."

***

"You ready?" I asked Chase.

We both stood waist deep in the water off Shell Cove the following afternoon.

"You don't need to do this." Chase had tried to talk me out of the test the entire drive. Said he didn't need proof, said he liked me no matter what, which I interpreted as whether I was nuts or not. Which made me even more determined to show him the truth.

I was glad he hadn't been scared away by my

confession. Other people, people in my past, had reacted funny when they discovered my abilities. Chase had proven his integrity, unlike Aunty Eva.

My mood disintegrated like crushed shells. Aunty Eva had been like an angel, appearing one day out of the blue when I was six. She'd greeted me with a hug, something I didn't remember ever receiving from her sister, Carlita.

Aunty Eva had moved into my small bedroom and we'd stay up late talking and laughing. She seemed to actually like me, not just put up with me. She listened to me, unlike her sister. I could tell Aunty Eva anything.

After a few weeks, we were closer than I would ever be with Carlita. So, I told Eva about my abilities.

"You're such a silly little girl. Dreaming of being a real mermaid." Eva had laughed at my claim.

"I'll show you." And I did.

I dove in the tank and stayed under for twenty minutes. I asked her to lift a five-hundred pound weight, which she couldn't, and then I lifted the weight while in the water.

Her face had turned white and she'd mumbled an excuse about needing to talk to Carlita. Dripping with water, I followed behind and listened at the open trailer window.

Aunty Eva had spoken in high rushed tones, "With those weird abilities we could take Pearl to Las Vegas or Hollywood."

"Don't you think I've thought of that," Carlita screeched back.

"We could make millions." Aunty Eva's voice quivered.

"People would assume we tricked them if she was on

television or a big production. They wouldn't believe it was unique." Carlita's answer sounded stilted, like she was lying.

"We could put Pearl on one of those reality shows, where they follow her around." Aunty Eva thought I was a freak. My limbs trembled. She believed I was different in a weird way. "I could be her agent. We'd make bucks."

"No." Carlita stood firm. "I won't expose her like that."

At the time, I thought that maybe Carlita did care about me and my happiness. But now I understood the reason. She was afraid the authorities would discover her deception. Uncover the truth. Like I had.

Chase splashed me with water. "Let's forget about this."

"No. I want to show you." I didn't repeat the words *I can breathe underwater* for fear he'd bolt.

Not only did I want to prove to him I hadn't lied but I wanted to share this part of me hoping it would create a special bond. A tighter connection. Maybe I was being stupid, but I had to know how he'd react, before getting closer.

I handed him an old circus stopwatch. He lay on his stomach on the floaty air mattress, positioned the facemask on his face and stuck the snorkel in his mouth, then he gave me the thumbs up sign, even as he shook his head.

He still didn't believe me. Thought this experiment was a waste of time.

We submerged and Chase clicked on the watch. I crossed my legs and sat on the sandy bottom. He floated on the surface so the breathing tube stayed out of the water and watched.

Faking a smile, I waved counting down the minutes in my head. Counting down to the beginning of our new relationship. Or the end.

He still might not believe me. He might think it was a trick. He might want me to prove my ability over and over and over again.

He could react like Aunty Eva. He could want to take advantage of me. He could think I was a freak.

I gritted my teeth together. Too late now. I'd made my decision. We were here. And soon I'd know his reaction.

There were always going to be people, like Aunty Eva, who learned about my abilities and believed I was strange. And maybe I was. But this is who I am, this is me. And if I was going to ever get close to Chase, I'd have to show him the real me. Good and bad. Freaky and un-freaky.

I scooped my hands into the sand and let the grains filter through my fingers. A portion of a nautilus shell caught in my palm.

The shell reminded me of one the circus owners possessed. As a child I'd been fascinated by the dazzling colors coming from inside that shell. I'd never seen anything like it. Their nautilus glowed and I'd climbed on the arm of the couch to reach for it.

When I picked up the shell warmth filled my two hands and my heart. I swore I heard waves slamming the shore and music tickling my eardrums.

"What're you doing?" Carlita had shouted from the doorway.

I'd lost my balance and tumbled to the floor, scraping my elbow and bruising my knee. She hadn't cared.

Instead, she'd snatched the shell away. "Don't ever touch this again."

Not that she'd given me the opportunity because she hid the shell and I'd never found it.

Chase tapped on the stopwatch bringing me out of my memories. The hands indicated five minutes had passed. I put up my hand and spread my fingers indicating five more.

He tapped the watch again.

I folded my arms in a stubborn pose and nodded. Then, I pointed at my chest and said, "I'm fine." Not that he could hear me, but he should be able to read my lips.

In the mask, his eyes sharpened. The lines around his mouth tightened as if he bit on the snorkel too hard. He reached out and grabbed my arm and pulled, trying to get me to come up.

Again, I shook my head. I wanted to prove without a doubt my abilities. I'd finally decided to share my secrets, share myself, and I wanted him to believe me. Believe in me.

Every few seconds his gaze traveled from the stopwatch to me, making sure I was all right. Another five minutes passed. He tapped on the watch again and held out his hand which had pruned in the water. I put my smooth hand in his letting him pull me to the top.

He dropped my hand, took off the snorkel and mask, then leaned his elbows on the mattress. Red lines circled his forehead from the pressure. His expression was unreadable.

I hung onto the end of the mattress, gripping the plastic between tight fingers. Holding my breath like I was under water, I waited for him to say something. Anything. With each silent second, dread pooled in my tummy like an anchor ready to sink.

Chase rubbed the red grooves. "I. Can't. Believe. It."

"You can't?" My chin dipped. "I'll stay under longer."

If nothing else, no matter what his ultimate reaction, I wanted him to believe me. I wasn't going to run away from who I was any longer.

"No. That's okay."

"I didn't fake it."

"Yeah, I know. No possible way for you to fake that. Especially when you opened your mouth to talk." He slid his hand around my neck and reached under my hair line.

At least he wasn't afraid to touch me. Unlike others.

A shiver skated across my neck. I wanted to lean in to his gentle touch. Until I realized he was searching for a breathing device.

"What's your secret?"

A blackness overwhelmed me. My thoughts turned dark. He thought I was a liar and a cheat. "I showed you my secret. I can breathe underwater."

"But how'd you do the trick? No one can hold their breath that long." A wave knocked him on the side of the head, kind of like I wanted to.

"I wasn't holding my breath. Did you see me smile?" I fake-grinned showing all my teeth. A real smile was impossible at the moment. "It wasn't a trick."

"But I don't understand-"

"Let's go on shore." I hoped some of his shock would wear off once he processed what I showed him. He held the proof in his hand—the stopwatch. Plus, he'd seen everything firsthand.

After swimming back to the beach, we sat down on the blanket we'd laid out when we arrived. I handed him a towel and then used another to dry off. Like I was on trial, my skin felt sensitive to each rub of the terrycloth. The air between us charged with silence.

"How did you do it?" Finally, the questions started again. He still thought it was a trick.

"I don't know. I've been able to breathe underwater for forever." Maybe the more times I said it, the easier it would sink in for him.

"Why can you do it?" His voice whispered each question like he was afraid to speak out loud.

"Genetic deficiency?" I only half-joked. I didn't know why I could breathe underwater, had never questioned it until I turned sixteen.

Please don't say I'm a freak. Please don't say I'm a freak.

"Who else knows about this?"

"Just the cir...my parents." The last word tripped off my tongue. I might've called them my parents for sixteen years, but now I knew differently. Yet, I couldn't tell Chase about the circus. The humiliation I'd endured my entire life, how I'd been so docile to Bill and Carlita's demands, how I'd been on display.

"Where else can you breathe besides the ocean?" His eyes held a semi-crazy gleam. His lips moved in a disjointed pattern. "The pool, the bathtub, where?"

Remembering reading about how journalists always ask five questions relating to who, what, where, how and why, I let out a long, slow breath. I set myself up to be questioned, reporter or not. I braced for the onslaught. "Anywhere I want."

"What're you going to do about it?"

My stomach squeezed tight. Doubts about showing Chase collided inside me. "What are *you* going to do about it?"

"What do you mean?" Confusion worried his face. From my one question or all my answers?

"Are you going to tell anyone?" I twisted the towel in my hands, wringing the cloth like I wanted to wring his neck if he shared my secret. "Write me up for that big story of yours?"

"No." He leaned forward examining my face, like I was a unique specimen. "Do you want me to? You'd be famous."

"So would you." Almost as famous, or infamous, as me. I smushed my mouth and narrowed my glance, shooting daggers at him. I needed to tell him what I wanted. "I don't want anyone to know."

"Why?" His voice filled with awe and his ever-present curiosity. "You'd get on the national news, appear on television, maybe meet the President."

"I'd be stared at, disbelieved, thought of like a freak." My throat burned and my voice sounded raw. Being in the spotlight in the circus had been terrible, having the entire world focused on me would be unbearable. "Are you going to tell anyone?"

"Not if you don't want me to."

"Even if you could break a big news story?" I wanted to believe him, that's why I'd told him in the first place, but he wanted to be a reporter.

His faced appeared thoughtful. He rubbed his knuckles against my arm. The automatic shivers that usually accompanied his touch were absent.

"Not if it would hurt you." His tone softened. "I wouldn't do anything to hurt you."

"Really?" I so wanted to believe him.

But it was hard when he'd only known me a few

days, while my parents had known me *almost* my entire life and they didn't seem to care about my emotional or physical pain.

"Really." He shifted next to me and put his arm around my shoulders. "I care about you. If you don't want anyone else to know about your amazing ability then I won't tell. I'm honored you told me." He bent toward me and his lips touched mine.

***

I was so right to tell Chase.

Minutes later, floating on the small air mattress beside him, our nearly-naked bodies touching in several spots, I relived our long, glorious kiss.

Chase was the best kisser ever. Okay, he was my only kisser. But our secret, our pact, our connection had deepened, just like the kiss. Tingles cruised up my spine remembering his gentle lips on mine. And I couldn't wait to kiss him again.

The quiet waves rocked. Our feet and arms dangled in the water. Lying on the small raft, only our middles supported by the plastic pillow, we drifted in companionable silence.

I'd finally gotten the courage to share myself, the real me, and it had paid off in several ways. Chase believed me, he'd promised to keep my secret, and this demonstrated how much he cared.

I felt like I was floating, which I was.

Chase splashed me with water. "I should've brought the snorkel and mask out. There's a lot of fish swimming right here."

"I need a drink anyhow. Do you want me to get it?"

"You don't mind? I don't want to lose this spot."

"No problem. I'll be back in a minute." Possibly less.

I hadn't told him about my swimming speed. I'd save that for another day.

I pushed off the floating mattress and swam underwater until I reached the shallows. Getting to my feet, a shadow fell over me.

"If it isn't janitor-girl."

The brightness of my day dimmed. I peered at the cause of the shadow. Joe from the railing incident towered above. He wore black shorts and the same black hoodie. A bit hot for the beach.

"Cops questioned me twice about that stupid kid falling into the lagoon." His hard voice threatened.

I took a step back in the wet sand. "Oh?"

A few of Joe's buddies circled closer, like sharks going after fresh meat. Strange green splotches stained their clothes like an unknown disease. Water lapped at their untied shoes but they didn't seem to care.

"You put that cop Clayton up to it." Joe moved his arms from behind his back.

A gun with a long, narrow barrel pointed at my chest. A tube ran from in front of the trigger to the hand base. I'd never seen a gun like that before. Real or on TV.

"Wh-what's that?" An icy shiver slid down my spine. I didn't want to find out the hard way.

"Sure glad me and my boys were playing in the canyon above this beach." He scrunched up his face and growled. "What did you tell Clayton?"

"I didn't tell him anything." I held my hands up, showing Joe I wouldn't make a fast move.

Which was a lie, because if I could dive in the ocean without a shot being fired I would. The water barely went to my ankles when the waves rushed in. I needed more water.

Joe jerked the gun. "Why'd Clayton ask me about balancing on the rail? I didn't tell him."

The gun looked real, lethal. Black metal, with a scope. A bit on the futuristic side with the tube thing, but I knew nothing about weapons.

My mind scrambled for a way out. Sweat broke out on my upper lip. I glanced at the sky. "Other people might've seen you do it. Why blame me?" I had mentioned it, even accused the boy's fall of being Joe's fault, but I didn't deserve to be shot for it.

"Pearl. What's going on?" Chase's words barely reached me above the noise of the surf.

I glanced back. Chase paddled the air mattress toward shore. My heart tightened at the idea of him coming to my rescue and yet, this was one incident that would be easier to handle alone. If I could only get Joe further in the water.

"Hey, that's the manager-guy from the mini golf course. Maybe he's the snitch."

I sucked in a breath. I didn't want Chase to be blamed for my mistake. "No, I'm sure he didn't-"

"Shut up." Joe stuck the gun against my ribs.

The barrel jammed into my skin. Yep, real metal. I froze in place not wanting to antagonize him further. Chase and the raft were about thirty yards out and I used my body to block the view of the weapon. I didn't want him to become alarmed. He had no way to defend himself working his way closer to shore.

"That orange raft would be a good target," one of Joe's friends egged him on. "Better than those sycamore trees behind the beach."

So they'd been shooting this gun in the park leading to the beach?

"I don't need shooting practice." Joe sounded offended.

"Come on. You missed that squirrel earlier."

Joe had shot at a squirrel. What other innocent animals had he harassed?

"Sink that sucker. Sink that sucker." The other guys joined the cheer.

My heart revved. I didn't know what kind of gun it was but Chase could be shot and it would be my fault.

Joe lifted the scope and straightened his arm. He squinted. The small muscles in his hand tensed. His finger drew back on the trigger.

"Chase, watch out!" I jerked my left elbow and bumped Joe's shoulder trying to throw him off balance.

Pop. Whoosh.

The shot wasn't loud as if air whooshed around it, kind of like a nail gun. I screamed anyhow. My eyes glued open like the lids were stuck, waiting to see if Joe still managed to stay on target even with my elbow jab.

A whitish-round bullet hit the raft and exploded. A blob of green marked the raft.

My knees buckled with relief. "What kind of gun is that?"

"Sink that sucker. Sink that sucker." All the guys cheered again.

"Paintball gun." Joe raised the gun and pointed. "My friends and I like to go paintballing."

At least the gun didn't shoot bullets. "If you shoot paintballs all the time you don't need to shoot at Chase."

"Wimp." Joe's cruel laugh scratched down my spine.

I jumped forward and pushed Joe harder this time. His fight was with me, not Chase.

Joe swatted at me. "Get her." He commanded his

buddies.

The three of them surrounded me, grabbing my arms and waist. Chase stroked harder now, trying to reach the beach faster, to come to my rescue. I kicked and squirmed trying to escape while Joe's friends laughed.

Joe pulled the trigger again.

The pop sounded louder this time. More ominous.

The paintball hit Chase in the head. A green splotch appeared on his temple.

Chase's eyes rolled back into his head. Then he slipped off the raft.

Chapter Nine
Seriously Stingy Sitch

Chase sunk under the waves.

A loud rushing filled my head with all sorts of awful scenarios. My heart stopped, then thumped wildly. The friction from my heart caused a static charge to shoot through me, spurring me into action.

Without thought to Joe and his stupid paintball gun, I jerked out of the other guy's arms, ran through the shallow surf, and dove under the surface. The salt hit my face like annoying gnats, which was unusual, but right now, everything bothered me.

I'd heard stories about how dangerous paint gun pellets could be, how they shouldn't be toys at all, how idiots like Joe should never possess one.

I swam as fast as non-humanly possible and reached Chase as his body hit the sandy bottom. His eyelids were closed and his mouth open. His body lifeless.

I placed my hand over his chest and felt his heart beating in a slow rhythm. He wasn't dead, just unconscious. The pellet must've hit a vulnerable spot on his head.

Relief swelled like the waves. I grabbed him beneath the shoulders and dragged him back to the air mattress. I draped him on his side over the orange plastic, and then cleared his air passages.

He choked up water and then sucked down air. Gasping, he breathed on his own. I ran my hands over his forehead where the green paint marked the spot and felt a large, red bump.

Chase winced and he blinked several times. He was conscious but his gaze appeared cloudy and unfocused.

I scanned the beach. We were still thirty yards out but Joe and his buddies stood on shore watching. The gun was nowhere in sight, but that didn't mean it wasn't hidden behind his back. I didn't want to find out if they meant to cause further trouble.

Chase moaned. Goosebumps appeared on his exposed arms. I had to get him out of the water and going through Joe and his goons would only take more time.

"Can you hang on a bit longer?" Literally, because he hung over the air mattress.

"I can swim on my own." His voice sounded weak, shaky. His eyelids closed again and my worry ratcheted up.

"No. Let me tug you back to shore."

Making sure he was balanced, I gripped the plastic edge of the air mattress and swam further out to sea. With my speed I could round the edge of the cove and land on the next beach in minutes. I wouldn't need to fight Joe and on dry land I could assess Chase's damage.

At the end of the cove, the waves intensified ripping at the raft in my hand. Waves tumbled over my head and smashed onto the rocks near the cliffs. Ocean spray made the top of the raft slick. We were at the furthest point, rounding the tip before entering the next cove.

I loosened my grip and then gathered more plastic in my fist, but didn't slow my pace. The raft scrunched up with the waves and the weight increased. The air mattress was flat, lifeless. All the air had leaked out and I could no longer use it to hold Chase.

Breath whistled out of my lungs. I could handle this. He was breathing, kind of alert. I had super strength. No problem.

"I'm going to hold you like a lifeguard." I turned on my back and positioned Chase above me keeping his head high above water. His skin rubbed against mine and I shivered. He was ice cold.

"I like when you hold me close." His words slurred together.

Either that pellet hit him extra hard or the cold water was affecting his speech.

A high-pitched screeching filled the air. A sea otter circled us, ducking in and out of the waves. I wondered if it was the same sea otter with the green paint.

Green paint.

The same color shot at Chase. Joe must've been the culprit who hurt the sea otter, too.

The little guy next to me screeched again.

"Out of my way. This time I'm trying to get to shore." I put my hand by Chase's nose and mouth. Hot breath blew on my hand. "Not far now Chase. How ya doing?"

"'kay." He sounded weaker.

A second sea otter joined the first. The pair swam in circles so fast it made me dizzy. If they were warning me, I wished they could tell me what was wrong.

Sudden, painful stinging on my leg alerted me to more trouble. I slapped at the pain but didn't feel anything on my calf. Another stinging pain hit my thigh. I rubbed the spot where tiny bumps formed on my skin.

I studied the water and noticed whitish-clear tentacles surrounding us. Lots of them, possibly hundreds.

Jellyfish.

I didn't know if any of the deadly jellies lived in the Pacific. Of course, Chase had mentioned strange occurrences, so who knew what was normal. In my life nothing.

I'd finally shared a large piece of myself with someone who accepted me and then, because of me, he gets injured.

The stinging sensation spread across my skin. I had no way to protect myself or Chase. He'd be a floating feast for the jellies.

The sea otters screeched, clamoring for my attention again. They swam together and...kissed? They were kissing or breathing into each other's mouths. Kind of like CPR, but otters didn't know how to do CPR. Then, they both dove deep under the surface.

They wanted me to go deeper in the water to escape the jellies. But Chase couldn't breathe underwater like me. He'd die if I took him under.

The otters resurfaced. Their tiny heads nodded up and down. They came close and kissed again.

I sucked in a sharp breath. The cold air hit the back of my throat and I coughed. Impossible. The sea otters couldn't know about me, couldn't know what my breath could do. Brandon had been too young to realize, but there had been one other.

My mind went back to a different place, a different

emergency.

About six months before I'd run away, Alonso, the circus's general handyman had been fixing a leak in the largest pool. An older man with a bald head and a long, grizzly beard, he'd been one of the few people who'd been nice to me, who spoke to me like I was a regular kid.

I'd been hiding at the bottom of the pool, my escape when I wanted to think or be left alone by the circus owners, when I heard a large splash. Alonso fell into the pool, hitting bottom. His arms and legs thrashed. He didn't know how to swim, but the pool wasn't that deep and all he needed to do was stand up and he'd be fine.

I glided over to help. It was then I noticed his long beard caught in the cracked plaster of the pool bottom. He was stuck.

Alonso yanked on his beard trying to free himself, but nothing worked. I tugged on his legs but he didn't budge. His entire body was completely submerged. I let go and swam to the surface for help.

No one was around. No tools lay about that I could borrow. If I ran for assistance, it would be too late.

I'm still not sure what made me do what I did. Instinct? A need to help a kindly old man? But I dove back into the pool and squirmed in front of Alonso between him and the wall of the pool. He was unconscious and didn't have much time. I placed my mouth over his and blew into him. It wasn't a kiss, more like blowing up a balloon. Like CPR, without the resuscitation part.

One breath was all it took. Alonso opened his eyes wide. Real wide. Fear flashed. His mouth opened but he didn't choke. He could breathe underwater. Like me.

He held up his hands to ward me off. Like I was going to hurt him. He tried to shrink away from me. The expression of terror on his face made me swim away. This time when I reached the surface, the knife thrower was setting up to practice.

"Help! Alonso is stuck under water."

The knife thrower grabbed one of his knives and dove into the pool. He sliced off Alonso's beard and dragged him to the surface.

Everyone said it was a miracle he didn't drown. The knife thrower was hailed a hero. Alonso never mentioned what had transpired between us.

That night, I saw him get in the pool when he thought no one was around. He went underwater and emerged seconds later with a disgusted look on his face. "Dios. I can't do it."

I guessed he couldn't breathe underwater anymore.

From that day forward, whenever Alonso and I passed each other, he'd cross himself and mutter, like he was saying a prayer. He treated me like I had the plague or was the devil. He never spoke to me again.

Loneliness settled into my chest. Alonso had been kind, but after breathing into him he'd been cold and distant.

Another jelly stung my arm. I plucked it off, still struggling against the waves.

The jellies multiplied around us. We were swimming in a sea of jellyfish. They were so thick I barely saw the surface of the water. My body tensed. At this rate, we'd both be a mass of swollen flesh when we reached the shore. And who knew if infection would set in.

Chase had three jellies stuck to his chest alone. I swatted at them and tried to swim faster. My heart raced with the need to beat this jelly attack and my skin tingled from the stings.

"Chase, are you feeling any stinging?"

He didn't respond. Maybe he was too cold to feel the sting.

Turning him around to face me, I examined his handsome face. His now pale skin made his wavy brown hair seem darker. His lips had a bluish tint from the cold Pacific. If he didn't die from the jelly stings, he'd die from hypothermia.

I didn't have a choice. I had to do something. If Chase freaked out like Alonso and never spoke to me again, I'd deal with it. Right now I had to save both our lives.

Swallowing the fist-sized lump in my throat, I placed my mouth over his and blew my warm breath into him. Blew my special breath into his lungs and his veins. Blew my magical breath to save his life.

Holding him around the waist, I let our bodies sink into the water. Once his head was covered, I put my hand to his chest. His heart still beat. His lungs moved in and out. I relaxed with the rhythm of his chest moving up and down.

Chase could now breathe underwater.

At least temporarily.

I dragged him down to the sandy bottom where there were no jellies. Similar to my nightmare, only this time I was the one dragging a person underwater. I didn't know how long my breath would last so to be sure, I placed my mouth against his again and blew.

As our lips touched, his body stiffened. I stared into his blue orbs, bright and clear. Chase was alert.

And his expression reminded me of Alonso's.

I gritted my teeth, waiting for his reaction. The beating of my heart went on a holding pattern. Would Chase fear me?

"No."

Chase's lips moved but no sound came out. Yet I could hear him. Or at least understand him.

"Did you understand my question?"

Just like the otter.

This was impossible. I'd never spoken to anyone underwater before. Then again, I'd never been with anyone underwater before for any length of time.

He reached for his throat. An expression of horror froze on his face realizing what was going on. "What's happening to me? What am I doing underwater, breathing, like you?"

"I can explain." I tasted bitterness in my mouth and it spread through my veins. Would Chase keep his distance? Would he cross himself every time he saw me at the Boardwalk?

He wiggled against my hold and I let go. My heart squeezed with the imprint of his fingers. I might've just let him go for good.

His gaze darted about. "How did you do this?"

I shrugged my shoulders. "It was the only way to escape."

"What're we doing down here? At the bottom of the frickin' ocean?"

Somehow, I heard panic in his thoughts. Which confused me even more. I understood him, but his lips weren't moving. We were talking, but we weren't. And not only did I understand him, but I heard his tone of voice.

"Calm down."

"You want me to calm down? I'm who-knows-how-deep under the Pacific Ocean without scuba gear or a submarine. What the heck happened?" His entire body thrashed.

"You were hit by a paintgun pellet and lost consciousness. I had to get you away from Joe, and then the raft sank, and the jelly fish attacked—"

"Oh my God, am I hearing your thoughts?" His face grew even paler.

"Yes, you—"

"Did you turn me into a...a you?" He'd picked his words carefully.

Or not so carefully. Each word ripped like a shark's tooth. My chest squeezed tighter, trying to suffocate or insulate my heart. "Temporarily, I think."

"How temporary?"

"That's why I breathed into you again. I don't know how long it lasts." I turned away from him before he fled. He was still my responsibility. I'd gotten him into this situation and I planned to get him out. "We should head back to the beach before the jellyfish find us."

As the otters predicted, the jellies weren't near the bottom of the ocean.

His fingers touched my bare shoulder. "I'm weirded-out."

At least he wasn't afraid to touch me. "You probably think I'm cursed." My lips quivered, imagining his rejection.

"No, just...different." He swam in front of me. "I mean this is crazy, but cool." His voice sounded excited like this was one big adventure.

Chase took my hand and we swam toward shore. He wasn't afraid of me like Alonso, and he still wanted to be close to me. Maybe this would turn out okay. Maybe this wouldn't be the end of our relationship. I could hope.

"Will I all of a sudden start to choke?"

"If you do, squeeze my hand and I'll breathe into you again." This was the first time I'd used my breath to keep someone under water. Normally, I tried to get them out.

"I like that idea."

"It's not a kiss." I shivered thinking of Alonso and the boy.

As we swam closer to shore, I could tell Chase became more at ease with his change. He started to point things out.

"There's a school of fish. There must be hundreds."

"Doesn't that look cool where the rock juts out?"

"I've never seen seaweed like this before."

I became more comfortable with my action of breathing into him. We'd needed to get away from Joe and escape the jellyfish. We were safe and heading toward another cove, and eventually home. Chase hadn't completely freaked. He didn't turn away from me. Things were going to work out.

Chase grinned. "This is so cool. Can you imagine what my friends will say?"

Sharpness plummeted my gut like it had been knifed with a serrated edge. Telling one person would lead to telling others. Too many people would find out. My secret would be exposed.

The grin grew happier, but to me it became sinister. "I'm going to write the most amazing, in-depth—haha, get it? In-depth?"

My tummy revolted at his lame joke. Shaking started in my toes and crawled up my body, slicing in spot after spot like I'd been shocked by a sneaky eel. A coldness invaded my soul.

Chase's smile mocked me. "I'll write an in-depth first person exposé."

Chapter Ten
Prized Prisoner

Exposé.

As in exposure.

Of me.

Explosion after explosion burned in my gut, gnawing away at my insides, carving out my stomach like he had my heart.

All Chase's promises and assurances were lies. All his charm false. All his caring phony.

I had to get away from him, from his backstabbing betrayal. I picked up the pace of my strokes. The jellyfish were gone and we weren't too far from shore. He could surface and swim to shore by himself.

Or drown.

I didn't care.

Well, I did care. And I couldn't leave him in the ocean. What if my power stopped working on him? I'd dragged him into the water, I'd make sure he got out.

Even if I didn't want to but kinda did.

A tingle of awareness tickled my spine adding to my

anger. Someone was watching. I didn't see anything unusual but the feeling of discomfort wouldn't go away. Hurrying to shore with Chase, I searched the murky water in between the seaweed and rock crevices.

Of course, the tingles must be part of my anger toward Chase. No one could be under the water monitoring us. Ridiculous.

Once in the shallow waves, I stood and stomped onto the beach. We were a few hundred yards from a rock cliff we'd need to walk around to get back to Shell Cove.

"Hey." Chase called from the surf. "Let's stay in the water for awhile." His morph from nice guy to jerk was complete.

From compassionate to conceited. From charming to cad. From caring to clueless.

I slammed my hands onto my hips. My body heated like a volcano. I wanted to explode. Instead, I kept my words hard, precise. "Why? So you can get more ideas for your exposé?"

He rushed forward trying to jump over the waves. Stumbling, he fell using his hand to break his fall. But he didn't stop moving toward me. "You have to understand, not only can you breathe underwater but you can make others breathe underwater, too. It's incredible."

"Not so incredible when it's taken advantage of. Used and abused." Okay, that one specific power wasn't abused because I'd never told Bill and Carlita.

He halted a step away from me. Raising his hands, he reached out. For me.

Like I'd ever hold his hand again. My eyes burned but I refused to cry in front of him. I scrunched up my face and swallowed the hard ball of tears down. I took a step back.

Drops of water slid down his tanned chest and I hated that I noticed. "I'd never take advantage of you."

Yeah, right. Only an hour before he'd promised not to tell anyone my secret. Now, he was planning on writing a news article.

"Take me home." Turning, I headed up the beach.

"Pearl." Chase ran after me. He snatched at my hand. "You have to understand this is a huge deal."

I yanked my fingers from between his, severing all contact. "I thought we were a big deal. I was wrong."

"But—"

I held up my hand to stop him from talking. I didn't want to hear his reasoning. I'd heard it all before from Carlita and Bill. Either I'd be laughed at or taken advantage of. Chase didn't understand that.

We reached the small path leading to the road where we'd parked the car. My anger made me walk faster.

"Listen, what you can do is amazing." His tone coaxed trying to convince me to change my mind. "I want you to think about the possibility."

There was nothing to think about. Nothing to consider. Nothing to say.

"Don't say another word. It will only make me angrier." I opened the car door, got in, and slammed the door closed.

The entire drive back to Mermaid Beach was silent. He tried to start a conversation several times, but I'd plug my ears and sing nonsense. Childish I know, but I didn't want to hear what he had to say. I didn't want him digging a deeper hole for himself.

I wished I had my driver's license so I didn't need to endure his company. If I had my license I could go wherever I wanted whenever I wanted. I wouldn't be stuck at this beach with Chase, wouldn't have to demand he take me home, wouldn't have to sit in a silent car during the drive back.

The day I turned sixteen, I snuck my birth certificate out of Bill and Carlita's private papers to apply for my driver's license. The lady at the Department of Motor Vehicles laughed, told me the birth certificate was a fake, and asked who would ever name their kid Pearl of the Sea Poseidon.

Shaking with anger, I confronted my *parents.* "Is this why you didn't want me to learn to drive?"

"How dare you steal from our filing cabinet." Carlita's face burned red, matching the dyed color of her hair. "Stay out of our things."

"The birth certificate is mine. Or I thought it was mine." I flapped the useless piece of paper in her face. "It's a phony."

"Pearl, dear." Bill always tried to make up for Carlita's anger, but I think he feared her himself. His small stature and ego couldn't go up against the exact opposite. "Yours was lost, in a fire."

"Lies."

"Don't talk like that to us." Carlita leaned forward showing her overly-large chest emphasizing the threat in her voice. "Don't make me punish you."

"We're your parents." Bill tried to assure, but I didn't want to listen.

Usually I cowered, but not this time. "Are you? Are you really?"

I'd always had doubts. I looked nothing like either of them. They both had reddish hair, while mine was blonde. Carlita was short and stout and Bill was just short. I wasn't a giant, but I wasn't small. They were greedy and manipulative, and I hoped I was neither.

"You're being insolent." Carlita swung her arm and her hand connected with my left cheek.

I staggered back. My fingers reached up and touched the raw spot. "You're not very good parents."

"How dare you?" Carlita screeched. "We've done everything for you."

Everything and yet nothing. I was their goose with the golden eggs. I kept giving and giving and all I'd gotten in return was... I thought about it a second. Based on what I'd discovered, I'd gotten nothing from them but lies and Carlita's verbal, emotional, and now physical abuse. Anger twisted to rage. "I'm the star of your stupid show. I've been working every night for as long as I remember. I've never had a normal life."

"Ungrateful little wretch." Steam seemed to seep from Carlita's head. "We took you in. Fed you. Clothed you. And all you do is mouth back."

I had never mouthed back, until now. Rage burned like a forest fire. "Took me in? Took me in?"

"Carlita." Bill tried to calm her down.

I glared at him. "What does she mean by took me in?"

"You're not our child," Bill sank down onto the metal kitchen chair. "You were left to us."

My entire life swished before me. As I suspected, everything I'd thought about myself was based on a lie. Probably several. "Who? Who left me?"

"Bill, shut up."

He shook his head but kept talking. "An old man paid us to take care of you when you were a baby. Said he needed to return home and couldn't take you with him because of the danger. He said he'd be back before you were two years old."

"What happened when he came back?" I held my breath.

"He didn't."

My breath whooshed out. My spirits plummeted. The old man didn't want me, either.

"Before he left you, he told us about your...unusual abilities."

Carlita turned and pounced on Bill. "Shut your trap. She's ours and no one can take her away."

At that moment I knew what I had to do. Carlita would never let me go. Not when I was sixteen or eighteen or even twenty-one. No one could take me away, but I could run, sneak away, escape.

***

Chase dropped me off at the Boardwalk after an uncomfortable silent ride. He'd tried to convince me again that telling my story would be good. I ignored him.

When I got back to my tent, I should've packed my things and ran, but I needed the ocean to cleanse the bitterness from my skin. Besides, if he wrote his article it would take awhile to get published. There would be people who didn't believe him. That's when my freedom would be curtailed. I'd be constantly watched.

That's when I'd have to leave Mermaid Beach.

I stripped off my shorts and shoved them into the string bag I brought, leaving it on the sand. I waded into the water. The waves welcomed and revived me. I squished my toes into the wet sand and then, kicked at the waves with my foot letting the refreshing splashes invigorate my spirit. The seagulls skimmed the surface searching for a meal. I inhaled the salty air and tried to relax.

Letting myself sink into the water, my body adapted to the ocean's temperature as if I had an internal thermostat when I swam. Once I'd breathed into Chase the goose bumps had disappeared from his body. My breath must've not only let him breathe, but warmed him inside.

He didn't deserve my warmth.

I swam faster and farther trying to burn off my hurt. He said he'd never take advantage of me, but that didn't mean he wouldn't write the story. Tell the world about me and my abilities. Change my life for the worse.

Awareness tingled up my spine, similar to what I'd felt at Shell Cove with Chase. I peered around trying to see something…anything.

It was too soon for the word about me to spread. And no one knew I was out here. Silly. No one could be here miles from shore, under the surface.

I was alone.

I'd always been alone.

My heart bruised with the single thought. Even more alone now, with Chase knowing my secret and willing to tell the world.

Still, my heart pounded in my ears. Louder than all the natural sounds around me. Even with my abilities swimming alone was dangerous. I'd proved that the other night. Before any other catastrophe stalked, I needed to head back. To think about my immediate future.

I flipped around and cruised past a pile of fallen rocks and boulders.

"Don't be afraid." The voice entered my brain the way Chase and I had communicated.

My arm jerked. "Huh?"

"Don't be afraid. I'm a friend."

I stopped swimming and spun around. My tummy tumbled over itself. "Who said that?"

"I did. Over by the rocks."

If I was imagining voices, the voice answered back.

I scoured the pile of rocks. "Who are you?"

"I'm like you." The voice sounded male, if that was possible. "I can breathe underwater, too."

My heart pulsed in a strange, new rhythm. My chest puffed as if it filled with petrified air. My entire body tingled with anticipation and a bit of fear. "What? Where?"

A guy emerged from between two large boulders. He wore blue swim trunks that blended with the water. His dark black hair hung a little too long, a little too wild. No snorkel or scuba gear was in sight.

He raised his hand in a slight wave. "I've been watching you."

Chapter Eleven
Ragin' Revolt

I wasn't alone. The thought pounded through my head. My impossible dream had come true. I wasn't the only one. There were others who could breathe underwater like me. A thrill shot through me like fireworks in the sky, sprinkling across my skin.

"Who are you?" My thoughts sounded light, tentative. The thrilled sprinkles changed into itches of tension and fear. "Why were you watching me?"

"Needed to confirm you're one of us." I liked that he didn't move forward. He seemed less threatening that way. "I'm Finn."

"How can you breathe underwater?" Maybe I could learn the reason for this ability. Some genetic mutation, a top-secret science experiment gone wrong.

"You're new here."

"Y-yes." I backpedaled, putting more distance between us. Something about him put me on edge. I balanced on my toes, ready to make a break.

"Do I make you nervous?"

I shook my head. A lie.

Finn held both his hands up in a surrender gesture. "Would you be more comfortable talking above?" His gaze shot to the surface.

"Yes." I wasn't sure why. I loved being in the water, but I still didn't have a handle on reading other people's thoughts. Could they *hear* everything I thought or only what I wanted them to?

"I'll meet you on shore." He kicked his feet and headed toward the beach leaving me to decide whether to follow.

Not that I had a choice. I needed to go back to the campground. And I needed to know more about Finn.

When I reached the shore, Finn sat near where I'd left my clothes. I jogged to my bag, took out my shorts and put them on, not wanting to be so exposed to a stranger. Ridiculous since he already saw me in my swimsuit and said he'd been following me around, possibly for days.

"Why were you following me?"

He appeared to be my age, maybe a bit older. His fit body didn't show an extra ounce of fat. Solid muscle. He was attractive but for some reason I didn't react.

Maybe because he wasn't Chase.

I surveyed the area hoping Chase would appear. Then, mentally kicked myself for the thought. He was going to betray me. I didn't need or want his help.

Finn stretched his arms, and then leaned back against his elbows in a non-threatening way, almost too casual, like he wanted me to be comfortable around him. "What's your name?"

"Pearl."

"We don't find many strangers who can breathe underwater."

I sucked in a lungful of air before spewing out the word, "We?"

"My people." He flung his black hair back in a practiced move.

People, as in multiple. Not just him and I. There were others like us. Lots of others. "Do all *your people* breathe underwater?"

"Yes."

Shock and hope cascaded through me like a cold, refreshing waterfall. Chills of anticipation splashed my skin. "There are more of us?"

He angled his head. "Where are you from?"

"Florida." In my excitement I answered without thought, for once being completely honest.

"What about the guy you were with today at Shell Cove? Is he from Florida too?" The questions shot out like accusations.

I didn't care. I was happy to meet someone who could breathe underwater. I'd answer all his questions. "Chase Thomas. He's from Mermaid Beach."

Finn had watched Chase and I swim earlier. That must've been the awareness I'd sensed.

"I've never seen him that deep in the water."

I didn't want to talk about Chase right now. "Well, he can't...he can't breathe underwater like us." This was the weirdest conversation. And yet, I wanted it to go on and on. I'd finally met someone like me.

Again the sprinkles spread across my skin. The thought of not being alone, of having others who understood my issues, burst again and again, lighting up my insides like a lighthouse.

Finn's body stilled. The too-casual smile disappeared from his face. He spoke slowly, "I saw him."

"I sort of breathed into his mouth." I stared down at the ground. Heat washed through me wondering if I'd broken some rule. "So he could swim with me."

"What?" Finn jerked into an upright position. "That's impossible." His gaze roved up and down my body like searching for an explanation.

"Can't everyone do it?" I angled my head to study him. If no one else could make others breathe underwater I'd still be different.

Still be a freak in a world of freaks.

"Not that I know of." He sounded tight, guarded. Maybe he wasn't as intelligent about *his people* as he'd claimed.

I needed to get information. "Where do all of your people meet? Is it like a club or a secret society? How many of us are there?" My voice rose with each question. Blood pumped stronger through my veins. I didn't care if we all didn't have the same skills, *his people* could breathe underwater therefore they were *my people*.

I fisted my hands trying to control my excitement. So many questions to ask, so many people to meet.

"Whoa. We're not a club." He rolled his shoulders. "I guess you could call us a secret society. But only secret to the air-breathers."

"Air breathers?"

"Humans who can only breathe air. Who don't have a choice like us." He sounded all-superior.

Which I guess in a way we were.

"Do a lot of us live on land?" Maybe that explained how I was adopted into an air-breather family.

"Not by choice." His voice hardened.

"How did we get our skills?" *Please don't tell me I'm a science experiment gone wrong.*

134

"It's in our genes. You inherit it." He spoke like he was explaining science to a five-year-old.

"I was adopted." Another truth told. "Where do you live? Where do our people call home?" I bounced up and down unable to wait to see everyone, to meet others like me, to learn how they lived.

"Underwater."

I swallowed. "All the time?" I loved the ocean but to be under all the time, to never see the sun.

"You'll love Free Atlantis." The words sounded tight coming out of his mouth.

I ignored his mixed signals. The name, Free Atlantis, sounded like the thing I searched for—freedom. My brain clicked with all the possibilities, while the insides of my tummy swished. Everyone lived there. Meaning my parents or people who knew my parents or even some type of distant relatives lived there.

"Would you like to visit?"

"Yes." The word fell out of my mouth like a hushed whisper.

"Let's go." Finn stood up. His actions appeared decisive, like he'd made up his mind about me.

"Now?" I squinted at the waning sun, at the fog rolling in over the ocean. The scent of cooking on the campground grills reached the beach.

"Things are quiet now. A good time to visit." He held out his hand.

"Do you mean because there are no whirlpools or jellyfish attacks?"

"Those weren't natural disasters." He angled his head and studied me as if he wanted to say more.

I pulled back. "You saw me and you didn't help?"

His face whitened. "You got caught in one of those?"

"Yes, I—" I didn't understand. "You didn't see me in trouble?"

"No." He studied the sand. "There have been a number of whirlpools in the area lately." He seemed to pick his words with care.

"That aren't normal or natural." I knew this from Cuda, and now from Finn's comment.

"Correct." He searched the ocean's horizon. "If we're going to go to Free Atlantis, we should go now."

I studied his face. I wanted to go, needed to go, but caution held back my impulsiveness. "How far is it?"

I scanned the tents sticking out between the trees. If only I could tell someone I was going. Tell Chase. My back straightened and I pulled my shoulders back. I couldn't tell Chase anything anymore.

As if Finn sensed my hesitation, he said, "You'll be fine. You're one of us."

I liked the sound of that. Belonging. "What if I have problems?"

"Let me know." He held his hand out farther.

I stripped off my shorts and left them in a pile on the hill leading to the campgrounds. Putting my bag on my back, I nodded. "How do you talk underwater? In Free Atlantis."

"Same as before, when we first met."

Walking toward the water, I tripped on the sand. "Can you hear all my thoughts?"

His mouth dropped open and he gawked. "No one taught you?"

"No." I'd had no one to show me.

"How did you learn about breathing underwater, and the other things you do?"

"Instinct. Trial and error." Bill and Carlita's terror

training.

"Our communication is like talking. Your thoughts are your own but when you want someone to hear you, your brain just does it. Like flipping a switch." He used his free hand to demonstrate. "I've never had to explain it to anyone before. I kind of grew up talking underwater."

Another way I was different. "There haven't been any others who've been lost?"

Finn was silent. His expression became stern. The brown of his pupils darkened. His lips thinned. "There have been rumors..."

***

We traveled straight into the deeper waters of the Pacific and then south. Even at our super-speed, the journey took over two hours. I was too busy sightseeing to pay much attention to the time or our exact location.

The ocean grew darker the deeper we traversed. The sunlight didn't penetrate the water. Shadows moved among us. Finn didn't take much notice, but shivers scratched down my spine—a warning of danger or my own stupidity.

Agreeing to go with Finn, a complete stranger, wasn't the smartest thing to do, but I needed to know where I came from, and possibly where I'd stay. Plus, when Chase reported my story I'd need a place to hide.

My extra-sensitive eyes showed the terrain morphing from smooth and sandy to mountainous. We swam over and around deep crags and high peaks, like my emotions swam around my excitement at finding others like me and my sadness at Chase exposing me. The water grew warmer.

"Why is it so hot when we're so far below?" The heat didn't affect me, but I could tell the temperature had risen.

Finn spared me a quick glance. "We're nearing thermal vents."

"Where?" I'd read about thermal vents near the Galapagos Islands. Surely, we weren't that far.

"West of Acapulco, Mexico."

I hadn't realized I'd crossed an international border. "Do I need a passport?"

"No." Guess he didn't get my joke or he didn't have a sense of humor. "We're almost there."

The back of my neck tingled. Fear intertwined with excitement like a rope, the lines twisting back and forth and over each other.

The harsh environment wasn't welcoming. I couldn't see living down here, didn't understand why people would want to. But if *my people* were here, then I needed to consider it.

White flakes floated past in a fast stream like they were being blown our way. The flakes multiplied and covered every surface. It was an underwater blizzard.

"Finn? What's with all the flakes?"

"Bacteria."

I wondered about this bacteria. Was it germy bacteria? Poisonous bacteria? Flesh-eating bacteria?

"Is it dangerous?"

"No. A new vent must be forming. They grow fast where the tectonic plates are shifting." That was the most he'd *said* the entire journey.

Like he didn't want to reveal anything to me in advance. Or not at all.

Finn stopped near a ridge and pulled out a bandana from his swim trunk pocket. "I need to blindfold you."

My tummy had churned the entire trip. Now, it jolted.

"Why?"

"The location of Free Atlantis is secret. Only citizens know how to find it."

"But I thought I was one of you?" Maybe acceptance wasn't as easy as having the same abilities. Maybe there was a test or a pledge of allegiance.

"The leaders need to be assured of your loyalty before divulging our location." He sounded all official-like. He swam behind me and raised the bandana.

My nerve endings tingled. Bubbles rose in my stomach like a shaken-up soda. I didn't like this. "Why is it such a secret?" Most free societies didn't keep their location hidden.

Finn huffed bubbles of air out of his mouth. "I don't want to give you a history lesson right now, but there are Royalists who cling to the old ways and believe in superstition and myth."

"What myth?" I asked only to delay my decision.

Finn's frown added lines around his mouth. "The myth says Atlanteans must wait for three princesses to return before confronting air-breathers about the destruction of the ocean. In the meantime, our people suffer from famine and wasted resources."

I felt for their plight. "There must be something Atlanteans can do."

"Not with the current Royal Regent in charge. Over the years he's taken away rights and trodden on the lower classes."

Sounded like the Atlanteans had issues like the rest of the world. My belly heaving, I digested the new information. "Maybe visiting Free Atlantis isn't a good idea."

"Do you want to turn back? Now?" Finn's thoughts

sounded incredulous but wary, all at the same time.

A battle of my own waged in my mind. If I turned back, I'd have traveled this far for nothing. I was almost there and nothing had happened yet. Finn had been nothing but nice and informative. A benign tour guide. Chase would disapprove.

To prove him wrong I'd go. "Okay. I'll go."

Finn tied the bandana around my head, covering my eyes. "Take my hand."

I slipped my hand into Finn's. No tingles shot up my spine like when I touched Chase. No warmth from a special connection. No panic.

Finn was an okay guy. I wasn't attracted to him. He was taking me to meet others like me. I had to take this risk and trust him.

Kicking off, I let Finn lead me to who knows where.

Chapter Twelve
Captain Charisma

When Finn slipped the blindfold off, I felt like Dorothy entering Oz. Except my Oz wasn't nearly as colorful.

I blinked a few times before adjusting to the red eerie light in the darkness of the water. It had been inky dark by the underwater mountains, now a strange, orange-red glow emitted from the ground in a series of caverns. Small, round vents shot black smoke into the water. Dark coral clung to the bottom, while tube-leafed plants swayed in the current.

The view wasn't what I expected. Nothing like the beautiful ocean I played in. It looked like something out of a post-apocalyptic movie. Steam poured into the water, a sulpher smell fouled the area, silent people trudged by like automatons.

Now I understood why my parents left.

Finn puffed out his chest. "Welcome to Free Atlantis."

"Is there an Un-Free Atlantis?" I hoped that didn't

sound sarcastic.

"Unfortunately, there is. A man with a military-precise bearing approached us." He studied me. "Is this her?"

"Yes, Captain Fisher." Finn saluted. "This is Pearl, the girl my father told you about."

My startled gaze settled on Finn. I hadn't realized I'd met his father. Definitely not underwater. So where? "Nice to meet you."

He continued to scrutinize me. His military cut blonde hair turned up at the edges like he tried to control the curls. He held his body stiff and rigid, which was hard to do underwater.

I wiggled in place, playing with the rope straps of the bag hanging around my shoulders. Something about his bearing and the way he examined me left me feeling icky.

"No one's seen her before now?"

"No, sir." Finn straightened his shoulders like he was in an army.

I guess that would be Navy seeing that we were under the ocean.

"I didn't know there were others like me."

"Show her around." The captain dismissed us, but his glare followed.

"Who is he?" I tried to keep the dislike out of my thought.

"One of the most courageous leaders of Free Atlantis. He risked everything, even his family, for our cause." Finn sounded over-impressed with the guy. "He's the leader of the Free Atlanteans and will steer us to victory."

"Victory over these supposed-princesses?" Finn

might not want to give a history lesson, but I needed to know what I was getting involved in, especially since Finn's zealousness bordered on devotion.

"Lost princesses."

"Lost how?"

"When the continent of Atlantis was destroyed—"

I sucked in a breath? Or water? "I thought Atlantis was a myth."

"No. It was real." Finn shook his head. "Out of anger, Poseidon destroyed the continent. When he realized what he'd done he saved some of the inhabitants."

"The princesses?"

"The princesses were placed in special pods and whisked away for their own protection. Loyal regents watched over the pods and were supposed to bring them back as toddlers so they could train for their royal duties. Only one of the regents returned."

My heart rattled. The story was similar to my own. But no way was I a princess. If all Atlanteans thought of air-breathers like Finn did, they'd never allow a grandchild of Poseidon's to live above the ocean, especially with people like Bill and Carlita. "And the others?"

"No one knows." Finn's eyes narrowed, watching my reaction to the story. "Unless the Royalists are keeping their existence a secret."

"Does Captain Fisher think I'm a spy for the Royalists?" That would explain the blindfold.

"Of course not." Finn flashed an insincere smile. "I wouldn't have brought you here if he did."

"I'm good at keeping secrets." Mostly, anyhow. My thoughts veered to Chase. To stop thinking about him I asked another question. "What happened to the other people of Atlantis?"

"The inhabitants started a new colony."

"Here?" I scanned the area.

Strange white crabs crawled on the ground. Pencil-sized worms wiggled through the mud. Darkened plumes swayed like a dim field of poppies.

The idea of living here creeped me out, and yet I needed to seriously think about it. If I wanted to live among *my people* I'd need to live in Free Atlantis.

"This is our temporary base."

"Whew."

Finn glared at me. "We're revolutionaries fighting for our cause, for the right cause. A little discomfort is worth it. There are people unhappy and dying. Un-Free Atlanteans struggling to survive under an evil Royalist government. Soon we will return to our real home."

"Where is your real home? What's it like?" It must be better than this place.

"The continent of Atlantis is gone forever but those who survived the destruction founded a new underwater home under an island. A beautiful place where sunlight and fish are plentiful."

My unease lightened. This is temporary. When they defeat the Royalists then everyone would return home. Maybe I'd be ready to go with them. "Do the Un-Free Atlanteans know a group of brave revolutionaries are fighting for their freedom?"

A sneer crossed Finn's face. "Oh, they know. Princess Cordelia and her gang of thugs try to keep them in the dark, try to keep them clinging to a myth that Poseidon's progeny will return, but we're much wiser."

So, Poseidon was real too. Surprise puffed out of my mouth in bubbles. Nodding, although not sure I believed,

I continued to peer around. People swam by at a slow pace, ducking the blasts from the vents. I pointed. "More thermal vents?"

"Our power source since we have no access to the sun."

I shivered. Even temporarily living without the sun would be difficult.

Finn swam forward and I followed. "The caverns are safe and deep. We can fit a few families or living groups in each one." He nodded toward an entrance and then swam into the dark opening.

Minimal light showcased the interior of the cavern. I followed. Not that there was much to see. A few rocks acting as chairs. Holes in the sand where people appeared to sleep. Cut-outs in the wall holding shells and clams. It reminded me of cave shelters used by early man.

I might live in a tent, but I think I had more creature comforts than these people.

Swimming behind him, a group of children rushed up and hugged me. Their words of love and welcome reached inside and touched my heart. They seemed painfully-thin but they appeared happy and healthy.

Finn high-fived each of the kids with a brilliant smile, enjoying their playfulness. I liked the happy-go-lucky Finn better than the serious-out-for-war Finn.

Not like-like him. I'd given my heart, and my trust, to Chase and he'd crushed it.

My crushed heart contracted. Pain radiated outwards like my heart wanted the rest of my body to suffer. Holding my unhappiness inside, I forced a serene, pleasant expression on my face.

Finn led me out of the cavern and a woman approached us, bowing her head. She handed me a closed clam the size of a large hand.

"For you." She tapped the shell and the clam opened revealing a ball-sized pearl.

These people didn't have much, but they welcomed me with hugs and gifts. Their kindness warmed my soul. "Thank you." I put the shell in my bag.

Finn pointed at a long, slimy fish. "Surprisingly, food down here is plentiful."

The rib cages showing through the children's skin didn't live up to Finn's statement.

"Air-breather scientists haven't discovered chemosynthesis yet, which replaces photosynthesis."

Definitely didn't want a science lesson. It was time to ask the question I'd been holding back, the reason I'd agreed to visit Free Atlantis. "So, if I wanted to find someone here, where would I look?"

"Who are you looking for?"

"My biological parents."

***

Finn showed me into a large cave that twisted and turned deep under the ocean floor. It reminded me of a bomb shelter.

"This is where the captain's office is located and where whatever records we have are kept." Finn swam ahead of me. "There's probably not much. Most of the historical records are kept at Princess Cordelia's castle."

All the workers in the cave ignored us. In fact, after the initial burst of greetings—almost like a planned welcoming—most of the people had gone about their business.

Finn stopped in front of a wall of shelves filled with large clams. "Why the urge to find your parents?"

"I only found out when I turned sixteen that I was

adopted. And I just found out from you that there are others like me."

"What can you tell me about your background?" Finn opened up one of the clams that had hundreds of paper-like seaweed sheaves inside. "You said you're sixteen, right?"

"Yes." I peered over his shoulder amazed at how they kept records. Paper wouldn't last long in water. "I was told that an old man gave me as a baby to the people who raised me. He said he'd come back and get me before I was two." I gathered my emotions and locked them away like the pearl in the clam before telling Finn the rest. "He never came back."

Finn's head jerked. "Was this man your father?"

"I guess." I gave a half-shrug. "I really don't know."

"This isn't a good idea." He slammed the clam shut and grabbed my hand. "Let's get out of here."

"But?" I couldn't give up now. I was so close. "There's another reason I need to find my parents or a relative."

He tapped his foot in the water and little bubbles rose between us. "What?"

I bit my lip unsure of how much to tell. "Remember Chase?"

"The air-breather." Finn's nose and lips scrunched up in a disgusted expression.

"He's a reporter and he's planning to write an expose about me." Speaking of Chase's betrayal made my lips tremble.

"I'll tell the captain. He'll know how to deal with the ocean scum." Finn started to swim away, but I grabbed his arm.

"The story is about me. Chase knows nothing about

Atlanteans." A crack spread through my aching heart, increasing the pain. "If I discovered my background, found a relative, I could move in with them and get away from Chase if he goes through with exposing me to the world."

Finn's expression set in hard lines. "The Free-Atlanteans will deal with him."

"No." Even though I was angry and disappointed in Chase I didn't want him harmed. "I'll talk to him again, convince him not to write the story."

"He still knows about you so he's dangerous. All air-breathers are."

I didn't need Finn's doubts about Chase. I had enough of my own. The sooner I got back, the sooner I could convince him not to do the article. I wasn't sure how I was going to talk him out of the story, but I'd find a way. I had to.

And while I was thrilled to find people similar to me, how much were they really like me? My nerves skittered when I thought about joining complete strangers. I'd lived on land my entire life, saw the sunshine almost every day, everyone I knew was an air-breather. Would the Atlanteans even accept me?

So far, I didn't have a great track record. No one at the circus had been my friend. Bill and Carlita called themselves parents, but they acted like slave owners. I was still new at the Boardwalk and hadn't really tried to make friends. Except for Chase.

Everything ached, from my heart to my toes to my head, when I thought of the loss of his more-than-friendship.

But he wasn't the reason I was going back. No, not at all. I did need to see him, but only to convince him to not write the article. And if I couldn't, I might not have a choice about returning to Free Atlantis.

"If I can't get any information, I should go." My bruised heart knew I couldn't flee my problems on land. I had to try to change Chase's mind. "It would be great if you'd look into my background based on what I told you."

Finn gave me a superior-look, as if he knew something that I didn't. "These are your people. You should stay."

I sympathized with the Free Atlantean cause and I so wanted to belong, but I couldn't disappear. Maybe Chase would at least worry. "I've got a job to get to in the morning and I need to talk to Chase about the article."

"You can't trust him." Finn judged based on whether a person could breathe in water or not.

"You don't even know Chase." I never should've told Finn about Chase's plans.

He glanced down one of the narrow caverns. "It's not safe to go back now."

I wasn't sure why the danger had increased. We were still under the deep depths of a dark ocean, still watching for sharks and rogue royalists. I needed to get away by myself for a while. Think about all I'd learned. "I need to go back."

"You're staying."

"Excuse me?" I hoped he heard the sarcasm. He acted like a bossy big brother. I was tired of taking orders from Bill and Carlita, and now my boss at work. I refused to be told what to do by a guy I just met. "Are you ordering me to stay?"

"We need to keep an eye on you." At my sharp look, he continued. "We protect all Free-Atlanteans, keep them safe. It's part of our job."

I arched a brow. "What exactly is your job?"

"I'm part of the Free-Atlantean army."

"How many people are in this army?"

Finn again glanced down the darkened cavern. "That's, um…top secret."

"How many people in the Royalist army? In fact, how many Atlanteans are there in existence?" I wanted to learn something about my people, even if I learned nothing about my parents.

"After the destruction, there were only a few thousand Atlanteans left. Over the centuries, we've increased in numbers." Finn swam toward the exit of the cavern.

I followed. "How many Royalists compared to Free-Atlanteans?"

"Numbers don't matter." His shoulders stiffened. "What matters is the free will of the people. There's no need to wait for three spoiled princesses in order to take control of our destiny."

I stopped at the cavern exit. "I thought you didn't believe in the princess myth?"

His lips puffed out. His eyes pulled back into their sockets. "I don't."

"But there is a princess in the Royalist castle right now. If she's a real princess, why doesn't she stop the oppression?"

"Oh, she's real all right." He said it like he knew her personally.

"So if she's real, why couldn't the other two be real? Just like I once thought Atlantis was a myth, why couldn't the three princesses story be true?"

"Because they were supposed to arrive when they

were toddlers to be trained for their royal duties. Only Cordelia and her regent showed. If the other two were real, they're probably dead or they would have been here by the time they turned sixteen." His gaze flew up to mine. A spark of light flashed like he'd just had a bright idea, then dulled. "The point is, real or not, Atlanteans should not be held back, oppressed, treated like slaves." His speech sounded rehearsed.

Or maybe he'd repeated a speech by the captain.

"Either way, I don't see how it can be more dangerous now than it was two hours ago." I crossed my arms. "I need to go."

Finn held out his hand, but dropped it when I didn't take hold. "It's late and we don't know where the Royalists have spies positioned."

"I'm going home." Weird, how I already thought of Mermaid Beach that way. Pushing my shoulders back, I tried to sound tough. "Are you taking me or do I need to find my own way?"

Chapter Thirteen
Back To The Beach

Thank God Finn changed his mind because finding my own way would've been next to impossible. Stupid me hadn't paid attention.

After he talked to, or more likely got permission from the captain, Finn blindfolded me again and took me out of the Free Atlantis base camp. When we were far enough away, he removed the blindfold.

I noted the mountains turning into hills, the strange rock formation we swam through, and a huge trench in the ocean floor. This time I paid attention the entire way home.

If I needed to escape to Free Atlantis, I'd know how to find my way to the general vicinity.

What seemed like hours later, we surfaced near the campground beach. I thought Finn would swim away but he walked with me to where the beach ended and the campground began. "Sorry I tried to force you to stay."

Nodding, but not in agreement, I gripped the straps of my bag. I hoped the large clam the woman gave me was still in one piece.

"I want you to know that I argued for bringing you back here. I know how much you wanted to come home." Finn took hold of my free hand.

"Really?"

"We take watching out for our kind seriously."

I examined our connected hands and felt nothing but kindness. I stared into his friendly, brown eyes. "I appreciate that, but I've been looking out for myself my entire life."

Maybe belonging to a group was too restrictive for me. Maybe I was better off alone. But I didn't believe it. I was concerned they wouldn't accept me with my differences, even though the differences were fewer compared to air-breathers.

I longed for acceptance and understanding. Wished for a family. I thought I'd found something with Chase. And I'd been wrong.

Confusion collided in my mind. Pain pinched like lobsters nipping at my toes. A crazy daze of befuddlement swirled. I wanted different things from different people and everyone had always disappointed me.

"Just know if you ever need help, I'll be around." He dropped my hand, knowing his charm wasn't working on me.

"Thanks. I should get some sleep." I didn't tell him my tent was only a few yards away, and he didn't ask.

"We don't like to advertise our existence or our secret location."

"The blindfold kinda gave that away." I glanced at the ocean, at the calm way the waves hit the shore. "Are you going all the way back tonight?"

"No. I need to talk to..."

"Talk to who?"

Finn's gaze glazed over. "You gave me some things to think about. I'm going to follow up on that old princess myth."

Every girl's dream would be to discover she was a princess. A smile drifted onto my face at the fanciful thought. Of course, Finn said the other two princesses were probably dead.

My smile flattened. Maybe being a princess wouldn't be so fun after all.

***

Even though I was exhausted from my overnight-underwater travels, I was up early in the morning. Nervous energy spurred me on. I got dressed for work and jogged to the Boardwalk. It wasn't excitement about work that had my stomach jumping and my heart aflutter. It was talking to Chase, or trying to talk him out of doing the story. And to be honest, it was about seeing Chase.

Which I hated.

I shouldn't ache to see him. He was going to betray me. I should hate him and everything he planned to do. And yet, I couldn't stop the jittery tingles shooting up my spine. I couldn't fool myself into believing it was because of our upcoming confrontation.

I didn't know where to find him, but figured I'd ask at the office. As I was walking up to the back door to Mrs. Fowler's office, Chase walked out the door.

"Chase." His name whispered off my lips.

"Pearl." He turned toward me with his arms open. "Where were you last night?"

I wanted to rush into them, feel his strong arms wrap around me. "Huh?" My confused expression must've reminded him of our fight because he dropped his arms.

"I stopped by your tent about ten. I wanted to finish our discussion."

The bang of a window shutting made me glance up. "What's above the office?"

"The owner lives there in an apartment." His face stiffened. "Do you have time to walk on the beach?"

"Sure." I wanted to get this conversation over with and I didn't want prying ears on the Boardwalk to hear.

He took hold of my arm and wouldn't let go, unless I fought him, which would be ridiculous and overly dramatic. So, I let him lead me past the rides and down the steps to the sand. "I hated how we left things yesterday." He dropped my arm and continued walking.

"Me, too." My heart unwillingly softened. My feet squished in the sand.

"You have to understand, I was excited about what you showed me. What you could do."

"You promised not to tell anyone, but now you plan to write an article about me." The betrayal renewed, ripping my heart like it had been gutted with a serrated knife. I had to remember I was here to convince Chase not to write the story. I couldn't be whittled down by sweet talk and explanations. "Now you plan to tell the world."

"Your skill could help people." He stopped and turned to observe me. A gleam of enthusiasm lit his face. "Scientists could study—"

"Study *me*? Analyze *my* DNA? Dissect *me*?" I didn't want to be studied under a microscope anymore than I wanted to be put on display at the circus.

"No one would dissect you." His voice sounded less-sure.

"You don't know that. Look at what greed does to people. What about military operations? Can you imagine what terrorists, or even the C.I.A., could do with my ability?" I'd thought of all these scenarios before. When I'd made the decision to run away, I'd considered Washington D.C. to basically offer myself as a science experiment, but each scenario evolved into a nightmare of torture that eventually left me dead.

Instead I'd followed my heart and ended up in southern California. I loved Mermaid Beach and the life I'd planned to build for myself. And now I'd found people like me.

"Like what?" He sounded more curious now.

I get that Chase is a reporter but I was telling him my biggest fears and he was just curious?

"Oh, I don't know." My patience hit its limit like the surf slamming into a cliff. "How about an army of underwater breathers?" Like the Atlanteans. "Who don't need to worry about expensive equipment or refilling air tanks. Or a new tourist industry where once the expensive fee was paid, I'd breathe into people so they could explore the ocean without inhibitions." I raised my arms to emphasize my point. "There's a dozen more at least and they all involve using me to make money. I'm sick of being someone else's gold mine."

Chase studied me. Sympathy shown in his gaze. He seemed to finally understand all the ugly possibilities.

He sunk to his knees on the sand. His head hung low "You did the same thing to that little kid Brandon, right?"

I jerked my head down in a nod.

"Does he know? Does his mother?"

"I told you, it wears off. The boy is too young to

realize what happened, and his mom won't let him near water for awhile."

I plopped on the beach, my anger draining with my energy. Tired of fighting, tired of hiding, tired of pretending.

Free Atlantis was looking better and better.

"How many other people have you breathed into? How did you discover it?"

After explaining about Alonso, I asked, "Do you understand why I don't want anyone to know? Between being thought of as unusual, a prize, or a scientific experiment I'd go crazy."

"I guess." But he didn't sound convinced.

I heaved a huge sigh. Maybe it was time to give up, run away again. I thought I'd stopped running, made a stand here in Mermaid Beach to make a life for myself, to live the way I wanted. But trusting Chase had been a mistake.

My anger was gone. There was nothing left inside. I felt empty. "Go on. Write your story, but I won't be around to prove it's true."

"Where are you going?" His sharp tone told me he wasn't expecting that response.

I chuckled at the thought of actually telling him the truth. "Does it matter?"

"It matters to me." Chase scooted closer.

Part of me wanted to move away from him and part of me wanted to move closer, knowing I'd never see him again. I was so weak. "If it mattered, you wouldn't be telling the world about my secrets."

"Surely, others know." He picked up a handful of sand and measured it in his palm. "This Alonso guy. Your parents."

My head jerked up. The circus owners had known some of my abilities, but not all. "They abused my skills. That's why I ran away." I clamped my lips tight.

"Ran away from where?" His voice softened and his fingers traced a line on my thigh.

His Prince Charming act wouldn't work again. I'd divulged enough for the day. I wanted him to understand how writing the article could affect me. And possibly him if the Free-Atlanteans found out. Not that I could tell him that part.

I swatted his hand off my leg. "I told you my parents and I don't get along."

"But you're eighteen, so it's not running away. It's leaving home." He sounded so logical.

But there was nothing logical about my life. I shook my head trying to clear it. All the lies and half-truths mixed together. Completely confuzzled, I brought the subject back around to my purpose. "Are you going to write an expose about me? No one will believe you without proof and I won't help. I'll be gone."

"I don't want you to leave." He grabbed my hand and this time held on tight. "I don't want to lose you. Although for even thinking of writing the story you probably hate me."

"You're not going to write the story?" I leaned forward showing my eagerness.

"No. I'm an idiot." He kicked at the sand, disgust filling his voice. Not disgust at me, but at himself.

Hope coursed through my chest like a rush of waves in an underwater cave. If he didn't write the story, I could stay in Mermaid Beach. Take the time to learn more about the Free Atlanteans and this battle they're fighting. My decision to live with them wouldn't be rushed.

"Do you hate me?" His please-like-me tone crept into my heart, breeching the barriers I'd built.

"Are you going to tell anyone about what I can do?" I kept the hope out of my voice.

"No. I promised I wouldn't." He rubbed his thumb against my skin. His gaze sought out mine and connected. "And I promise again. I will never tell anyone about you and your amazing skills." He sounded like he was making a solemn vow.

And I wanted to believe him.

"I admit I got excited about the idea, but I won't say anything. We'll keep it our secret." He squeezed my hand tight. "Do you forgive me?"

The hope rushed through the barriers around my heart. The walls crumbled at his hurt-lost expression. I hated seeing him like this. My instincts told me to trust him. He hadn't actually done anything yet. Just got over-excited about his experience. I should believe him.

"Yes."

"Can I have a real kiss now?" In other words, he wasn't asking for my underwater-breathing-breath. He wanted a kiss from me. An emotional connection to show all was forgiven.

I wanted that connection, too. Chase was the one person I'd had a bond with. The one person I believed in. The one person I trusted.

His slight lapse was over. He wouldn't betray me again.

My heart pulsed in anticipation. I wanted to show him all was forgiven. I wanted to feel that closeness and electricity.

I parted my mouth. His lips descended onto mine.

Our mouths, the perfect fit. His firm lips tasted salty and sweet.

His light touch sent tremors through my body and shivers across my skin. Heat spread through my veins. The varying temperatures mixed and mingled like lava from an underwater volcano pouring into cool water.

He ran a finger across my cheek. "I swear I will not tell a soul."

"Thanks." I felt our closeness in my heart.

We both scanned the ocean, catching our breath at our near miss.

"The experience was one I'll never forget." Chase spoke gently like treading on quicksand. He recounted some of the special things he'd seen that deep, putting names to sea life I didn't have a clue about.

While I might have underwater skills, he could be my tour guide. "How do you know so much about the ocean?"

"I've lived in Mermaid Beach my entire life."

"Where?" I didn't know much about Chase beside the fact that he'd worked at the Boardwalk for years and was going to college in the fall.

He continued to stare straight ahead. "I live with my aunt in an apartment near the Boardwalk."

"Where are your parents?"

"My parents died when I was eight." He fisted his hand in the sand. His brows knitted together in a frown. His body stiffened beside me. "That's when I went to live with my aunt."

"I'm sorry." I nestled closer to him.

We sat for awhile in silence, our hands entwined, both in our own melancholy thoughts. The seagulls squawked and the waves lapped at the shore. Until recently I thought I had parents, not very good ones, but parents all the same.

"What are you thinking about?" He placed his arm around my shoulders and tucked me against his solid body.

I nestled closer, appreciating his strength and support. "My parents." I spat the last word out.

"You said they abused your skills." His flat tone told me he believed me but wanted details.

Details I didn't know if I was ready to share. "Yes." The memory refreshed the pain, the hurt, the betrayal.

"How?"

"It doesn't matter." I didn't want Chase knowing about the circus or my past life. Too embarrassing. "They weren't my real parents anyhow. I recently discovered I was adopted."

Not legally.

"Are you going to search for your biological parents?"

I steadied my gaze, my eyes moist. The questions I'd asked last night hadn't helped.

Even Finn didn't want to help. He'd shut up tighter than the clams stored with the information.

If only I could find where the Royalists lived. I bet they kept detailed records. I could find my history. Find relatives. Maybe even find my parents.

"I wouldn't have a clue where to start."

Unless I could find the Atlantean castle.

Chapter Fourteen
Security Snafu

Later at work as I was changing garbage bags around the Boardwalk, I was paged to one of the rides for an emergency clean-up. The line wound out the front entrance of the log ride and around the building. Chase was feeding rope through stanchions to keep the crowd under control. He waved and my day got a little brighter.

The ride manager showed me the tunnel where the jam occurred. "We're holding all the logs until we get this fixed so don't worry about getting splashed." He pointed out the narrow metal ledge I should walk on.

I entered the tunnel. Multi-colored lights lit the inside. The ride was supposed to be scary but it was brighter than the caverns the Free Atlanteans called home. I edged around the corner, scanning for the spot where the slow-down happened.

Water flowed about three-fourths deep in the blue painted flume. Two metal rails, or tracks, dissected the bottom. Wrapped around one of the rails was a large, black, plastic trash bag. The bag was partially full.

I pinched at the garbage bag with my pick-up tool trying to wrestle it lose. The pincher slipped off the bag and I fell backward. My back scraped against the rock-like tunnel.

Ouch.

Shaking off my pain, I glanced around. No one could see my feeble attempts at unclogging the flume. The tunnel blocked any questioning eyes. I was tired and had too many other tasks to finish before clocking out.

I peered around a second time before sitting on the edge of the ledge. I took off my shoes and then slipped inside the flume.

The flow came to my waist. I placed the net downstream to catch any garbage that came loose. Bending at the knees, I reached down taking hold of the bag and tugged.

The bag ripped.

With my hands I fished out plastic water bottles, an old baseball cap, even a shoe. I grabbed both ends and tossed the bag onto the ledge. That's when I noticed the metal chain wrapped around one of the glides.

With a slow twist of my head, I again scanned the area. No one could see me. Not the manager, not the people in line, not even Chase below. My shift was almost over and I wanted to go home. I needed a nap. I didn't need more questions.

Pushing doubt aside, I gripped the metal chain and using my powers yanked with one sharp pull. The chain split in two. I took the pieces and shoved them into the bottom of a new garbage bag. Then, I took the old garbage bag and whatever trash had leaked out and covered the chain. Grabbing my shoes, I dripped my way over to the log ride manager to let him know the job was done.

I made my way to the large dumpster near the side of the office with still dripping clothes. I lifted the heavy lid and let go of the bag. It hit the bottom with a clunk.

"Miss Seidon." I jumped at the use of my fake name and dropped the dumpster lid. The lid fell with an echoing thud.

"I need to speak with you," Mrs. Fowler called from the front office window.

"Me?" My bones ached with exhaustion from work, from the anxiety over my discussion with Chase, from my all-night underwater traveling.

"Yes, you." Her firm voice didn't brook argument.

I dragged myself into her private office all the while muttering to myself. She closed the door with a slam.

Standing in front of the wooden desk, I shuffled my feet back and forth.

Mrs. Fowler examined me with a curious expression. I avoided her gaze and stared at the mountain of paperwork on her desk which had grown since my last visit.

"How did you do that?" Her voice sounded disbelieving, incredulous.

"Do what?" She'd seen me throw garbage bags in the dumpster before.

She moved forward, toward me. "You broke a metal chain with your bare hands."

My heart thudded like the dumpster lid. "What are you talking about?"

"I saw you on the security camera." She waved her hand at a television monitor, right next to a large portrait of a much younger Mrs. Fowler and a boy.

"What security camera?" Mentally slapping my

forehead because I'd been so concerned about a person seeing me, I never thought to skim for a hidden camera.

"I was working on the accounts in my office when I heard the log ride was shut down and decided to take a look." She patted her bun which wasn't as neat as usual. "We've got cameras in all the hidden nooks and crannies and tunnels to make sure no one on the ride is goofing around." She lasered into me. "I zoomed on you in the flume. I saw you break the chain with your bare hands."

A flash seared my lungs and panic burned. I had to think of something, anything to save my secret. "It's not what you think."

"I'm flabbergasted. I don't know what to think."

"The chain was...the chain was..." Rusted? Corroded? Unlinked? "Plastic. The chain wasn't metal. It was a toy. Like from a Halloween costume. And it already had a cut in it, so, it was pretty easy to snap in two. Anyone could've done it."

Mrs. Fowler's eyebrows rose high enough to touch her hairline. "Plastic, huh?"

***

Hurrying to the time clock, I thought about the last glare Mrs. Fowler had given me. She didn't seem to buy my explanation of a plastic chain, yet she'd let my leave her office. Nigglings of doubt crawled over my too-tired body. I was too exhausted to think about it.

Chase met me at the end of my shift. After giving me a quick kiss, he asked, "Any plans for tonight?"

"Sleeping."

He rubbed my temple with a gentle thumb. "Where did you go last night that you're so tired?"

Between the kiss, the mini-massage, and my mushy brain, I wasn't thinking clearly. "Free Atlantis."

"What?" Both his brows rose, similar to Mrs. Fowler's surprised expression earlier.

Oops. I'd promised Finn to keep Free Atlantis a secret. But the Atlanteans knew about Chase. Threatened him. He needed to be told.

A new burst of purpose and adrenaline poured through me like I'd drunk a gallon of coffee. I glanced around to confirm no one could overhear our conversation. "Are you off now?"

"Yes."

Weird how we always worked the same shift. "Walk me back to the campground and I'll explain."

Decision made. I trusted Chase. I was going to tell him about last night.

With a nod, Chase took my bag and slung it over his shoulder. We started walking. "Explain away."

"This is super secret confidential." I peered around to be sure no one could hear. Walking on my toes, I couldn't contain the news. "I met someone last night."

His body tensed next to mine. "Who?"

"His name is Finn and he's...like me." I tried to whisper but I couldn't douse my excitement. "There are other people like me, Chase. Ones who can breathe underwater. In fact, they live underwater and I met some of them. Finn took me there." My voice rose higher with each word.

Chase stumbled to a stop. "A strange guy took you to an underwater city?"

"Not a city, exactly. It's more of a base."

"What kind of base?" His I-can't-believe-what-you're-telling-me tone raised in a question.

I rushed to explain. "You see there's this battle going on under the Pacific, which could be the reason for the unexplained phenomena, that the rest of the world doesn't even know about." I filled him in on the Free Atlanteans versus the evil Royalists.

His unbelieving expression changed to an incredulous look highlighted by his arched brows and wide eyes. "Where is this base located?"

"Somewhere off of Mexico at the bottom of the ocean."

Chase snorted. "You're saying you swam all the way to an underwater military base off the coast of Mexico last night?"

With his disbelief in full-force, now probably wasn't the time to tell him about my super speed. "Yes."

"Describe it." His demand put me on edge.

Nerves swam in my veins like Olympians in a race, pulsing back and forth and back and forth doing laps of indecision. Of course he didn't want details for an article. He was just worried about me.

"Well, it was a mountainous area. The depths so deep there were sea creatures I'd never seen before." I debated how much detail to give. The more details given the more dangerous the trip sounded. "Thermal vents shot heat and stuff."

He turned to face me, his gaze shooting accusations of lies. "Don't you think a military base would've been discovered by the Mexican government or the U.S. government or any of the marine biologists or scientists studying the ocean?" He spoke like I was a complete moron.

I didn't like it. I'd told him and showed him fantastical things. Why didn't he believe this one?

"It's well hidden," I forced contempt into my voice.

"I'll rent a boat and you can show me." Not only

didn't he believe me, he dared me.

"A boat would never work." I wanted to show him I'd told the truth, wanted to breathe into him right this second and swim to the base to prove I wasn't making anything up. But...

"I don't know if I can find it again, without Finn." My stomach spasmed knowing what he'd want to know next, not sure how to explain.

"Why not?"

I huffed out a defensive breath and tried to make is sound unimportant. "He blindfolded me."

It sounded stupid now, but at the time I was driven by my curiosity, by my need to meet others like me, and by my anger at Chase.

Chase let my backpack drop off his shoulder and it hit the ground. Green flashed in his eyes. "You let some strange guy blindfold you? And then let him take you to who-knows-where?" He reached out and placed a hand on my shoulder, holding me in place. "You don't know what his intentions were."

The weight of his hand was like a judge's mallet, deciding right and wrong. I shook off his patronizing hand and shoved down my fears from last night. "He's like me."

That should explain it all.

"You trusted him, without any doubts?" Unlike me, he seemed to leave out.

"I had doubts." Lots of them, but the need to know won out.

Chase's lips smirked into an ugly line. "Even if he is 'like you' that doesn't mean he's a good guy. You said yourself there's a war going on. What if he's on the wrong side?"

"He isn't." I remembered my unease at the base, how the captain had examined me. Still, Chase didn't know what he was talking about. He hadn't met Finn, couldn't judge him sight unseen.

Kind of like how Finn judged all air-breathers.

I reached out and touched Chase's arm. "There's something else."

"What?" The word shot out of his mouth like a bullet. "You're leaving with this guy, who probably has superpowers like you, to live under the ocean?"

"Don't be ridiculous." I forced a slight laugh because the option had definitely been presented.

"Then, what?"

I had to warn him. "They know about you, Chase."

His casual shrug appeared stiff. "So these, Atlanteans," he said the name in a sarcastic-way, "know I exist. I assume they know about the world above the ocean."

Frowning, I didn't like how he made fun of what I'd told him. He wasn't taking it seriously. "They know that you know. About me."

"So?" His voice challenged.

"I, um…" Here came the tough part. "I sort of told them you planned to write an article about me and they weren't happy."

"What're they going to do? Come out and drag me under the ocean?" He blew the entire thing off.

Another huff. This one frizzled with frustration. "I told them I'd talk to you. Convince you not to write the story."

His gaze narrowed as if he'd come to the wrong conclusion about my motivation. "And. You. Did." He crossed his arms. "Is that what this morning was all about? You wanted to guarantee I didn't write the story. Is that why you kissed me?"

"Yes. I mean, no." He was confusing me. "I did need to convince you not to write the story, for my sake, and for your sake, too."

"Have you ever heard of freedom of the press? Do they not have that in *Free* Atlantis?"

"I don't know. The point is, you're not going to write the article. They won't come after you. And everything is fine between us, right?"

His phone shrilled an interruption. Chase glanced at the number. "I have to take this." Uncertainty still showed on his face. I don't know if he didn't believe me or didn't understand why I'd gone with Finn.

My shoulders slumped. Would I have to prove everything to him?

He shoved his phone in his pocket. "Mrs. Fowler has an emergency she needs me to take care of."

"Now?"

"Yes."

"What about us?"

He shook his head staring at the ground. "What about us?"

Now he was being obtuse.

"Are we okay?"

"Sure, we're okay." But he sounded like he was anything but okay. "You go off on a stupid excursion all night long with a strange guy. What's not to be okay about?" He turned and started to walk away.

"Chase." My voice broke. My eyes burned with a telling sensation. I didn't want him to see me cry.

If he wanted to walk away from this discussion—fine. If he thinks I acted rashly—too bad. If he thinks I betrayed him—well that's nothing compared to how he almost betrayed me with the article.

I picked up my backpack and walked away, heading toward the campsite. I refused to glance back. Refused to see if Chase looked back at me. Refused to be hurt more because if he didn't look back I'd be crushed.

Sniffling, I sucked down the damp ocean air. Chase didn't understand. He hadn't seen Free Atlantis, how those people lived and struggled. Sure, the captain was creepy, but according to Finn he led the revolt. The man had a lot of responsibility.

Yes, it had been stupid of me to go with Finn, but everything turned out okay. Except for with Chase.

I shouldn't have told Finn about Chase writing the article either, but it was done.

I passed the barbecue grills by the campground. Mr. Plankson lectured someone inside his office, his angry but non-understandable words carrying through the open window. Tears streamed down my face. Brushing them aside, I climbed into my tent. I didn't want anyone to witness my hurt.

Chase didn't believe me. Or if he did believe me, he thought I'd acted recklessly. And maybe I had.

But he hadn't seen how the inhabitants of Free Atlantis had welcomed me like one of their own, given me a gift.

I reached deep into my pillowcase and took out the present the old woman had given me. Maybe I should've brought the clam to show Chase. Then, he would've believed me.

Opening the clam, I heard the music of the sea and relaxed.

A palm-sized pearl sat in the cushion of the shell. I'd

never seen a pearl this big. I picked up the pearl and held it to the light.

A line, almost like a crack, ruined the luminescent beauty of the pearl. My gaze followed the crack until it reached a corner. The crack made a right turn.

A perfect, ninety-degree right turn.

My breath caught.

The crack turned downward and then left. A rectangle. Not made by nature, but by man.

I pressed against the rectangle with my finger. The panel popped open like a jack-in-the-box door.

My lungs wheezed. My pulse tapped. My heart stuttered.

I thought my imagination had boosted my memory. I was wrong.

The dazzling lights of blue and gold danced around the tent, brightening the interior. The lights were vibrant like I remembered. They were the same lights that came from the shell Bill and Carlita once owned.

The small nautilus inside the pearl called to me as theirs did. I found it just as familiar, just as intriguing, just as mysterious.

Chapter Fifteen
Coy Clam

With shaking fingers, I reached inside the pearl and took out the small nautilus tucked inside. The shell was a miniature version of the one Bill and Carlita had placed on the mantel. The same shape, the same twirling lights, the same magnetic force.

My chest squeezed tight with all the memories. Mostly bad memories. As a kid, the large nautilus had always called to me like a magnetic force. I'd been fascinated by the shell's shape and color and essence.

I brought the new nautilus closer to my face and examined its beauty. The rough outside appeared like a normal shell. Ridges highlighted the various chambers. Lines swirled in varying directions.

The inside fascinated. Swirling colors formed and reformed shapes. Sparkles of light shot through the center. I swear I saw images of oceans and beaches, of coral castles and exotic fish.

The sound of the ocean poured through the shell. I put it to my ear and listened.

"Millennia ago as Atlantis sank," a voice boomed from inside the shell.

I dropped the nautilus. The shell bounced along the canvas tent bottom and rested against my backpack. Staring at it, I tried to catch my breath.

Had I really heard a voice?

I pinched the shell between my two fingers. The lights sparkled again, the ocean sounded. I scrunched up my face and leaned back. I brought the nautilus closer, even though I was fearful of what might happen.

"Millennia ago as Atlantis sank into the depths of the sea, King Atlas cocooned his three infant daughters in special pods and sent them across the globe to carry on his legendary line. When the time is right, the girls will be born into the human world for their safety. Reunited as children, they will be raised to understand their duties and combine their powers to prevent a similar disaster from befalling future Atlanteans, and all mankind."

My hand fell to my lap while keeping hold of the shell. I sat still, afraid to move. Afraid to breathe too hard. My mind digested the legend I'd just heard, a legend I'd heard before from Finn. Only his version wasn't positive.

Finn said it was a myth. That Princess Cordelia's followers had been fooled into believing a fairytale.

Lying down on my sleeping bag, I clutched the nautilus in my hand. My eyelids dipped closed. My body gave in to exhaustion. My mind pictured an underwater world saved by three lost princesses.

Dreams took over from my imagination. I saw a massive earthquake and people scurrying to protect themselves and their families. A man with a crown carried a baby and placed her in a shell pod.

The baby was me.

**

I awoke the next morning with an ache in my heart. My eyes felt dry, my throat scratchy. My head hurt from a restless sleep.

The dreams had seemed real. As if I'd really lived them.

Which I found hard to believe. The myth Finn and the shell told me must've implanted in my brain creating my princess fantasy.

The nautilus lay beside me. I picked the shell up and searched for the pearl to hide for safekeeping. Odd that the woman who gave it to me had chosen a pearl—my birthstone and the very thing I was named after.

I popped open the panel in the pearl, slipped the small nautilus inside, and tucked both away in my bag. Then, I picked up the clam. That's when I saw the additional strange lines inside the bottom of the shell.

They weren't straight lines and right angles like on the pearl. The etched lines were crooked and wavy. Like a rough sketch.

A few of the lines looked like waves. One appeared to be a mountain range. I turned the clam upside down. The outer edge of the drawing appeared to be the southern California coast.

I sucked down a ragged breath.

The drawing was a map.

"Knock, knock." The sides of my canvas tent shook and so did my body.

I tucked the clam behind my back. "Yes?"

"It's Chase."

I bit my lip not knowing how to respond after the way we'd left things last night. Was he angry or was I?

175

"Will you come out and talk to me?" His voice sounded unsure.

I picked up the clam and shoved it in my pocket. Then, I unzipped the front flap of the tent and crawled outside. I didn't know what to expect or what I'd tell him.

Chase wore board shorts and a swim shirt. His brown hair was tussled and I wanted to run my fingers through it.

"So, um, how'd you sleep?" The casual question seemed to cover nervousness.

"Okay, I guess." I ran a shaky hand through my own hair, unsure what to do or say.

"I'm sorry I got angry yesterday, but I worry about you." He raised his arms up about to put them around me, but then dropped them. "All alone. Sleeping in a tent. Going with strange guys to strange underwater places."

"You believe me now?"

"I always did. I mean," he scuffed his foot in the dirt, "the tale was incredible, but I know with you things will always be unusual." He jerked his head up. "In a good way."

"If you believed me, why the sarcasm?"

"It was more anger than sarcasm." He grabbed hold of one of my hands and squeezed. "That fact that you went away, blindfolded, with some strange guy."

"I was safe with Finn."

"Hindsight."

"You have to understand why I needed to go. I want to find my real parents, find out where I came from." My stomach tightened thinking about my goal. "And I didn't make-up with you yesterday to sway you about writing the article. I don't want you to write the story, but more importantly, I don't want to fight with you."

"I don't want to fight with you either." His eyes warmed. "Will you forgive me?"

I took a tentative step forward wanting to see every tiny movement on his face, needing to read what he felt. "Do you understand why I need to keep things quiet? Everything."

"Yes." His rough hand took hold of both of mine. I liked how they looked intertwined. "I'm sorry for being a jerk."

"It's okay." I didn't want the I'm-sorry-session to go on and on. It's over. We're okay. That's all that mattered.

"Kind of completely off the subject, I did a little research last night." A self-satisfied smile slipped onto his face. "Based on your descriptions you might've traveled to the East Pacific Rise. Although how you got there and back in one night by swimming, I don't understand."

"What's the East Pacific Rise?"

"It's an undersea mountainous area west of Mexico where thermal vents have formed." He crossed his arms. "But it would be impossible to withstand the heat."

I stepped closer to him, close enough to feel the warmth from his body, close enough to smell his fresh scent, close enough so no one else could hear. "After I breathed into you, were you cold underwater?"

He stood silent for a second. "No."

"My body adjusts to water temperature. So did yours."

"To temperatures as high as 400 Celsius?"

I bumped my shoulder against his. The weight of pressure, confusion and excitement lifted with the slight contact. "I didn't burst into flames. If you even could burst into flames underwater."

Silence stood between us. His gaze was unfocused as if in deep thought. "I guess I'll buy that. It's not the strangest thing you've told me."

Maybe now he'd start accepting things without doubt.

"What do you have planned for today?" he asked.

My earlier excitement resurfaced. "An adventure."

"What kind of adventure?" His lips quirked in a cute-guy smile.

"Are you working today?"

"Nope. Got the entire day off."

"So do I." I opened my hand to display the clam laying in my palm. "Since you've possibly found where I went the other night, I've got another place to find."

"You can find those shells all over the place. Although that's a big one and in excellent condition." He kissed the top of my head. "You want to go shell hunting?"

My head tingled. A simple touch and sparks sprinkled through my entire body. Our camaraderie and connection had returned. Things could get back to normal. Or whatever was normal for us.

"No." I placed my other hand over the clam and using my fingers, I opened the shell with care. "I want to find this."

Chase bent over my opened hand and examined the inside of the shell. "It a map."

I pointed to one of the lines. "That looks like the coastline. And this appears to be an island."

"Atlas Island." He ran his long finger over the grooved surface. "Where'd you get this?"

"A woman, at the underwater base, gave it to me." I scrunched up my facew waiting for his reaction.

"She just handed you a shell? Did she know it had a map inside?"

"Maybe she didn't know." I didn't mention the pearl with the hidden compartment or the wondrous nautilus inside. For some reason, those items felt more personal to me. Like by sharing them with Chase I'd betray another Atlantean secret.

He ran his fingers over the one spot. "This appears to be Atlas Island. You can feel how the island surface is dug out. It's the only place like that on the map."

"So, we should go there?" Energy skyrocketed. To be so close to this mythical place, my mythical place, and possibly my future home. "Atlas Island isn't that far away."

"There's no 'X' that marks the spot."

I slapped him on the arm, feeling the lightness of his mood. "We're not searching for treasure."

He angled his head and his brows rose in that familiar way. "What are we looking for?"

"The possible underwater location of the Royal Atlanteans."

***

Water sprayed my face as Chase and I stood by the railing of the ferry from Long Beach to Atlas Island. Our drive from Mermaid Beach had been filled with logistical talk and excited theories. He didn't quite believe everything, but he didn't *not* believe either.

I squeezed Chase's hand. "Nice of Cuda to let you borrow his truck so we could get to Long Beach."

"He asked a lot of questions about why we both had the sudden urge to see Atlas."

"What did you tell him?" I held my breath praying he didn't tell Cuda my secret.

"That you were new to the area and wanted to explore."

I nodded glad Chase hadn't spilled. "Sounds reasonable."

"And partially true." Chase laughed. "Could you imagine if I'd told him the truth? He'd think we were crazy."

Laughter bubbled up and lightened my soul. I couldn't imagine doing this alone. Sharing this adventure with Chase meant more to me than all the tuna in the sea. "I think sometimes we are crazy."

I needed to show how grateful I was. For supporting me, for believing me, for keeping my secret.

I stood on tiptoes. His masculine lips were directly across from mine. I leaned forward. Nothing separated our mouths but a sliver of air. I touched my lips to his.

Felt the sizzle.

Tasted the sweetness.

Sensed our connection.

This was the first time I'd initiated a kiss. The first time I'd reached out. The first time I'd displayed my feelings directly. I kind of liked it. A lot.

Chase responded. Holding me tighter, the pressure of our mouths increased and so did the intensity of my feelings. I wanted to stay like this forever.

When we separated, Chase squinted. "A sea otter."

The little creature swam in circles on the left side of the ferry.

My stomach twisted. Whenever an otter appeared, water emergencies happened. Before the whirlpool and when the jellyfish attacked.

"Cute." There was no enthusiasm in my voice.

"There's another." He pointed.

Double trouble.

"Two more."

The otters swam around and around. They chattered and moved their paws in an agitated fashion.

I checked the sky and then stared deep into the ocean water. Nothing unusual.

Tingles spread down my back. I couldn't shake the doomed feeling that had darkened all the light inside me. "Something's wrong." The otters were a sign.

"What're you talking about?" Chase spared me a you-really-are-crazy look.

"The otters. I can't talk to them while I'm out of water but they're trying to warn us."

"Excuse me? Did you say talk to them?" His earlier you-really-are-crazy look multiplied. "Like talk to the animals Dr. Doolittle style?" He leaned away from me.

Huffing out a breath, I wanted to scream with his predictability. He didn't believe me again, but I didn't have time to get angry or explain.

I scanned the surface of the ocean scanning for trouble. "They understand me and can answer yes or no."

Chase laughed. "You're kidding, right?"

"No, I'm not." I kept my tone flat and serious.

The laughter wiped off his face. "The otters are playing. It's what otters do."

"Ladies and gentlemen," an announcer came over the loudspeaker. "We're experiencing mechanical difficulties on the ferry."

I shot Chase an arched-brow in a know-it-all style.

"Okay, I believe you can talk to the otters." He held up both hands in an understanding gesture. "But how

181

could otters know about mechanical difficulties? They know nothing about the workings of a boat."

The announcer continued, "Please do not panic, but proceed to the emergency stations near the exits of the boat. Crew members will be handing out lifejackets for every passenger to wear."

"Do you think we're sinking?" I gripped Chase's hand glad to have him to hold on to.

We followed the other passengers to get our lifejackets. "The ferry is still moving at a fast clip."

"You'd think they'd slow down for an emergency." My tummy tumbled, feeling a little seasick.

The group in front of us rushed to get their jackets. An elderly man carrying a cane struggled to get his vest on. A couple of teens joked around about death.

A man kissed a woman on the lips. "This is not a good sign to begin our honeymoon."

"I don't know how to swim," a pale woman confided to her friends.

A mom helped two young kids snap on life vests with shaking hands.

A tear ran down the little girl's cheeks. "Mommy, are we going to die?"

"Of course not." The mom's voice sounded tremulous. "Stay close."

"We're going to crash and end up in the ocean and be eaten by sharks." The other child shouted.

"Be quiet." The mom took both their hands.

My stomach revolted. I stared at the little girl and boy. If we sunk I'd be okay, and I could save Chase. But there were possibly a hundred passengers on board. I couldn't save everyone.

How could I possibly choose?

Chapter Sixteen
Ferry Folly

Like playing God, I'd decide who to breathe into first.

I'd decide who to save.

I'd decide who would live and who would die.

My head swirled. With white knuckles, I gripped the brass rail. My stomach heaved. I couldn't let all these people die.

Chase grabbed one of the crew by the arm. "What's happening?"

"Engine malfunction. We can't slow down and we've almost reached Atlas Island."

"Are we going to crash?" Chase's voice rose. The tension between the two men, between everyone, encrusted the air.

The man jerked away and hurried on.

"Not if I can help it." There had to be a way to stop the ferry. I unsnapped my life vest. Purpose filled my every move.

"What're you doing?" His face paled.

I slapped the life vest into his arms. "I'm going to stop this freaking ferry."

"How?"

Pulling back my shoulders, I fisted both hands. I couldn't let this water disaster hurt hundreds of people. Especially, since this accident could be my fault. Chase was right. Water disasters did happen around me. "I'll figure something out."

"You're crazy. One person can't stop a huge ferry." He gripped my arm, stopping me. His chin jutted with determination.

"I forgot to tell you," I jerked my arm out of his grip, climbed onto the rail and swung my leg over. "I have super-strength too."

His Adam's apple moved up and down. His gaze glazed and then cleared. "Take me with you." He unsnapped his life vest and took it off.

Decisive. No questioning if what I said was true. But I didn't have time to rejoice in his reaction.

"No way. The dive from here is way too steep." I didn't want to be responsible for his possible death or injury. And I couldn't delay any longer.

"I've dived off the cliffs near Mermaid Beach before and survived. I can do this." His hard tone told me he wouldn't give in.

"But—"

He dropped the vests to the deck. "I'm diving in whether you breathe into me or not. You are *not* doing this alone."

I stared into the blue steel of determination and then swiveled my glance to the churning water below. My tummy churned, too. "What if you get hurt?"

"I won't." A promise he didn't know if he could

keep.

The churning in my stomach flipped and flopped. Like my mind. How could I risk his life? "Have you ever dived off of a moving ferry into the ocean before?"

"Have you?" His brow arched in challenge.

"No, but I've done platform diving." I remembered the crowds excited oohs and ahs. How I'd hated it. But this time, hopefully, no one would see.

"And I've done cliff diving. Into the ocean." He stomped his foot onto the rail and swung a leg around. "I have more experience than you."

My mind wavered. Not give Chase my breath and have him go for it anyhow—dive in and die. Or give Chase my breath and have him possibly get hurt on the dive. "Chase—"

"Do it now while no one is watching."

People scurried toward the emergency exits. No one paid attention to two teens sitting on the rail. On a normal trip, we would've been yelled at or apprehended.

"Come on. Now's our chance." Chase lifted his second leg over the rail. The stubborn expression on his face told me I didn't have a choice. "Do it."

I liked the idea of not going alone. But with that comfort came fear because Chase was a frail human in the ocean. He wasn't like me.

Expediency fought with worry like a pulley in my soul. Leaning into him, I didn't have time to convince him to stay. His unique scent mixed with the salty ocean air. My lips touched his and I breathed my special breath into his mouth, blowing as much of my power as possible to keep him safe. "Ready?"

"A real kiss first. For luck." He leaned into me and touched his lips to mine.

I enjoyed the real kiss, much more than giving him my breath. This kiss was special. It wasn't a means to an end, but a promise. My lips tingled from his quick touch.

And then his mouth was gone. I opened my eyes and beheld his shiny blue ones, knowing the kiss meant as much to him.

Together, we both stood. Dove.

The water slapped me in the face. Hard. I let the momentum from the dive take me down deep. The entire time I scanned for Chase. My gaze roving. My strokes frantic. My nerves tightening. I hoped he'd survived the dive. I hoped he wasn't scared or hurt. I hoped we ended up close to each other.

"Pearl?" I heard my name carried on the current.

"Chase." I scoured the bottom. "Are you okay?"

"What a ride!" He sounded like he'd just gotten off the roller coaster on the Boardwalk.

I swiveled around following the sound of his voice, needing to see him. "Where are you?"

"Over here." He swam from behind a section of jagged rocks. A smile flashed.

"Oh." I rushed over and landed in his arms, reveling in his touch. "I was worried."

"Me, too. About both of us." He held tight and kissed me on the forehead. "Where's the ferry?"

With both of us safe and his arms around me, for a second I almost forgot our purpose. I glanced up and listened. The sound of the ferry's engines came from a spot west of us. Our deep dive and the ferry's speed hadn't carried us too far in the other direction. "This way."

We swam toward the ferry.

"What's the plan once we reach the ferry?" Chase's

question gave me a boost of confidence. He respected that I was the expert in this arena.

Except, I wasn't.

My heart quivered. "I don't know."

Chase kept his pace even with mine. And I was swimming pretty darn fast. Did my breath not only let him breathe underwater but give him speed, too?

I sliced deeper and faster. "We need to think of something."

"There's the ferry." He pointed at the churning water up ahead caused by the boat's engines.

Just like the churning in my stomach because I still didn't have a plan. The quivering in my heart increased to spasms of uncertainty.

We kept pace with the ferry. The engines ground together and the noise reverberated across the ocean. The ferry above jerked and then, changed direction.

"It's heading to sea." Chase's voice held an edge of panic.

The same panic echoed inside me. "That's good." The ocean floor was sandy and smooth here, but I saw rocks in the distance. "That means it won't crash into rocks or Atlas Island." It gave us more time.

A mechanical whirring and heavy clinking noise echoed under the waves. Several large anchors attached to thick, metal chains dropped out of the backside of the ferry. When the noise stopped, the anchors dragged across the bottom but did little to slow the boat.

"The anchors aren't helping. What can we do?" Biting my lip, I controlled the rush of fear and adrenaline. Controlled my insecurity. Controlled my scream. I'd risked everything to come down here, even risked hurting Chase, and now we couldn't figure out a way to help.

"Grab onto an anchor and use the super strength to stop the ferry." He sounded so decisive, committed. Like no matter what happened we were going to sink or swim together.

Which I loved and hated. Because I didn't want to sink. I didn't want him to sink. And I didn't want the ferry to sink.

My chest thumped echoing the fall of the anchor. "I don't think I'm that strong."

"Together we are."

"What?"

"Remember when you said I wasn't cold in the water because of your breath." His confidence grew with each word he spoke.

"Yes."

"And just now I kept up with your swimming pace."

"Super speed." The words rung in my head.

"So, why wouldn't I have super strength, too?"

So logical. But my life wasn't logical. Nothing worked as planned. "What if you're wrong?"

"You said it yourself, we have to try something."

We didn't have a lot of time. The ferry would eventually hit something. "Okay. Let me go first."

Maybe on my own I could slow it down. I raced after one of the anchors on the right side. Every time I reached out, the anchor bobbed and jumped ahead. It was like trying to catch a spawning salmon, except the anchor weighed a lot more. I felt stupid.

"It's like baseball." Chase swam beside me and cheered me on, listening to my instructions that I should grab the anchor first. "Watch the anchor."

I swam ahead and stood in the path of the chain and

massive anchor. My best chance was to catch the anchor coming toward me, like catching a ground ball in baseball. My chest throbbed with burning heat, heaving in and out and in and out.

In order not to get clonked on the head, I had to catch the anchor while ducking the chain with precision. I held my breath, even though I didn't have to, and waited.

The anchor hit a rock and angled left. I shifted position and then held out my arms like I was waiting for a hug. The metal smashed into my chest. Sharp pain shot through my ribs. I grabbed the anchor by the hooks ripping my skin. The anchor slipped in my grasp. It yanked me forward.

"Ahhhh!" A scream tore out of my throat.

"Drop it." Chase lunged toward me. His mouth pulled into a grim line. "Just drop it."

"No." I clutched the anchor to my chest and held on with all my super strength. I stuck my heels in the sand and dug them in deep, refusing to give up. "I got it."

The boat didn't even slow down.

"My turn to catch an anchor." His trying-to-sound-playful tone couldn't be pulled off. He swam to the other side of the ferry.

"Be careful." My fingers already hurt from the tight grip I had on my anchor. I kept my gaze glued to him in case he needed help. If he got hurt, I don't know what I would do.

He swam behind the anchor on the other side, seeming to calculate the bumps it would take. Then, he picked up his speed and darted to the right. He reached out and grabbed the anchor like it was the end of a rope in a tug-of-war game.

"Got it." He readjusted his hands and dug his feet

into the sand.

A smile leaked onto my face. Guess he played more baseball than I did.

The boat slowed but didn't stop.

All of our efforts weren't helping. My arms shook with the effort of holding on. My heels felt scraped and raw. I didn't know about Chase, but I couldn't hold on much longer.

"Playing with ferries?" Finn swam toward us. "Doesn't sound fun to me."

"Grab an anchor." Everything inside me celebrated. Assistance had arrived. Surely, Finn would help. "We're trying to stop the ferry."

"We?" His tone changed when he spotted Chase.

"You got a problem with me, Finn?" With his quick mind, Chase realized who the stranger was.

After all, how many guys do I know who can breathe underwater?

"I'll do formal introductions later." We didn't have time to argue. "Finn, please grab an anchor and help us stop the ferry."

"You're with the guy who's going to write a story about you? Not a smart choice." His tone was slow and censuring.

He had no right to question me. "It's my choice. Besides, he's not going to write the article."

"That's right." Chase chimed in.

"You better not." Finn dove at the anchor between Chase and I. He grabbed the hooks in one swift swoop. The ferry jerked and slowed down almost to a stop. But not quite. Even with three of us, we couldn't stop the coming catastrophe.

"What happened?" Finn asked.

"I don't know." I gritted my teeth. "We were taking the ferry to Atlas Island."

"Why?"

First, I shot Chase a look willing him to keep quiet about the shell map, then I answered, "I, um, wanted to see the island. Anyhow, the ferry had mechanical difficulties. It couldn't stop or slow down. I couldn't let it crash."

"So you brought an air-breather along?"

Chase smirked at Finn. "I wasn't going to let Pearl stop the ferry alone."

Finn's gaze narrowed at Chase, but he didn't say anything. Instead, he turned to me. "I can't hold this anchor forever."

"Do you have some place more important to be?" Chase goaded.

"Be nice, Chase." I didn't want to play referee. "What do you suggest, Finn?"

I'd take any ideas. The pain in my arms was nothing compared to the panic in my chest.

"We could hook the anchors to a big rock."

"If we could find a big rock without the ferry smashing into it first." I pictured the little girl with the tears running down her cheeks. The old man with the cane. The couple on their honeymoon. My chest heaved panic to pure terror.

"Good point." Finn sounded like this was a casual conversation, not like hundreds of lives could be lost.

A noise, like a bubbling sound, filled our silence. I squinted trying to see if there was a new danger. A black smudge grew bigger on the surface and threw a shadow over our location.

"What's that?" I pointed with my chin.

Chase scowled at the darkening slick. "Looks like oil or gasoline."

"If you and those air-breathers ruin another portion of our ocean..." Finn's tone scraped with disgust.

"An oil spill?" I studied the concentration of sludge hanging around the back of the boat. "The ferry is dumping their fuel tank."

"That's got to be it." Chase agreed.

Buoyancy filled me like I was floating on water, not sunk down at the bottom. "Once they're out of fuel the ferry will stop."

"And we can let go of these stupid anchors and I can be on my way."

"Are you in a hurry?" Chase's reporter tone returned.

Which reminded me. "Finn, why were you swimming around Atlas Island?"

"Usually I avoid the area, but I was looking into something."

My thoughts whirled. "Are you spying?"

"What? That's stupid. Why would I come this close to the enemy?"

"I meant spying on me, but since you mentioned it, is this the base for the Royalists?"

"Not a base." Finn's tone had an edge, like he didn't want to explain further.

"What are you doing here?" Chase's question sounded like an accusation.

"You shouldn't be down here at all, air-breather." There was no respect in Finn's tone.

Chase pressed his lips together, but didn't say a thing.

"If Atlas Island isn't a base, what is it?" I wanted information, not a fight between the two of them.

"Atlas Island is where Princess Cordelia holds court.

It's where all the Atlanteans lived until the split."

"You mean war." Chase used the same tone of accusation.

Finn shrugged his shoulders trying to appear nonchalant. "Split, war, battle. It kind of depends on your point of view." He didn't sound as confidant about his cause.

"Have you changed your mind?"

"What does it matter what I think?"

"Killing people for a cause is war." I hated the thought of hurting and killing other people. I hated even more that I'd finally found people like me and they weren't peaceful.

"When did the war officially start?" Chase asked the relevant questions getting the facts straight.

"It hasn't. Yet." Finn actually gave Chase a straight answer. "More like skirmishes or sabotage up to this point."

The guys were chattering on about a war that was relevant but not important at this moment in time. The ferry had to run out of gas soon. I couldn't hold on to the anchor much longer and the more time these guys spent together the more likely they were to come to blows.

Chase jerked his head at the ferry that was almost stopped now. "Was the ferry sabotage?"

My heart thwacked. I hadn't thought of that. Maybe this wasn't an accident. Maybe the ferry's malfunction and the war were related.

"Why would either side want to hurt air-breathers?" Awkwardness filled my lungs. I didn't like calling them that, it sounded negative.

Again, Finn shrugged. "Did you tell anyone in Mermaid Beach you were going to Atlas Island by ferry?"

"A lifeguard friend of mine." Suspicion darkened Chase's expression. "Is Pearl a target?"

I opened my mouth but I couldn't speak. Couldn't even form words.

Finn glanced up at the shadow of the oil slick and the ferry. "Not that I'm aware of.

That's not much of answer." Chase's voice grew tougher, more accusatory.

"Why would I be a target?" I needed to calm them both down.

The boat stopped. The chains attached to the anchors quit pulling and loosened up. Like a yellow light, cautious optimism flashed inside me.

"Think we can drop these anchors?" Finn sounded like he wanted out of here, possibly away from Chase and I, and our questions.

"Me, first." After all, I'd been holding on the longest.

I held the anchor away from my body and dropped it. Sand swished from the bottom. The boat didn't rush forward.

"Air-breathers, second." Finn made it sound like Chase was second class.

Chase ignored him and dropped his anchor. Then, Finn dropped his anchor. The ferry stayed in one place, rocking with the waves.

"We did it! The three of us." I slapped my hands together to emphasize my point that it had taken all three of us. "We saved the ferry."

"More air-breathers still alive." Finn tried to sound cruel but he didn't.

"Better than war-mongering Atlanteans." Chase crossed his arms and glared at Finn.

So much for celebrating our success. "Guess we're free to go."

"Only the truth shall make me free." Finn's sarcastic tone touched a warning off in my head.

Before I could ask what he meant, he dashed deep into the ocean.

***

Atlas Island was an oasis of calm compared to the calamity, and then victory, we'd experienced under the ocean. Palm trees swayed with the light breeze drying my hair. Beach chairs lined the soft sand. No car noise on the island, just the humming of golf carts and the cawing of seagulls.

Chase and I took off our wet clothes. We sank down onto a couple of free beach chairs and the let the sun dry our bathing suits. He took my hand and our arms dangled between. With his strong hand in mine, I felt more powerful now than underwater.

"Are you tired after all of that?" I wasn't, but I didn't know how it would affect Chase.

"Why didn't you tell me about your super strength?" Anger tinged his flat voice.

"Why be angry now?" My weary voice held back my surprise.

"Anger wouldn't have helped in an emergency situation." Logical as always. "What else haven't you told me?"

I flipped through my old responses from sarcasm to rudeness to downright lies. I couldn't use any of those with Chase. He'd been good to me.

Like a gong announcing my intention my heart pounded. My pulse picked up speed. My veins throbbed.

Honesty.

While I'd shared parts of myself with Chase, I'd never told him about my upbringing. If I really liked him, and I wanted to have a real relationship with him, I'd need to be straightforward.

"Even though I had adoptive parents," who didn't treat me like their child, "I've always had a hard time sharing things about myself. I didn't have any friends." The admission cut across my heart. I pressed my lips together trying to keep my emotions in check. He didn't need to know I was a total loser. "Probably because of my abilities. I didn't want people to find out about my special powers." Well, Bill and Carlita didn't want people to know for fear of losing their source of cash.

"But you told me about breathing underwater." Chase dropped my hand and crossed his arms, taking a stand-offish stance. "Super strength and speed aren't all that miraculous after that."

"I know." My gaze shifted away.

"Do you have something else to share?"

I licked my suddenly dry lips. What to shut up about and what to share? "I'm not proud of what I did in my past."

"Anything illegal?"

"No." Except running away and lying about my age. Working in a circus wasn't illegal, just embarrassing. Yes, I was dancing around the truth. I wanted to tell him, really I did, but what would he think of me?

And, my past wasn't all that important.

"Then, I guess it doesn't matter to me." He took hold of my hand again and squeezed.

Not the normal inquisitive-reporter-keep-pushing-until-he-gets-answers Chase, but a willing-to-wait-until-I-was-ready Chase.

I wanted to melt against him, feel his strength. "You're sure?" Our connection seemed to be solid even without all the facts.

"Someday, when you're ready you'll tell me. I can wait until then." Scanning the busy marina, he stayed silent.

So, he knew I had more to tell. I bit my lip. Indecision swelled up and down like the waves. If I told him everything, would he think I was strange? A freak like everyone else who knew? I wasn't willing to take that chance.

"Don't you think Finn coming across us in the middle of the ocean was a little too coincidental?"

I smiled, glad the previous subject was closed. I loved how Chase's mind always returned to a puzzle. Stretching my neck, I was unwilling to admit my own doubts. "Possibly."

"He confirmed Atlas Island was where the Royalists lived."

"Yes."

"And Finn is against the Royalists." Chase chipped away at the coincidence theory.

I squirmed in my chair. "He was."

Chase turned facing me. His sharp gaze cut like diamonds. "Did you ever think maybe *he* caused the problems on the ferry? Maybe *he's* not your friend? Maybe *he's* dangerous?"

Each question dropped in my mind and plopped in my stomach. Even though I wasn't sure of Finn's loyalties, I trusted him. I think. "He showed me others like me. He might've blindfolded me to take me to the base, but he returned me home." With an argument. "He helped us today."

Chase ran a light finger down my cheek sending tingles across my skin. "I worry about you. Even with your super abilities, you're vulnerable." His tone went from soft to hard. "I don't want Finn taking advantage of you."

"He won't." I would never let anyone take advantage of me again. "It's just, I'll always be grateful to him for introducing me to Atlanteans."

"Grateful enough to blindly follow him?"

"Follow him where?"

"Into battle without knowing the facts."

Chapter Seventeen
Distressed Damsel

Did Chase mean a battle between him and Finn?

The way they argued I wouldn't be surprised. I was not a contest. Chase and I were together. Finn knew that. "What battle?"

Chase squeezed my hand tighter. "Finn's talking about a war."

"A war that doesn't involve me."

Chase leaned forward. "You know about their world now. They know about you." His soft, warm voice showed his concern. "You're bound to be affected."

"Pearl."

"And there's Finn's battle cry now." A know-it-all-disgust filled Chase's voice.

"Pearl." Finn rushed toward us waving his hands. His bathing suit dripped and his hair flipped back. An expression of urgency covered his face.

Probably similar to the look I wore when I'd been holding the anchor and he'd showed up. Something was wrong.

Chase stood and placed his hands on his hips, his stance like a warrior.

I stood, too. Could Chase be right? What was Finn's problem? And was I obliged to help?

"Pearl, you have to come with me." Finn puffed out the words, bending at the waist as if not used to running on land.

"Come with you where?"

"The Royalists are on emergency alert." He straightened, still huffing between breaths. "We need to find out if they're preparing to attack the Free Atlantis base first before—"

"Before you attack them?" Chase's smug expression changed when I glared.

"You shouldn't know any of this." Finn's lips protruded from his face in an angry pout. "How much more does he know?"

"Enough to warn her not to go." Chase took hold of my hand to show Finn we were united.

I was glad Chase was on my side, that he wanted to protect me, but I had to hear Finn out. Guilt twirled in my belly for betraying Atlantean secrets. The knowledge might put Chase in danger. Tiptoeing around Finn wouldn't help. "What could I possibly do?"

"We need to sneak into the palace and see what's going on. Find out what their plan is. Then, one of us can stay and lookout while the other reports back to base." Finn kept glancing around as if afraid of being caught.

"Why do you need me to help? Surely, there's someone else you can ask?"

Finn seemed to consider my question. His pupils moved up and down and then connected with mine. "I don't trust anyone else."

"What?" My mouth hung open.

His gaze shifted to Chase and then back to me. "I can't trust a Free Atlantean with this task. And no Royalist would trust me."

"Everyone's chosen sides?" There was no Switzerland in this war.

"Everyone."

Except me. Finn didn't need to say it. Like I was missing an essential game piece so I couldn't play. But because I wasn't in the game I'd be fair.

"Why should Pearl help you?" Chase's hand tightened around mine. "It sounds dangerous."

"Just information gathering."

"I'm not a spy." And I wasn't ready to choose sides.

"I helped you with the ferry. You can help me now. Please." His normally firm voice pleaded. He sounded desperate.

His desperation pulled at my heart. Finn had been good to me. He trusted me. He wanted my help.

I huffed out a breath not wanting to follow him blindly like Chase mentioned. It was like I had an internal battle going on inside of me, similar to the one being fought under the ocean, and I didn't know which side to choose internally, either.

"All were doing is seeing what's going on, right? You're not going to tell the captain about this?"

"Not unless they're planning an immediate attack. The base is completely unprepared for that. Many people would die."

I didn't want that on my conscious. "Only if Chase agrees to come with us."

"What?" Both guys said together but with different intonations like an off-key boys' choir.

"Are you willing, Chase?" I didn't want to force him to endanger himself again.

He raked over Finn before turning back to face me. "If you're going, I'm going."

"But he's an air-breather," Finn protested. "He shouldn't even know about us. He shouldn't get involved."

Chase angled his chin. "I'm already involved."

With me, I hope. "Take both of us, or neither."

***

Chase and I followed Finn as he scrambled around the rocks at the far end of the marina. Surf pounded and sprayed water into the air like a natural fountain. He dove into the waves and then surfaced a few yards away.

I took Chase's hand and we climbed down into the ocean taking one rock at a time. I worried about exposing him even more to this underwater world, especially the way Free Atlanteans thought about air-breathers. But I was glad he was going to be by my side. "Ready, Chase?"

His confidant nod showed he trusted me and wanted to protect me. A happy warmth settled in my soul.

I placed my mouth over his and breathed my special breath into him. When I emptied my lungs, I moved away. "Go under."

Chase let his body sink into the ocean like an anchor.

Finn watched us, an expression of bewilderment and fascination on his face. He might be an underwater breather but he appeared frightened by my abilities.

My happy warmth chilled. I shivered. Even in this world of water breathers, I'd be different.

Chase tugged my ankle and I slid under the water to meet him. He held out his hand, and I put mine in his.

Together, as a team, we swam to where Finn waited.

An unsmiling Finn led us into the mouth of an underwater cave. I watched his every reaction. Because of Chase's suspicions and my thoughts that didn't add up about Finn, I had to wonder whether this was a trap. But it was too late now. I'd agreed and we were here.

The strong rock had been cut down by even stronger waves rushing in and out for eons. The sight made me and my powers feel insignificant, like the shells and algae clinging to the rock.

Going deeper into the tunnel, my eyes automatically adjusted to the darkness. Clams settled at the bottom of the cave, next to a dull-orange anemone and green moss. A black sea hare darted past.

"This is awesome." Chase pointed at a large school of rainbow fish. "I can see in the dark."

"Do your other abilities transfer with the gift of your breath?" Finn's amazement reconfirmed my worst fears.

I was different. Strange. An anomaly.

"Chase doesn't get cold. He can swim fast and has super strength underwater like us."

Finn studied me and then switched to Chase. "Can he breathe into an air-breather and change them?"

Chase choked out a laugh. "I've never tried."

"If that were possible wouldn't there be hundreds of turned air-breathers? I turn two friends and you turn two friends, etc." I remembered how shocked Finn was when I'd told him that Chase wasn't one of us. "Didn't you say you've never met any Atlanteans who can breathe into other people?"

"No, I haven't."

"But I can make air-breathers breathe underwater. Why can't others?" The princess myth crossed my mind again. I immediately doused any royal thoughts. Every isolated, friend-less girl in the world dreamed of discovering she was special.

I wasn't special. I was a freak.

And just because Finn hadn't met anyone exactly like me didn't mean they weren't out there.

"You're…" He turned his head to study me. "Different."

Freak.

"Special." Chase jumped in like we were having a completely *normal* conversation.

"You mean she didn't tell you about the princess myth?" The accusation that I'd told Chase everything was clear in Finn's tone.

"No."

Finn quickly summarized the princess tale. "The regents were supposed to return to the new Atlantis after the princesses came out of their protective cocoons so they could unite and rule together."

"How long have you waited?" Chase asked.

"Centuries."

"Why did your people suddenly get impatient?" Chase's curiosity and a little distrust showed in his tone. "If Atlanteans had waited centuries, what's one more?"

"You wouldn't understand air-breather." Finn swam a bit faster.

"Then explain it to me. I'm a willing student. I'm sure Pearl would like to know, too."

Finn spread his fingers wide and let water trail between them. "The regent in residence has become more and more power hungry while the ocean has become more and more polluted. The regent refuses to confront the air-breathers. If we don't do something soon, our homeland—all the oceans—will be permanently damaged."

I let Finn's message sink in. It was more than about the legend. "Do you believe in the princesses or not?"

"I believe Cordelia is a princess." He gave me another intense stare. "About the other two... I don't know."

The cave narrowed and grew darker. Places on my bathing suit snagged on the wall. Several tunnels branched off in all directions like an underwater maze. A chill settled over me. I didn't know if I could find my way out.

As if Chase and I were on the same wavelength, he asked, "How'd you find this place? How do you know your way around these tunnels?"

"I played here as a kid." Finn sounded less grim. "Until the revolt, I lived under Atlas Island with my father."

Bewilderment fuzzed my brain. "You said it was light where the Royalists live."

"It is, but it's always dark in the tunnels. That's what made it fun." Finn flapped his feet. "The palace and homestead are lighted by electric eels that have been harnessed."

"Cool." Chase swam ahead of me and caught up to Finn. "What were you doing by the ferry this morning?"

Finn shook his head like he couldn't believe he was going to explain. "I was swimming to Atlas Island when I saw Pearl in trouble."

"Quite a coincidence." Chase countered.

Finn swung his head and hit a rock jutting out of the wall. "Darn."

"You okay?"

"Yeah." Rubbing his head, he kept moving as if he didn't want a simple injury, or Chase's questions, slowing us down.

"Why were you heading to Atlas? Aren't they your enemy?" Chase sounded like a good prosecutor, making his case. Or a good reporter digging for facts.

"I was following a hunch. I didn't know Pearl would be on the ferry." Finn glared at Chase. "She has no need to take a ferry."

A shiver ran down my spine. Not from Finn and Chase's exchange but the deeper we went, the darker it became. No plants grew in this area. The shells clinging to the wall appeared ancient and vulnerable. I never would've thought this fun.

Chase let go of my hand and broke off a strange shell I'd never seen before. "Souvenir."

"Tourist."

I laughed at the sound of disgust in Finn's tone.

We took another passage heading further down. The walls here were smooth as if they'd been scraped with a tool. And the current didn't seem to flow in any specific direction.

"We're almost near the castle entrance. Keep your voice down." Finn instructed.

"How far away can people hear us?" On land, everyone knew how far a whisper carried. This whole communicating without actual sound confused me.

Finn moved his head back and forth. "Same distance as a normal conversation. Unless you're shouting in your mind."

"Is there a reason for me to shout or scream?"

"Only if you're caught and tortured by Royal Guards." Finn's answer was unexpected. He sounded like he spoke from experience, like he'd been tortured by Royal Guards.

"Are we going to meet Royal Guards?" Maybe my attitude had been too cavalier, agreeing to this journey.

Chase swam in front of me in a protective way. "Why haven't we come across any guards? This is a palace and there's a war going on."

"Most of these passages are secret. Only a few of the kids who played in the palace knew about them."

So, Finn played in the palace. What rank did his family have before switching sides?

***

After another ten minutes, the passage we traveled grew narrower and narrower. The tunnel ended in a small hole, like a porthole on a ship. I squeezed between Finn and Chase and peered into a previously unknown world.

I gasped. Bubbles escaped my mouth. The palace was bright, sun filtering through the water. Those eels must put off a lot of electricity.

The grand hallway was sculpted out of coral. Not brownish, dull coral but vibrant white and pastel pink coral. The walls were fine filigree carvings with fancy cuts and curlicues. Lavender, bright orange and turquoise anemone made patterns on the ground like they'd been planted to replicate a design.

Starfish evenly spaced apart, clung to the wall. Coral polyps, with their sac-shaped bodies, spread out tentacles in search of food. A crystal chandelier made of glass and shells hung from the coral ceiling and swayed with the water instead of a breeze.

"Epic." Chase's expression must've mirrored my own awe-struck-ness.

Exotic fish, ones normally not living off the

California coast, swam past. Like an over-sized aquarium, orange-striped clownfish, bump-headed parrot fish and long-nosed butterfly fish darted right and left. A lion fish floated right in front of our noses. The three of us leaned back to avoid its poisonous spine.

A seaweed door swished open and two similarly-dressed men emerged. Blue with gold stripes down the side, their swim trunks looked like a uniform.

"Royal Guard." Finn answered my unspoken question.

Stiffening, I held my breath.

As the men approached, their conversation became clear.

"What areas have been searched?" The man with four stripes on his suit asked.

"My men have searched the dungeons, the open passages, and the ocean immediately surrounding the castle." The guard with only two stripes answered.

"Did anyone see her leave?"

"No."

"Have you questioned those around her about whatever crazy plans she may have made?" The first guard continued questioning.

The second guard nodded. "No one seems to know anything."

"Alert all the troops. With discretion, send men to search the beach and marina above." He pounded his fist into his other hand. "We can't let her escape."

The two guards moved further away and we couldn't hear anymore.

"Who are they searching for?" Sorrow for this unknown girl wove into me, braiding with my own feelings of fear and rejection. An entire army searched for her. "Why is she so important?"

"I don't know." Finn's serious face appeared deep in thought. "I thought they were planning an attack but it seems like they're trying to locate someone. Guess this little mission was unnecessary."

"Should we help the guards find whoever she is or help her get away?" For some reason I wanted to help this unknown girl.

Chase peered out the hole. "These tunnels make a great escape route."

"Excellent point." It was the first time Finn had ever complimented Chase. I wanted to write it in the history books.

A sudden high-pitched scream filled the water.

I froze. Now, I knew how far a scream traveled. A chill traveled the length of my body.

Chase and Finn stilled beside me.

The seaweed doorway twisted. A limb pushed through the green weeds. Then a girl's body held by the two guards from earlier.

"Unhand me." The girl commanded in a firm tone. She wore a golden bikini with a short, green flared skirt. Long, thick, brunette strands of hair stuck out of her elegant bun.

"Just because you're a princess doesn't mean you're in charge.' The guard sneered at her.

"I should be in charge." Her tone sounded sophisticated. Royal. "You can't treat me like this."

"It's for your own good, Princess Cordelia." The guard with the four stripes held her arm.

I sucked in a breath. She was one of the real princesses from the myth. The tale was real.

"For the good of Atlantis Captain I need to find—"

The captain slapped Princess Cordelia's face. Her mouth made an O-shape.

Chase fisted his hand as if he wanted to protect the captured princess. Finn stiffened beside me like he was in shock.

Fake or real, she didn't deserve to be slapped. I snarled wanting to defend her, too.

"You will do what you are told." The captain scolded. "A war is about to commence and we need you safe and in the palace."

She struggled against her captors. "If we produce proof—"

"Be a good princess and get that silly stuff out of your head. The Separatists will never listen."

I watched them lead her away.

My stomach sank. My skin tightened. I wanted to fight the guards. Our situations were similar. Princess Cordelia was being used for her position and powers. Similar to how Bill and Carlita had used me.

We'd both run away. Only I'd been successful.

She was a prisoner in her own kingdom.

Chapter Eighteen
Star Shocker

I didn't know why I felt a connection to Princess Cordelia. We came from different backgrounds. Our success in running away differed. She'd aligned herself with the Royalist side. Of course, since she was a princess she probably didn't have a choice.

I shot an accusing glance at Finn. The Royalists called Finn and his people Separatists, not Free Atlanteans. What was the real definition? I knew Finn thought himself a Free Atlantean. The real definition probably depended on your point of view.

And I didn't have enough facts to make a decision.

"They're out of sight." Chase edged further into the hallway to spy on the Princess and her guards. "We should go after her. Help her."

I liked that Chase wanted to assist someone in need. His heroics warmed me inside.

"Too dangerous for the three of us, especially Pearl." Finn focused on me with a peculiar expression. "I'll follow Cordelia and find out what's going on."

"Why would we trust you?" I grabbed Finn's shoulder. I wanted to help the princess, not hurt her. "You're a Free Atlantean, or Separatist. Whatever the true label is."

"I know the tunnels." His fierce expression tried to intimidate. "And I know Princess Cordelia. We played together as kids."

"You did?" My stance toward Finn softened.

"I'd never hurt her." His voice caught. His expression softened. Warmth and sorrow lit his pupils.

"How do we know that?" Chase sounded protective like Finn.

"You don't." Finn crossed his arms and glared. All the passion in his expression gone.

Chase seemed to consider. "You're right that three of us can't follow her. Together we'd be caught."

"I know the tunnels and the palace. I know the politics. I know Princess Cordelia. I should go and make sure she's okay."

Chase nodded and took hold of my hand. "We're both new to this entire situation and don't know who the players are. We should let Finn go."

"I don't know." No matter how silly, I felt somehow responsible.

Chase held our entwined hands up and pointed at Finn. "The princess is in her own castle. I'm sure she's fine. Let Finn check it out and he'll get back to us. Right, Finn?"

Finn's slight nod showed he wasn't paying attention. Worry lines creased his forehead as if trying to figure out how to get to Princess Cordelia. "Can you guys find your own way back?"

I recalled the narrow passages, the choice of tunnels,

the complete darkness with no identifying marks. A claustrophobic panic set in. My lungs squeezed tight. How would we get out?

"I can." Chase squeezed my hand and I sensed his confidence. "I wasn't being a tourist. Breaking off those shells was like laying bread crumbs in case we got lost. Or were abandoned."

Chase truly was my hero. I could rely on him, trust him.

My stomach bubbled, unsettled about the situation with Princess Cordelia, but both guys had a point. There was nothing I could do for her. My presence might even endanger her.

After wishing Finn good luck, Chase and I swam through the tunnels and out the cave. I was so glad to have him beside me, guiding my way.

***

The next morning, I walked to the Boardwalk with a feeling of something hanging over my head. Princess Cordelia's state of affairs worried me but I knew so little about Atlantean history and legend, I didn't know which side to believe.

Worry about Finn had also kept me awake. Even if I wasn't sure about his decision to become a Free Atlantean, or if everything he told me was true, I trusted him. And I believed he wouldn't hurt Princess Cordelia.

I also wondered where the other two princesses were and if, gulp, my situation was connected. The thought of me being anything close to royal was ridicu-mongous.

Who would ever believe I was an Atlantean Princess? I didn't.

As I clocked in, Mrs. Fowler approached me. "I'd like to speak to you, Pearl…Seidon."

Odd, how she paused before my last name. "I already clocked in."

"That's okay. Come to my office." Something about the way Mrs. Fowler's stare zeroed in on me like a target made the hairs on the back of my neck stand at attention, as if my hairs were a tiny army waiting for an unexpected attack.

I fiddled with the door knob. "Do you know where I can find Chase Thomas?"

"He's upstairs getting dressed." She waved in a general up direction. "He'll be down shortly."

I collapsed against the door to her office and almost fell over when the door moved backward and hit the wall. Everything in my mind moved, shifted. Jarred. Chase was getting dressed upstairs in the owner's apartment? In Mrs. Fowler's apartment?

"My nephew is always late for work." Mrs. Fowler took a few steps toward me. "I guess that happens when you're related to the boss."

My shoulders dropped. My ears popped. My eyes bugged out like I was an alien and didn't speak the same language. "N-n-nephew?"

She ushered me further into the room and closed the door. In my state of shock, I didn't protest. She pushed me onto the cracked leather couch and took a seat beside me.

Mrs. Fowler was Chase's aunt.

The aunt he had dinner with last night. The aunt he lived with. The aunt who insisted he study business instead of journalism.

Why hadn't I figure it out before? She called him on his cell phone all the time. She'd referred to him as *honey*. He was so deferential to her.

"Tea, dear?" She held up an old metal pot from the table in front of us.

"No." I sunk back further. The cracks in the leather pinched my leg so I knew this wasn't a dream.

Chase hadn't told me. He'd called her Mrs. Fowler, not Aunt Sarah. He'd never told me where he lived.

Each thought slapped me in the head. Stupid. Stupid. Stupid.

I'd told him everything about me. Well, almost.

"I have a business proposition for you." Mrs. Fowler poured tea for herself. "The Boardwalk has been struggling financially for years. We need a big attraction." She raised her hands and shook them like jazz hands. "An attraction that will draw crowds, bring families back to the Boardwalk."

I swallowed a lump of confusion, still thinking about Chase's deception, not comprehending what Mrs. Fowler said.

"In my late husband's day," her voice grew weary and sad, "there were lines for every ride and game. Our ticket sales were through the roof. We were known as a tourist destination."

I squirmed in my seat, not wanting to hear about the Boardwalk and its problems. I had enough of my own.

"Now," she picked up her teacup with shaking hands and sipped. "I can barely afford to fix the rides, pay the employees, or keep the gates of the Boardwalk open."

"Since he passed," her voice cracked. "It's just Chase and I. We've had a difficult time."

"I'm sorry." I truly was, but I didn't understand why she'd divulged the sad tale. At the moment I couldn't focus on what she said when a haze of anger smoked over Chase's omission. Why hadn't he told me he was

Mrs. Fowler's nephew?

"The Boardwalk is my late husband's legacy." She set her teacup down with a snap. Her voice filled with strength. "I need to save the Boardwalk for my husband's memory and for my nephew to inherit."

For Chase.

Her motivations were sincere, but I knew Chase didn't want to run the Boardwalk. That's the reason Mrs. Fowler pushed him into going for a business degree and not the journalism degree he desired.

"You know, you might want to talk to Chase about your plans for the future." I shouldn't be defending Chase when he'd lied. But the sooner I pointed out to Mrs. Fowler that this had nothing to do with me, maybe she'd let me leave. Then I could go find Chase and yell at him.

I didn't hate him because he didn't tell me his relation to Mrs. Fowler, but I didn't understand. Why keep it a secret?

"I have talked to him." She stood and paced in front of the couch. "This is what's best for the Boardwalk. What's best for Chase."

"What are you talking about?" I hadn't a clue what ran through her mind or why I was involved in the discussion.

Mrs. Fowler appeared to float while she talked, like she had a brilliant thought and couldn't wait to tell everyone. "A grand water show featuring a magnificent star who performs high dives from unimaginable heights."

Nausea crawled in my stomach.

"Who swims at swift speeds."

Tension pulled on my spinal column trying to stretch

my body to full height.

"Who defies gravity with her strength."

Every hair, not only the ones on my neck, stood at attention.

She held out her hands, palms up showcasing me. "You, my dear, will be our star performer."

Chapter Nineteen
Bewildered & Betrayed

I jumped to my feet. Pain sliced into my heart and ripped it apart. Finding it difficult to breathe, I panted in shallow gasps.

Chase had told his aunt. He'd told her everything.

For once in my life I'd been completely honest, well pretty honest, and I'd gotten screwed. Chase had used me, used his knowledge about me, and now wanted to put me on display like a circus freak.

Screaming inside, I wanted to run away once again, but knew I had to control the damage. I didn't want more people finding out about me and my abilities.

"I don't know what you're talking about." Lame, when it was obvious Mrs. Fowler knew more than I'd ever imagined.

She grabbed both my shoulders, her bony fingers digging into my skin. "You'll be famous. More famous than before." Her eyes glittered. "We'll print billboards, run advertisements. There will be interviews on radio and TV."

I shoved her hands off me, still feeling her nails clinging like a crazed fan. "I don't want to be famous."

"Everyone wants to be famous." She poo-poohed my denial, pouting her lips and waving my protest away with her hand. "You'll be like Esther Williams, Olympic swimmer and famous actress. And the Boardwalk will be saved."

"Who?" Not that it mattered. "I won't do it."

I crossed my arms, giving up on convincing her I didn't have the abilities. What was the point? Chase had witnessed everything. He'd probably given her a blow-by-blow account of our day yesterday.

Negative thought after negative thought dove from my brain to my chest producing a tidal wave of hurt. Had he faked his feelings for me? Was this all about saving his legacy? Maybe he'd lied about not wanting to work at the Boardwalk, too.

A sharp breath speared my lungs. What if he'd told her about the Royalists and Free Atlanteans? Were all those people in danger because of me?

And because of Chase. I refused to take all the blame.

The hurt flowed from my heart to my veins surging with power, building with anger. My muscles tensed. Rage and hurt mixed together like an explosive cocktail. He didn't care about me. He didn't care about me at all. He didn't want my love or affection. He was like everyone else in the air-breathing world.

The only thing he wanted from me was what I could do for him.

Like a punch in the gut, that thought spurred me forward. I rushed toward the exit. My hand gripped the door knob.

"Pearl. You've got a gift and you should use it." Mrs.

Fowler sounded like Carlita with her I-know-what's-best-for-you tone.

I turned to glare. "You mean *you* want to use *me*." Fury simmered and burned. "I've been used my entire life for my abilities and I'm sick of it. I don't want to perform like a trick pony. I don't want to be on display. I don't want to be different or a freak. I'm outta here."

I turned and yanked the door open.

On the other side stood Chase. His instant smile lit my hot fuse.

"Hey."

Exploding, I lifted my hand and slapped him across the cheek. My fingers burned with the harsh contact.

His face flamed red. The white imprints of my fingers stood out on his cheek. "Pearl? Why—"

"Don't say anything." Internal debris landed in my stomach, smoldering. I couldn't listen to his phony explanations and lies.

"Wait—"

Not giving him a chance, I turned.

"Chase, let her go." Mrs. Fowler ordered, and he always listened to her. "Let her calm down."

There'd be no calming down. I fled the building and ran all the way to the campground.

Swiping at the tears, I slowed passing the office and continued to my tent. I sorted through my belongings, knowing I'd have to be quick. I didn't want to think about what had happened.

The sleeping bag and tent I wouldn't need for life under the sea. I shoved the clam with the pearl and nautilus inside my backpack. After stripping off my work uniform, I balled it up and threw it into the corner of my tent. Then, I put on my bathing suit and cover-up.

I opened the worn duffel bag with all my clothes. My fingers touched Chase's sweatshirt and my tummy seared. He'd told his aunt about me. He'd never reciprocated my feelings. He used me.

Although, I hadn't felt like I was being used. The searing tummy lightened. My gut instincts told me to trust him and they'd always been pretty accurate.

Up until now.

Pulling out his sweatshirt, I couldn't resist the urge to rub the soft fabric against my cheek. His scent filled the tiny space inside the tent. I breathed in deeply knowing I'd never see him again.

My heart contracted, squeezed tight. I didn't know if I could ever believe again. If I could ever love again.

Betrayed or not. My secret was out. I owed it to Finn and the other Atlanteans, Free and Royal, to warn them.

I tossed the sweatshirt aside and slipped out of the tent. Taking one last glance around, I touched the pearl necklace around my neck. The one constant in my life. The one I'd been given by my biological parents.

Most likely, the circus owners had lied about that too.

I'd run away from the circus.

And now, I was running away from the Boardwalk.

From Chase.

From all air-breathers.

***

Except this time, I wasn't actually running. I was swimming away.

I knew the general direction to go. I'd paid attention on the way back from the Free Atlantean base with Finn and thanks to Chase, I knew to head toward the East Pacific Rise.

Guess he helped with something. He helped my

escape from him.

Following the varying ocean floor surfaces, I soon found myself swimming between high peaks. The water warmed nearing the thermal vents and white flakes floated by. The trip had gone by quickly because my brain still steamed. My body used the negative energy to go faster.

Twirling around, I studied each direction.

An orange octopus waved its protruding arms.

Remembering one of my recently discovered skills, I asked, "Can you help me?"

The creature's small head seemed to nod between the large arms—arms so large they looked like elephant's ears.

I moved a little closer but not close enough to get hit. "I'm trying to find the Free Atlantean base. Which way do I go?"

The octopus shifted again. The creature's arms rippled with the current. One arm seemed to push out further pointing me in a southerly direction.

"Thank you." Kicking my feet, I was off.

Once I warned the two sides maybe they would unite behind a common enemy—Chase and the air-breathers. Then, there would be no war and I wouldn't have to choose a side.

The current changed. Green seaweed floated in front of me. The plant shimmered with a strange aura. I reached out to push the seaweed out of my way, but it circled around like a net, entrapping me.

Just what I needed. Suicide seaweed.

I hacked at the plant. Blood pounded through my veins. My pulse banged an angry rock tune. My legs and arms kicked out. I didn't have time for this.

The plant seemed to have a mind of its own. The long tendrils wouldn't release me like I was dinner.

Struggling against the seaweed, I squashed down my panic. I had to be realistic. The seaweed wasn't alive and it wasn't trying to trap me.

Grabbing a strand, I untangled it from around my face and shoulders. The slimy seaweed immediately wrapped itself around my arm. Like it was alive, the seaweed moved faster.

Slimy tendrils curled around my waist, my legs, and both arms. I struggled, but even with my super strength I couldn't unwrap the plant from me.

My breath came in shallow spurts. Chase was right, which I hated. Water emergencies did find me. How was I going to save the underwater world when I couldn't even save myself?

"What have I caught here?" The deep words penetrated my panic. Captain Fisher swam from behind a rock. "You're Finn's special friend."

My shoulders sagged and the plant loosened. Weird. "Captain Fisher, I'm so glad I found you. I need your help—"

He bowed. "At your service."

"The air-breathers know about me, know about us. We have to warn the Free Atlanteans, and the Royalists."

His eyebrows twisted into a question mark. "Royalists? Did they send you?"

"No." I shook my head and calmed myself. I must breathe, or water, or whatever it's called. "We have to warn them, too."

His eyes narrowed into adversarial slits. "Why have you come skulking near our base?"

"You have to listen." My tone rose. "The air-breathers know about us."

"Because of you."

I blew out a breath. I wouldn't place the blame on Chase. Even though he deserved it, I didn't want trouble for him. I hated him, but I still cared for him. "Yes, because of me. We have to do something. Warn everyone."

He scratched his chin. "Is this a plot cooked up by the Royalists?"

"No, of course not." I struggled against the seaweed and it tightened again. "What is this stuff?"

"An air-breather scientist developed it for me." The captain's smirk reminded me of a shark about to attack. "A new scientific development for use on our enemies."

I wasn't an enemy. I was a friend trying to sound a warning. "Let me out."

"Not a chance." The captain's pure-evil smile darkened his face. "You're existence needs to be kept secret. Now, you're my prisoner."

Chapter Twenty
Princess Problem

Blood pounded behind my eyeballs. My body trembled. Confusion rocked my mind. What was going on?

The seaweed tightened around my middle section. Fronds held my arms tight against my body and twisted around my legs. My body tensed like I was caught in shackles.

Regular shackles I could handle, I did have super strength after all. But this seaweed was tougher than anything I'd encountered on land. I twisted, trying to fight it off. The seaweed tightened.

I tried to stomp my foot but it became more tangled. This was absurd. "Why are you doing this?"

The captain swam around like I was a specimen. "Plankson told me about your special gift."

I stopped struggling, finally comprehending Fisher's comment. "The campground manager isn't an air-breather? He's one of us?"

Guess I was never alone at all. I just didn't know

about the others. The confusion twisted and turned and tangled like the seaweed choking me. I must not be observant.

"I know you can turn air-breathers. Your talent is quite unique." The captain didn't make it sound like a compliment.

"Who cares what I can or can't do? I'm trying to help you, to save our people." I was trying to save all Atlanteans and he had me trapped like a dolphin in a net.

I struggled more. Frustration scratched against my nerve endings, rubbing me wrong.

His harsh laugh boomed in my head and scratched down my spine. "If the Free Atlanteans found out about you, they'd never follow me."

"I don't want to be a leader." I was only a girl who recently discovered this entire new world.

"I've finally convinced them that the tale of the three lost princesses from Poseidon's line is a fraud. A fairy tale made up to keep them enslaved to the Royal faction."

I stopped struggling. The nautilus hung heavy in the bag on my back, weighed my body and my thoughts. "I've heard the story."

"If there aren't three real princesses, then they shouldn't follow Princess Cordelia, and her henchmen."

"What does that have to do with me?" A stopwatch ticked in the back of my head, an ominous countdown. The circuits in my mind fired but they weren't connecting.

"Your talent is so rare it might be recognized. Only Poseidon possessed it, and only one of his heirs would inherit it."

The watch exploded in my head like a sonic alarm

clock. The circuits connected but I still I couldn't think straight. Two and two together suddenly wasn't four. "What are you saying?"

"Isn't it obvious?" His scoffing tone announced he thought I was an idiot. "You're a lost princess, an heir of Poseidon, one of the legendary three who will join the other two to lead."

Stunned, I didn't know how to respond. The thought had crossed my mind, but my life wasn't anything like a fairy tale and wasn't going to get a happily ever after. Not if I couldn't get out of this seaweed. I must look like a ginormous tuna not a princess.

Hysterical laughter gurgled out of my chest and escaped my mouth. Bubbles formed a rising chain in the water. "Me, a princess? Impossible."

The captain's lips firmed. "As much as I wish it wasn't so, the facts are conclusive."

"You're insane."

Images bombarded me. The large nautilus Bill and Carlita owned. The fact they weren't my real parents and had used me like a trained seal. The pink pearl I'd worn around my neck since birth. My underwater skills and how they were more powerful in the ocean. The woman bowing to me at the Free Atlantean base and the gift she gave. My one special skill of *turning* an air-breather.

A skill only Poseidon possessed.

And my last name—Poseidon I mentally thwacked my forehead.

I'd always thought my last name was phony like my birth certificate. That Bill and Carlita had made it up for a public relations stunt for the circus.

I tried to reach up to clutch the pearl around my neck but the seaweed refused to let go of my arm. Puffing out my chest, I shot Fisher an I'm-better-than-you look. "If I'm a princess, I order you to let me go."

He smiled unevenly making his mouth appear sinister. "I don't think so."

I needed information, something that could help me escape, or something to convince him to let me go. "Which princess am I then?"

"Princess Cordelia lives with the Royalists. Then there's Pelagia and Marisabel." He ticked off on his fingers. "With your known name being Pearl and the skill you have, I believe you're Pelagia."

Uck. I couldn't even have a pretty princess name. Not that that was important right now. Escaping and getting more information had priority. "What does Pelagia mean?"

"Dweller by the sea. Which makes sense for you to have the talent you have."

I still found it hard to believe the whole princess thing. I mean, come on, me a princess? But maybe if I played along he'd let me go.

"Where's the third princess, Marisabel?" I couldn't believe I was Princess Pelagia. I'd led too crappy a life. But Fisher acted like I was a political prisoner.

"No one knows." He swam around again, studying me. "I'll deal with one princess at a time."

A cold spray of goosebumps scattered across my skin. I struggled against the seaweed some more. "What do you mean?"

"My air-breather scientist friend, the one who invented the seaweed, would love to study you, possibly dissect you." The captain examined me like I was already under a microscope. "He'd love to take care of my princess problem."

***

The captain held onto the seaweed net and dragged me behind him like a sack of sardines. I fought by creating drag in the water. I couldn't believe I'd come to save his Free Atlanteans and he treated me like a bag of garbage, but I should be used to it.

We traveled past the spot where I was blindfolded, and then past what I believed to be the entrance of the Free Atlantean base camp.

Using my teeth, I tried to bite through the seaweed strands but the gnawing had no effect. And the seaweed tasted like cleaning solution.

The captain kept glancing around, dodging between rocks and crags, and stopping suddenly to hide for a few minutes within a seaweed forest. He looked like a fugitive Santa trying to steal children's toys. Or more like the Grinch.

Nope. Just kidnapping me.

He finally stopped in what appeared to be a dead area of the ocean floor. No plant life. No sea life. Barren ground with black sand as if a fire had burnt through, which was impossible. He rolled a large, scarred rock off of a hole and peered inside.

"Get in."

My eyebrows shot up. "What?"

"Get in the hole."

The hole was about twenty-four inches around. Inside I saw nothing but blackness.

Kind of how my life was ending up. My heart blackened from Chase's betrayal. My mind darkened from my lost princess life. My body shadowed from my useless struggles.

I tried raising my hands in a helpless gesture, which

of course, I couldn't. "I can't get in. I can't even swim all tied up."

"Do as I say." The captain sounded royal. Royally pissed.

My heartbeat picked up its pace. Now might be my only chance. I bunched my muscles ready to take flight. If he untied my hands I could overpower him and swim away. "Untie me and I will."

"Not a chance." He grabbed the seaweed and positioned me over the hole.

The complete darkness below seemed to reach up and swallow me. Shivers racked my bunched body. "What is this place?"

"Dead thermal vent. We'll wait for my contact inside."

Using the edges of the hole for leverage, he pushed me down and then followed. I couldn't even struggle against him.

The water immediately dropped in temperature. Inside was darker than dark. I couldn't tell what skulked at the bottom. Even with my enhanced vision, I could barely see. It was like being blind.

The large, cave-like hole was surrounded on all sides by rock. Besides the tiny entrance at the top, there didn't seem to be another exit.

I'd shrivel and die in this shadowy hidey-hole. No one would know what happened to me. No one would care.

All-encompassing sorrow filled my frame, stretching my nerves to breaking point. My skin wanted to crawl off my body. There were so many things I still wanted to do.

Would Chase care? His betrayal had driven me to this drastic ending. A fissure formed in the middle of my bruised heart. The ache throbbed, pressing inside my chest. Did he even realize I was gone?

The captain continued to tug me down. He held the seaweed with one hand and seemed to be searching for something with the other. A click sounded in the darkness and a bright light burned.

He held a large, yellow flashlight in his other hand. "Air-breathers are good for something."

For flashlights.

And princess extermination.

Funny, how it would be an Atlantean to cause my downfall, not an air-breather. One of my own people causing me harm.

He wrapped the seaweed around a rock that jutted out and tethered me down to the spot. "Get comfortable."

His silence gave me time to think. All of this princess stuff was difficult to believe. I wasn't raised in luxury and had been treated more like a slave than royalty. I certainly didn't feel royal. Right now I didn't want to be. Being a princess meant certain death.

I squirmed in my bindings. "How long?" How long did I have to contemplate death?

"Not long. I received a message you were headed this way." He swam back and forth in front of me like a man pacing. "I'm surprised Plankson didn't beat us here."

I gasped finding it hard to believe Plankson was in on it, but I remembered how he'd watched me, how he'd insisted I clean litter from the rocks and how the seagulls had pushed me into the ocean. "Plankson tested me, didn't he? The whirlpool, the seagull attack, the ferry."

"The whirlpool was a small skirmish between forces, but the rest, yes. I couldn't rely on Finn's reports."

"Finn?" My chest tightened making it difficult to

breathe. Another betrayal. I could trust no one. I was completely alone. No family. No friends. No boyfriend. The fissure in my heart widened like the Grand Canyon I'd passed on my trip west.

And I'd let Finn go after Princess Cordelia. I shuddered at her plight.

"I'm not sure of Finn's commitment to the cause even though his father assured me he was loyal. I understand father and sons being on separate sides."

Confusion multiplied. "Who is Finn's father?"

"Plankson."

My head jerked. That's how Finn found me. Picturing Finn and Plankson in my mind, I now saw a resemblance. Their eyes and hair were similar, although Plankson's hair was grey and a few wrinkles lined his face.

The relationship twists I'd encountered today confuzzled my brain. Mrs. Fowler was Chase's aunt and they both had betrayed me. Plankson was Finn's dad and they both had tricked me.

"Any other familial relationships I should know about?' I tossed the question out with deep sarcasm, not expecting a response.

"Finn is your half-brother."

***

I swallowed the news like swallowing bad pills. The information went down like a lump of oyster, slimy but hard. I'd been searching for my real family, even mentioned it to Finn, yet he'd said nothing.

"Does he know?" My heart braced for the answer.

Fisher shrugged in an off-hand way like he didn't care one way or another. "I don't keep track of the latest gossip."

A drilling pain stabbed my heart. Another, more horrendous thought occurred. "Is Plankson my f-father?"

"Don't be ridiculous." Fisher snapped.

"Are Finn and Princess Cordelia related?" Finn couldn't hurt his half-sister, could he?

"No. You and Finn had the same mother. You and Princess Cordelia had the same father."

"Who is my father?" I might be dead soon, but at least I'd finally know who my father was.

"With your talent," Fisher snarled. "You're from Poseidon's line. King Atlas was your father."

My heart stopped beating for a moment. I had a father. A father who was a king. A father who was dead.

I was a princess. My heart re-started, picked up its pace like a strengthening hurricane. Hearing of all these family relationships connected all the dots.

Dots I'd been piecing together like a five-year-old doing and adult puzzle. I ran through the facts in my mind. My last name. My strange upbringing. My abilities. And the most solid fact of all—the one special talent of turning air-breathers—a talent only Poseidon possessed.

"So who is King Atlas?"

Fisher blew out a breath and bubbles rose from his mouth. "History, girl."

"But I don't know Atlantean history. I didn't even know it existed until a few days ago. If I'm going to die, I'd at least like to know why."

"King Atlas is Poseidon's son. He ruled Atlantis at the time of the great calamity. The selfish barbarian dispatched regents across the world to save his three daughters instead of his people."

Fisher believed King Atlas, my father, had been

selfish saving his own flesh and blood before his subjects. If I was one of the people he saved, I was glad. But I felt awful for all those who died. "But some Atlanteans survived."

"Thousands perished." Bitterness laced his voice. The lines on his face seemed to deepen.

"That happened hundreds, no thousands, of years ago." I did the mental math and things didn't add up. "I'm only sixteen, how could I possibly be King Atlas' daughter?"

"You were cocooned in a special protective pod. When the right time arrived, you were to be released into the world."

Like a chicken or a turtle.

Another freaky fact about me.

"How old are you? How old is Finn?" I examined my hands for wrinkles and age spots. My fingers trembled. "How old am I?"

"We age slowly underwater. Cocooned you didn't age at all. Any other questions?" Although he asked, I didn't think he meant to answer.

Sixteen years ago I was released from my protective shell. A chill cascaded down my spine and ended in the dark pit of my stomach. "Why now?"

"That is the big question." Fisher's expression grew thoughtful. "Princess Cordelia was released sixteen years ago as well. The timing couldn't be worse for the Free Atlanteans. We've been building our resources for the last couple of years and our all-out revolt will commence soon. Cordelia is taken care of."

A shiver ran down my spine and spiraled out of control knowing I was next.

"How is she taken care of?" My guilt multiplied. By

letting Finn follow her I could be responsible for Cordelia's death. Responsible for my half-sisters death.

My aching heart lifted in my chest. I had two half-sisters.

Two half-sisters I'd never meet. The lightness vanished. Replaced by shadows of death.

"You don't need to know the details."

Maybe the details weren't so important. Two princesses gone, or almost gone in my case. I tugged at the seaweed netting. One princess to go.

***

A rolling sound, like a ball going down a bowling alley, awakened me from my tense-exhausted-half-sleep. I had so many thoughts swirling inside my head and stabbing my heart, I couldn't focus on a thing.

Chase's betrayal.

Finn's relationship.

My half-sisters.

The captain's evil plot.

My father's improbable plan.

The dead thermal vent pitched into blackness once again. The captain had turned off the flashlight. He stood, ready for action.

A body pushed through the hole at the top.

"Plankson?" Captain Fisher responded. "What took you so long?"

"I've brought a present." Plankson's tone didn't sound merry, so I'm guessing the gift wasn't a good thing.

He tugged on something pulling it into the vent. A body. The person wore swim trunks, a blue swim shirt and a scuba tank on his back.

Recognition flickered sending a shock wave across

my skin.

"Caught him searching for her." Plankson pointed. "Rifled through her tent, then rented equipment and a boat. Headed in the direction of our base."

Coming after me?

Plankson jerked the guy's body closer. Strong legs and muscular arms flopped. His brown hair rippled in the water. His body twisted and I saw his face.

Agonized pain stabbed hundreds of points on my skin like over-sized pinpricks. I froze in complete shock.

Chase.

Chapter Twenty-One
Water War

Everything I felt for Chase tsunami-ed. Wave after wave of emotion pounded my heart, eroding any wall I'd tried to erect. All my hurt, all my pain, all my love washed through me. If he'd been gone a long time even my gifted breath couldn't bring him back to life.

"Chase." With my arms tied up, I swam toward his floating body. I leaned into him, kissing his familiar forehead and cheeks. The coldness of his skin frightened me. The tiny bubbles tickled my nose from the scuba gear's breathing apparatus.

I pulled back. Bubbles?

If there were bubbles, he was still breathing.

My chest lightened. Renewed hope burst through me. "He's alive."

"I only knocked him unconscious." Plankson's whiny voice morphed into a laugh. "He's alive until his tank runs out."

I checked the gauge on the canister attached to his back. Over half the air was gone.

"Why did you bring him here?" The captain's raised voice vibrated the water in the cave.

"Fool was planning to save her."

My heart warmed at Plankson's words confirming again Chase wanted to save me. Maybe he was sorry for betraying my confidence. Maybe he did care. Maybe he loved me.

A new feeling rushed through my heart. A feeling of joy. I had to save him.

"You shouldn't have brought the air-breather here. To her. To us." The captain flapped his hands around, clearly agitated.

"What was I supposed to do with him?" Plankson didn't understand the captain's anger.

"Leave him on the beach. Kill him. I don't care."

My hope and joy dashed, crumbled like castles in the sand. The captain didn't care about anyone. Not me, and certainly not an air-breather.

Relaxing my arms, the seaweed loosened and I inched my hands from beneath the seaweed tied near the top of my thighs. My wrists barely cleared their tight grip. Jiggling at my waist, I let Chase's body drift a bit away. With his head in my lap, I reached to slip the mouthpiece off.

"Stop her." The captain noticed my actions.

Before I could take off the mouthpiece, Plankson dove over and grabbed Chase's limp body out of my arms.

"Why? She was going to kiss him goodbye." His saccharine tone rubbed like sand in a fresh wound.

"She was going to give him the breath of life, turn him into one of us." The captain yanked Chase from Plankson and set him on a rock across the space of the dead thermal vent like Chase was a lifeless doll.

Only ten feet away, and yet so far.

The bubbles rose from his mouth apparatus signaling each bit of breath lost. Each precious second we had together gone.

The crumbles of my heart jolted and settled. I lost all faith. Neither of us would survive.

Plankson's face whitened. "You mean she really is... I thought Finn was making stuff up."

"She really is one of the lost princesses." The captain waved away Plankson's shock.

Judging his reaction and the captain's determination, I reconfirmed my earlier thought.

I was a real princess.

Daughter of King Atlas and granddaughter of Poseidon.

A lost daughter of Atlantis.

I'd understood the concept but hadn't accepted it yet. Logically, it made sense but inside me, inside my heart, I didn't feel like a princess.

I'd gone from slave and star of the circus, to custodian of the carnival, to princess of the Atlantean people. I'd gone from no history to tons of history. I'd gone from no heritage to royal heritage.

My head spun. Wave upon wave of future possibilities hit me. Or un-possibilities. Because I'd have no future.

My optimism dove like a heron for food. None of the three princesses would have a future. Would anyone even believe we were real?

"Idiot, not only do we have to get rid of her, we have to get rid of the air-breather." The_captain fisted his hands together. "The air-breather will be missed."

"I-I thought it was a legend." Plankson still hadn't recovered.

The captain's frustration showed in the way he shook his head back and forth. "For Poseidon's sake, you were married to her mother."

"What?" I wanted to jump out of my skin. "He was married to my mother? This is how Finn and I are related? Where is she? Does she know what you're doing to me?"

I had a mother. Another relative I knew nothing about.

"Your mother's dead." Fisher's tone was flat, cold.

A new sadness welled in my chest. My heart ached for the dreams I'd had. I'd never get to meet my mother. Never feel her arms around me. Never know her love.

A love I'd needed.

"I say, good riddance." Plankson swam around the vent like a caged animal. "She left me and our son when King Atlas crooked his finger. She wanted the prestige of royalty. Didn't realize how much she'd pay."

This was the man my mother married? Loved at one time? That didn't say much about her judgment.

I wanted to ask more about the woman who gave me life but Plankson's answers would be skewed. And I didn't want a negative picture of my mother, even if it was true.

"What's the plan to get rid of her?" Plankson's gleeful tone cut sharp across me. As if by killing me, he'd get revenge on my dead mother.

So not fair.

"I have a meeting scheduled with the air-breather scientist. He'll love my surprise." The captain shot me a conspiratorial smile like we shared a secret. "Until then we wait."

"What about him?" Plankson pointed at Chase.

"We'll wait and be entertained by watching the air-breather's tank run out and him expire. Permanently."

***

I couldn't sit and watch Chase die. The level on the gauge seemed to move with every second and my heart beat as fast. The seaweed choked my arms and legs and waist. I couldn't move. I couldn't get to Chase. I couldn't save him.

He wasn't innocent in all of this. He'd told his aunt about me. But I shouldn't have exposed him to my world, expecting him to keep this humongous secret.

I stared trying to will him awake. His body lay against the rocks, his head lolling to the side. His pale face and lips tinged a light blue. He could die of hypothermia before his air ran out.

My gaze followed the captain. He swam back and forth in between Chase and me, constantly on patrol. Never slack in his duties. I wanted to scream.

A slight movement from Chase caught my attention. I tried not to react. He opened first one eyelid and then the other.

He was awake. Conscious.

A second of lightness floated through only to be brought down by a weighty thought. Watching him die while conscious would be far worse for both of us.

Wishing I could take his place, I wanted to communicate my grief and sorrow but didn't want the captain and Plankson to know. I wished I could tell him how sorry I was we'd argued. In my anger, I'd classified people into categories. Chase wasn't an air-breather to me. He was special.

One blue eye opened and closed in a wink.

My head fell back against the hard edge of the cave. Not only was Chase conscious but he obviously was thinking. His thought process must be working for him to wink. Did that mean he had a plan?

The captain swam past and headed toward Chase. Chase's body stiffened.

The captain turned. Chase leapt from his position. He grabbed him around the neck. His legs circled the captain's waist like a wrestler. Bubbles flew, arms and legs collided.

My heart catapulted out of my chest, vaulting over my tonsils, and sticking in my throat. I had to help. Struggling against the seaweed, it tightened again.

Chase was sacrificing himself for me. He must've known he only had a short time left. He didn't realize I couldn't help him or couldn't escape.

"Plankson." The captain called for help.

Floating in the cave, Chase had his arm around the captain's neck in a choke hold. His face was red, his eyes bulging. He kept trying to swing his arms back to connect with Chase but he wasn't accurate.

I held my breath watching the skirmish, flinching with every blow.

Plankson grabbed a rock from the ground and swam up behind.

Two against one wasn't fair. I wiggled and twisted against the seaweed. "Watch out! Plankson has a rock."

Plankson raised his arm to hit Chase on the head. At the last second, Chase maneuvered around showing his back to Plankson. The rock came down.

The pinging sound of rock hitting metal echoed through the thermal vent cavern. The rock hit the air tank, not Chase.

I let out my breath in a whoosh.

A waterfall of bubbles escaped from the tank. The rock had put a hole in the metal canister.

Air escaped into the water.

Air that kept Chase alive.

I choked, strangling myself. The tank had a hole. Chase's air would run out even sooner. He'd die sooner. My heart would die with him.

Oxygen from the tank shot across the vent hitting me with unexpected force. The canned air sprayed my face, my body, the seaweed holding me prisoner.

The seaweed loosened. The plant disintegrated. The bindings flaked off like dead skin. The oxygen from the tank decomposed what ever magical force held the seaweed.

I was free. Exhilaration, like my own oxygen boost, filled me. I jumped off the rock and joined the fray. Chase had an advantage over the captain, so I went after Plankson.

I leapt onto his back and pulled his long, grey hair jerking his head back. I wanted to whoop-whoop with triumph. Through surprise, I got the upper hand.

He spun around grabbing hold of my leg and pulled trying to dislodge me. Our super-strength counter-acted each other. Neither one of us had an advantage. We circled like a carousel, round and round and round and round.

I kicked out to loosen his grip. My heel contacted with his stomach. He doubled over but righted himself. I kicked again and again, using all my built up anger and frustration to punish him.

Plankson stumbled. He lost his balance. I stumbled

with him. Together, we went down to the ground of the cave with him on top. He shifted his weight and used his legs to hold my legs down. His weight was too much for me to move, even in water. I was stuck.

Glancing over at Chase's fight, I saw the captain sink to the ground. Dead or unconscious I didn't know, but his limp body lay perfectly still. Chase had defeated him.

Pride spouted. Chase truly was my hero.

His arms dropped to his side. His eyes rolled back. He sunk down to the ground beside the captain, reminding me of the way the little boy Brandon had appeared when he'd been in the lagoon too long.

Chase might've won the battle, but he lost his personal war with water.

Chapter Twenty-Two
Awkward Accusation

No! My mind screamed. I struggled against Plankson. We'd come too far, fought too much for it to end now. Chase had beaten the captain. He couldn't die.

I reached out to Chase, but Plankson's body blocked my move. Bucking I tried to get Plankson off me. His arms scrambled, trying to pin mine down. My arms flayed like a windsock in a breeze trying to evade capture. My legs kicked and twisted beneath.

But all of this took time. Time Chase didn't have.

I swung my arms wildly. My hand encountered something solid. A rock. The rock Plankson had used on Chase.

Clutching the rough stone, I felt its weight in my palm. I glanced at Chase. He lay dying on the ground. No bubbles emitted from his breathing apparatus. No movement from his body.

A grief so strong quaked inside me. My internal organs quivered and collapsed. Chase would die. I'd probably die. Hundreds of Atlanteans on both sides of the war would die.

I couldn't lay here and let that happen. I had to try. Gripping the rock, I wielded it with all my strength toward Plankson. The rock pounded into his head. My stomach heaved. I'd never physically hurt another person before.

Plankson's body went limp. Forcing the upheaval of grief and fear and nerves aside, I shoved him off and slipped from beneath his body. I dove to Chase and ripped off the mouthpiece, placing my lips on his purplish ones. I breathed into him.

Please breathe. Don't die.

Another breath and then...

A slight movement in his chest. I eased away. His eyelids fluttered open and then widened. His skin warmed beneath my fingers. Color returned to his cheeks.

My earlier sadness and worry bloomed to light. Tears burned but they were happy tears. Tears of joy.

"Chase." I ran my fingers through his hair. "Are you okay?"

His lips weren't purple. They'd returned to their same kissable selves. "I think so."

I jerked my back straight and leaned away. He might've saved me, or helped me save myself, but he'd still betrayed me, telling his aunt about my abilities. Wanting to save Chase was one thing, wanting to kiss him again was completely wrong.

Pushing any warmth, any love, aside, I controlled the betrayal sure to taint my voice. I kept my jaw tight, my gaze cool. "We better get out of here."

"Yeah." Dazed, he undid the buckles holding the empty and useless tank.

I straightened and pushed off the sand. Chase was slow to follow. I wanted to reach out to him, to help him, but I needed to stand firm. I'd get him out of the ocean and then never see him again.

We came from two different worlds. We held two different sets of loyalties. We believed in two different meanings of love.

Like swimming out of a small, dormant volcano, I reached the top and used the edges for leverage to push through the hole. I bent down to check on Chase's progress. He was so close we almost butted heads. Stepping back, I let him wiggle through the hole on his own.

"This way." I turned to swim forward.

"Halt." The word came from everywhere.

A group of men advanced, circling around us.

My thoughts scrambled. I sought a possible escape. The rhythm of my heart picked up pace knowing that again we were in trouble.

Chase swam beside me and raised his hands in a cause-no-harm action. "We're peaceful."

The men wore blue swim trunks with gold stripes. Each of them held a weapon like a machine gun but with a sharp point. They were Royal Guards. And they were armed.

"Who are you?" A man with four stripes on his suit asked. He sported an orangish-red goatee on his chin.

My brain unscrambled. Maybe the Royalist side would listen. "We're friends. We've come to warn you that a few air-breathers," I shot Chase a look, "know about us and will soon tell the world. They will try to find us, hunt us down, experiment on us."

At the moment, with the harpoon-like guns pointed at

us, I felt hunted.

The man with the goatee jabbed with his weapon. "Why should we trust you?"

"Her information is false." Chase grabbed my arm, squeezing painfully.

My heart crushed into tiny pieces. Pulverized by his betrayal and now calling me names. How dare he call me a liar? I tried to jerk my arm out of his grip. "Listen to me, he's an air-breather from Mermaid Beach."

The men gasped. Their disbelief obvious by their dropped mouths and sunken cheeks. "What is this about?"

I held my hand to my heart. "I recently discovered I'm an Atlantean. Down below, in the vent," I pointed to the hole. "are two Free Atlanteans who held us both captive."

"Free Atlanteans?" The Goatee-guard snapped to attention. He pointed at two other guards who edged around the hole and then swam inside to check out my story.

Trying to calm my voice, I explained. "I came to warn them, warn everyone, that soon the land-bound world would know about our underwater world."

"That's not true." Chase's voice had a you-have-to-believe-me tone. "Pearl, I never told my aunt."

My heart stilled. My backbone wavered like seaweed in the surf. I so wanted to believe him, but I couldn't. "Mrs. Fowler, or should I say your Aunt Sarah, told me everything. She knew about my abilities and wanted to put me on display." Remembered pain stiffened my spine, made me stronger.

"Don't make snap judgments. I didn't tell her. She found out on her own. Researched you and your circus background." The intensity of Chase's gaze bore into me. His ocean-blue eyes appeared honest. Truthful.

I'd been so careful. I remembered her saying that I'd be more famous than before, yet I'd never told Chase about my circus background. "How did she discover the truth?"

"I don't know. I never would've betrayed you like that. I care too much."

"Enough of this drama." Goatee-guard raised his weapon.

As Chase had talked, little pieces of my heart had slipped back into place, almost making it complete. He'd risked his life to come after me. He'd fought the captain knowing he'd have no chance of coming out of the ocean alive.

"Who knows about Atlanteans?" The guard continued his questioning.

Chase raised his hand. His Adam's apple bobbed in his neck. "I'm the only air-breather who knows about you."

Goatee-guard's eyes narrowed. "How can you possibly be an air-breather?"

"It's a long story." Chase took hold of my hand and squeezed sending me strength. "We need to talk later." Meaning not in front of all these strangers.

I nodded. My emotions wavered between hopefulness and hopelessness. Between insecurity and rightfulness. Between love and hate.

The guards who'd gone into the vent surfaced. Alone.

"No one's down there," said one of the guards.

I glanced at Chase. His bewildered expression mimicked my thoughts.

"There must be another way out." Chase jerked

around, but the second guard stopped him.

Goatee-guard gave his attention back to us. "You called them Free Atlanteans which means you are not a Royalist."

I shook my head trying to clear my brain. "I'm not on anyone's side. I just discovered this world existed."

"Why call them Free Atlanteans then? Royalists, people on the correct side, call them Separatists because that's what they are. People who want to ruin our current form of government."

"It's what I was told by..." I didn't want to get Finn in trouble. He might've tricked me, but he'd helped me out and showed me the world where I belonged. If he kept his word and was helping Princess Cordelia, I couldn't endanger him, although I had my doubts about that, too.

"We'll sort out who's on what side later." Goatee-guard snapped his fingers. "Take them into custody."

***

Entering the Atlantean palace from the main entrance was much different than entering through the hidden tunnels. The guard house in front was cut from pinkish coral. The oversized gateway arched over our heads like a towering filigree barrier reef. The ornate walls of the palace were decorated with starfish and shells. And the varying colored anemone burst from the ocean floor in a mosaic pattern that would've put the Sistine Chapel to shame.

Except for the fact that we were captives and not guests, I would've been dazzled by the display of opulence.

Instead, I was overwhelmed with rolling emotions. Shock. Awe. Surprise. Fear. This should've been my home. Instead, it could become my jail.

Goatee-guard marched us through a grand foyer and then led us down a sloped hallway. The walls narrowed and became less decorative, more functional. Atlanteans passed in the other direction and stared. My skin prickled with their curiosity and disapproval.

Turning a corner, the hallway darkened. No coral decorated this area. The rooms were formed by large rocks cut into caves. Caves with bars for doors.

A shiver traveled the length of my spine. The guard had promised to straighten everything out. How long would that take? By our accommodations, possibly never.

Chase squeezed my hand as if understanding my fear. "Why are you bringing us here? These are cells. We've done nothing wrong."

Goatee-guard swiveled his head. He curled up his nose in distaste. "By being a supposed air-breather you've done something wrong by existing."

I couldn't let Chase take the blame. "I was trying to help by warning you."

"There's a war brewing." Goatee-guard stopped in front of one of the cell-like caves. "We don't know who to trust. Palace policy. Get inside."

One of the guards opened the bars and pushed Chase and I in. I stumbled against him and he held me tight. I clung, not caring how I seemed so needy. The bars slammed shut on us.

"We want to see a judge." Chase demanded. "A speedy decision."

I swam up and gripped the bars with white knuckles. Even my strength couldn't bend them. "How long will we be in here?"

"Until we determine whose side you're on. And what to do with the air-breather." Goatee-guard marched away.

His words sounded like a death sentence for Chase. My tattered heart bled. I'd believed he'd betrayed me, which led him to find me, which led him to die at least once. And possibly once again.

I squeezed my eyelids to shut out the image. We'd been through so much because of our mistrust. I should've confronted Chase about his aunt, not stormed off like a spoiled...princess.

Chase came up behind me and wrapped his arms around my waist. "I'm sorry."

I turned to face him. "You've done nothing wrong. I'm sorry I suspected you of betraying me and my secret. I should've asked."

"I understand why you might've thought that, especially with Aunt Sarah confronting you in that way." He ran a finger down my cheek, reminding me of better times.

Reminding me of all he meant to me.

"How did she find out? What type of research did she find on me? I'd been so careful. Changing my name, traveling across the country."

"She knew you'd saved that boy. She saw how you fixed the log ride." Chase leaned his forehead against mine. "I guess I got my sense of curiosity from her, because you intrigued her as much as you intrigue me."

"Oh?" I liked that I intrigued him.

"Aunt Sarah dug into your background and discovered internet articles about your circus act."

My shoulders dipped. She knew about me, knew about my past. Chase now knew about my weird circus life. Warmth raced to my face. He'd think I was a circus freak.

"Why didn't you tell me?" The hurt tone clashed with the softness of his hand on my face.

I bit my lip. I'd told Chase more about myself than anyone, but not everything. I studied the ground afraid to look at him. "I was afraid you'd think I was an abnormality. A circus freak. Or you'd want to take advantage of me."

"Like my aunt."

I lifted my head and stared at him directly, wanting him to see the painful truth. To know the real me, all of me, and to see his reaction. "Bill and Carlita, the circus owners, forced me to perform. They kept me away from other people, other kids. I was home-schooled and had no friends." I kept my tone flat, unemotional, even as feelings bombarded me and tore up my insides. "I'd been thinking about leaving for awhile. What pushed me over the edge was learning I'd been adopted."

Chase's expression softened. "I'm sorry you've led such a hard life."

I shrugged trying to shake off my own sadness. "I'm my own person now. Doing what I want, when I want. Except for the bars currently locking me up."

"I'm sorry I made your life worse." He twisted a strand of my hair between his fingers. "I never would've told anyone your secret. Since the moment we met I knew you were special."

"Special as in freak or special-special?" I hated how my insecurities invaded, tainted my view.

"Special-special." He leaned into me. Our lips were only inches apart. "Very special. So special, I couldn't stop thinking about you. And when I found your tent empty and Plankson told me you were gone…"

I moistened my lips with my tongue. My heart swooned in my chest. My love for Chase exploded like underwater fireworks sparkling inside and probably shined from my eyes.

"I had to go after you, to tell you what you meant to me." His lips touched mine in a slight caress. "And then Plankson grabbed me."

I held onto his waist afraid I might slip beneath his grasp. We'd had so many near misses. Loved and lost so many times.

Chase held me tighter. "I care about you." He kissed my cheek. "I want to be with you." He kissed the tip of my nose. "No matter what happens, I love you."

Three simple words set off the grand finale of my internal fireworks. Tingles of pleasure shot through my veins and exploded on my skin. Warmth wrapped around me like a comfy blanket.

His lips came down on mine again. Gentle at first and then the caress turned into an onslaught. I responded to his urgency.

Heat flashed through my body. My knees weakened. My heart rejoiced.

With light pressure, he opened my mouth with his tongue and dove inside. Our tongues tangled and twirled like a dance. He tasted like chocolate, and salt like the ocean we were beneath.

His body pressed against mine and my tummy tingled. My heart thudded as if trying to reach outside my chest to be closer to Chase. I wanted him to feel all my love.

"Lovebirds and kidnappers." Goatee-guard's familiar voice interrupted.

We jumped apart like guilty schoolchildren. My breath hitched. Heat flooded my face.

Chase wrapped his arm around my shoulders. "Kidnappers? What're you talking about?"

"Princess Cordelia is missing." The last word was a whisper. "Obviously, the Separatists are behind it. Since you're a Separatist, tell me what you've done with her?"

Chapter Twenty-Three
Royal Power Play

Finn, my half-brother, must've kidnapped Princess Cordelia. My instincts might've been right about Chase but they were wrong about Finn. But I wasn't ready to fink him out yet. Not until I knew for sure. I'd jumped to a wrong conclusion with Chase, I refused to make the same mistake now.

"We're not Separatists. And we didn't kidnap Princess Cordelia." Chase rushed to our defense.

"Maybe she ran away again," I added.

"How do you know about that?" Goatee-Guard leaned against the bars, his accusation sharp.

I stiffened and glanced upwards. Unwilling to tell him about the tunnels because we might need them to escape later, my mind sought an excuse or a reason. "Um, um—"

A scuffle at the end of the hall caught all of our attentions. Two guards pushed a guy with curly blonde hair forward. The guy didn't appear to be in custody but he wasn't on friendly terms either. "Let me see. I know people from Mermaid Beach."

Chase dropped his arm from around me and grabbed onto the bars. He squished his face against them. "Cuda?"

The guy broke away from the guards and swam over to our cell. Chase's lifeguard friend, Cuda stood before us.

And he was breathing underwater.

First Plankson and now Cuda. Was anyone living in Mermaid Beach truly an air-breather? No wonder I felt so at home there.

Cuda's mouth dropped open. "Chase? Pearl? What the heck? What are you doing here? I didn't know you were a—"

"I'm not." Chase shot a glance toward Goatee-guard. "But Pearl is."

Cuda examined me with renewed interest. "I wondered about her, after the whirlpool incident."

"What about you?" Chase's amazed tone matched the expression of wonder on his face. "You never told me. I mean, I knew you were totally into the ocean but I didn't realize how totally."

"I'm on a mission. One of my duties is to patrol the coast for signs of war." Cuda motioned to the guards. "Give us some space."

The guards moved back to the doorway.

"You need to explain to these guards that we're not their enemy." Chase must've been on the same wave length. "Pearl wanted to warn all of you—swimmers because she thought air-breathers, besides me, knew about your underwater world and were going to expose it."

"Which side are you on?" The expression on his face

was one of anticipation expecting a certain answer.

Funny, because even I didn't know my own reply.

"I'm not on any side. I didn't even know this world existed until a few days ago." I was repeating myself over and over. "I recently moved to Mermaid Beach from Florida."

"Were you always able to breathe underwater?"

I had to make him believe me. I had to tell the truth. He was the key to getting out of this cell. "Yes. Ever since I remember."

"What about your parents? Siblings?"

My throat swallowed the fresh rawness of hurt. "I was adopted."

Cuda pinched his lips together and then poked at Chase with a sharp finger. "What about you? I thought I knew you, that we were friends. If you're an air-breather, how are you able to be down here without an air tank?"

"Pearl did it. She can breathe into people and—"

"How many times?"

"What?"

"How many times has Pearl breathed into you?" Cuda regarded me.

Chase shrugged. "Four or five?"

"Ok-aay." Cuda crooked his finger at Goatee-guard. "These two are not Separatists. Let them go."

Goatee-guard's laughter sounded fake. "Why should I trust you? With your background."

"Leave my family out of it." Cuda sounded angry. "I've proved myself time and time again. Instead of treating them like prisoners, you should be educating them to our cause."

"Children, this is not a school or a playground." Goatee-guard spoke down to us. "We're in the middle of a war."

Cuda glanced at me. "Not yet we're not. Should I inform Princess Cordelia of your attitude?" Cuda's threat would've been more effective if not for the fact that the princess was missing.

"Obviously, you know where she is then." A look of superiority passed over the guard's face.

"What do you mean?"

"She's gone."

Cuda smirked with his own insider-knowledge. He bowed toward me. "Then, maybe you'll listen to another princess and her command."

***

A new realization hit. Hit so hard I almost fell over.

I should have power. Not, underwater-super-strength-super-speed power, but real commanding power, political power. When I spoke, people listened.

Well, I hoped they would. Commanding the captain hadn't worked.

"Release us." My order echoed through the small chamber and reverberated up my spine. I stood taller and straighter with my shoulders pulled back.

The guard shook his head. "I don't think—"

"In Atlantis, aren't the princesses the only royalty left? Aren't the Atlantean people waiting for the princesses to return? For my return?"

Cuda smirked and nodded.

Chase stood further back. Because he respected my new position or was terrified of me, I wasn't sure. I hoped the whole princess thing didn't change our relationship. We'd been through so much, we had to work it out.

"I've proved my identity by turning an air-breather

and_Cuda_concurs. Release us."

"I'll take responsibility for them." Cuda's confident-demanding tone showed he had some authority.

Goatee-guard's right cheek spasmed, but he took out his keys and unlocked the cell. I swam past him and Chase followed.

I felt different, stronger, more confident. "Since Princess Cordelia is gone, take us to whoever is in charge."

Chase and Cuda exchanged glances. They must've noticed the difference in me. I recognized a new feeling of power or status or someone deserving of respect. My chin tilted to a regal level. My shoulders pulled back. I stared straight ahead.

In the dark cave I'd accepted I was an Atlantean princess, but here in the palace I realized all that it meant.

We were led to the advisory chamber where the regent sat behind the desk. A silver-haired man, his maroon robes flowed behind him when he stood. "May I help you?"

The majesty of the room struck me, deep where my insecurities lurked. Maybe I was a princess by birth, but not by upbringing.

But I couldn't show weakness. I swam-strolled into the grand room and lifted my chin to an even haughtier angle. Again, the acting skills came into use. "I am Princess Pelagia."

The regent staggered back, disbelief stamped on his face. He put his hand to his chest. "Cuda, explain yourself. Who are these people?"

Cuda swam forward and bowed to the regent. "Regent Mollusk, she is one of the lost princesses. I've seen proof. He pointed at Chase. He is an air-breather she turned."

The regent twisted his lips together. His face blanched white. "Preposterous."

I almost laughed at the man's incredulous expression. "King Atlas was my father. Poseidon, my grandfather. You've been waiting for my return."

The regent's gaze traveled between me, Cuda and Chase. "We will expect proof." He studied me. His lips turned down in a frown. "You look like your mother."

My heart lightened. He knew my mother and didn't hate her. A million questions rushed to the forefront of my mind but I understood now wasn't the time. "Thank you."

He stepped around his desk and bowed. "Welcome Princess Pelagia."

"You may call me Pearl." A name I'd answered to all my life. "I need to take Chase to the surface. In the meantime, I'd like you to prepare a strategy for finding the missing Princess Cordelia. When I return, we will plot how to find the location of Princess Marisabel."

I portrayed confidence and calm, but inside I was happy dancing. Grooving to a new beat. An excited beat. A familial beat. A belonging beat.

Squee! I have sisters.

"Then we will approach the Free Atlanteans—"

The regent froze in place. His face whitened.

"I mean the Separatists, and show them the three lost daughters of Atlantis have returned. That we're united. The legend is fact. We shall avoid war. And the three princesses shall lead all Atlanteans to peace and prosperity."

Chapter Twenty-Four
Possession To Princess

With the setting sun at our backs Chase and I, guarded by Cuda, swam home to Mermaid Beach. It turned out, now that I was recognized as Princess Pelagia, a Royal Guard must be assigned for my protection. But since the regent insisted we keep the news of my return a secret, for my own safety, the regent decided that Cuda, since he already knew, would be most suitable for the role.

"I'm not sure I like the idea of strange Royal Guards following me around in the future."

Chase wrapped his arm around my shoulders. Together, we walked up the beach toward the Boardwalk. "Neither am I, especially if it's a guy."

"I might have a solution." Cuda followed behind us. "We need to test one last thing, but not in the ocean where there might be spies."

The idea of spies and war curled my stomach. Now that I understood the consequences and how it related to me, I had to stop this war from commencing. We'd told

Cuda all about Finn and our adventure under Atlas Island, how he'd followed Princess Cordelia. Cuda said he'd follow up on it which comforted me.

Cuda kept walking. "Is there another water source nearby? Like at the Boardwalk?"

"The lagoon at the mini golf course."

Where my underwater adventure had started.

If I hadn't saved the boy I might never have met Chase. I never would've divulged my secret and exposed my abilities to Finn. I might never have learned there were others like me and that I was a princess. I might never have gained the confidence I needed to stop running and hiding, to be myself, to stand up for myself.

Feeling good to be me, I danced to the mini golf course holding Chase's hand.

He punched in the security code to unlock the building. "Now what?"

"Legend says that each of the princesses has a special talent." Cuda pointed at me. "Yours is turning air-breathers."

"I can confirm that." Chase waved his hand.

I scanned the blue surface of the water. The edge of the pool still showed stains, but it was so much cleaner than before. "Now that the lagoon is scrubbed and refilled, I don't mind diving in again." It would be like coming full circle, like finding myself in myself.

"Not you." Cuda jerked his head toward Chase. "You."

"What?" Chase's entire body jerked to an alert position.

"If an air-breather is turned five times, the change becomes permanent," Cuda spoke with authority.

"Why five times?" Chase sounded a bit shaky.

"Poseidon wanted to confirm the air-breather he planned to turn was trustworthy with his secret before making the change permanent."

"What. Are. You. Saying?" Rubbing the pearl hanging around my neck, I glanced at Chase. Had I permanently changed Chase?

His face paled and his body wavered in place. His eyes were bigger than sand dollars.

"Poseidon bestowed the gift on humans he favored. We haven't seen it recently because you haven't been around." Cuda peered at me and then switched to Chase, "Chase may be an honorary Atlantean."

The curling in my stomach collapsed upon itself like a wave ending in a big wipe out. My entire body stilled before a spurt of sympathy drove me to action. I ran to Chase and grabbed his hands. "I'm so sorry. I didn't know."

"Why are you sorry?" A smile lifted the ends of Chase's lips. His expression softened.

"I changed you." Maybe he didn't fully understand the repercussions. "I involved you in my world. In a possible war."

"You involved me with you. With your new world." He squeezed my hand and pulled me forward. "With our new world."

His lips came down to mine sealing the deal. A deal that we would be together forever.

My tummy calmed but my heart sped up. I returned his kiss showing all my excitement and love and commitment with my lips. We didn't need words. Our touch, our emotions, spoke for us.

At Cuda's discrete cough, we pulled apart. "Sorry to interrupt but we should test the theory before making any promises."

"If this is for real," Chase squeezed my hand again before letting go and walking toward the water. "I'll be Pearl's personal Royal Guard."

"Really?" I squealed.

My boyfriend. My bodyguard. My best friend.

Cuda nodded. "After training."

Pure happiness floated through me. A lightness filled my insides. I had a boyfriend to protect me, a palace to live, and people to call family. More importantly, I found my true self.

I held my breath as Chase waded through the shallow end. He saluted before going under the surface. Cuda and I waited.

And waited.

And waited.

I edged closer to the lagoon. Peered in.

Chase was swimming back and forth on the bottom.

Five minutes passed.

"I need to check on him." I moved to dive in but Cuda held me back.

Ten minutes.

I was a wreck. I believed Cuda's theory but Chase had risked his life so many times for me. He didn't need to do it again. Not for this.

Finally, Chase emerged like a sea lion in a water show. Water splashing, a huge smile on his face. "I can breathe underwater! I can do it."

My lips jumped into a smile. We could be together all the time.

The door to the building banged open. I froze in place. Cuda didn't move either. Chase sunk to the bottom of the lagoon.

"What is going on in here?" Mrs. Fowler stormed toward us, her heels clicking on the concrete. Had she seen anything? "I'd call the police for trespassing but Officer Clayton is already here."

I leaned sideways searching behind her to where Clayton stood. Two other shadows stood by the open door. "I can explain." Although I wasn't sure how.

Chase emerged from the lagoon, water dripping from his body. "Aunt Sarah, we were goofing around."

"Chase." Mrs. Fowler scowled. "I can't believe you would break every rule you've known since you were a child."

"I'm not a child anymore, Aunt Sarah." The sympathy in Chase's tone was edged by firmness. "I'm eighteen. It's time I made my own decisions and my own rules."

"I've raised you since you were eight-years-old."

"And I appreciate all you've done." Chase stood in front of her, his bathing trunks dripping onto the fake Astroturf grass. His chin jutted out in a firm position. "I love you, but I need to be my own person."

"Do you plan to press charges?" Officer Clayton asked.

Mrs. Fowler took in me and Cuda, then stared at Chase. Love shown from her bright eyes. She opened her arms. "Of course not."

Chase went into his aunt's embrace and hugged her back, getting her wet.

I blinked a few times to get rid of the stinging sensation. Growing up, I'd never had that kind of affection with—

"I'd like to press charges."

Carlita.

Dread wove its way around my chest, squeezing the air from inside. I took a step back. My adoptive parents stomped into the building.

"She's a runaway," Carlita's voice shrieked. "Arrest her."

My heart slashed. Panic and pain ran through me like I should be running. My muscles bunched, ready to break into a sprint. I could slip past them and dive into the ocean only yards away. They'd never find me, think that I drowned. I could escape forever into my new underwater world.

Chase broke off the hug with his aunt and sidled over to my side in solidarity. "She's eighteen and can go where she wants."

Uh oh. My head dropped and I examined the ground. Fear ate away at the lining of my stomach. The sensation burned.

"She's sixteen." She advanced toward me like a jail warden. "And she's ours."

"Ours?" White, hot flashes exploded, punching a hole in my fear. "I'm not a possession. I'm a person." I'm a princess, but I didn't add the last bit.

If Carlita learned of my other world she'd find a way to take advantage of it.

Clayton raised his hands taking charge. "Everyone take a deep breath. Pearl, tell us everything."

"I'll tell you what happened." Carlita waved her arms about, pointing at me like a madwoman. "She ran away from the circus. She's the star attraction. Ticket sales are down. I'm taking her back." She reached out to grab my arm.

"Don't touch her." Chase stepped in front of me and knocked Carlita's hand away.

"If you put a hand on Pearl, I'll arrest you for assault." Clayton turned on Carlita. "I asked Pearl to explain."

"I am sixteen." I placed a soft frown on my mouth and angled my head begging Chase to understand. I searched for his reaction, hoping he'd still feel the same about someone two years younger.

He reached for my hand. Found it. Our fingers intertwined.

We were together. A couple. I didn't need to know anything else right now.

I swallowed my fear of Carlita. Fear I'd kept inside for sixteen years. Fear that had controlled every move I made. I had to stand up for myself. "I did run away from the circus, from Carlita and Bill. I always wondered why they'd treated me so terrible when I did everything they asked."

"Did they abuse you?" Clayton's gentle tone encouraged confidence.

"No." Carlita stomped her foot.

I stared her straight in the face, refusing to be cowed by her temper. I'd learned a lot about myself in the last few weeks. Grown as a person. Supported myself in the real world. Discovered my true home.

I firmed my mouth determined to tell all. "Not physically with beatings, but emotional and psychological abuse."

Carlita kneaded her hands together. "We're a family."

I slapped my chest outraged at her definition of family. "Family is in your heart, not your wallet."

"She's still under age. We're her legal parents." Carlita rummaged behind her for Bill's hand. "We're taking Pearl back to Florida."

"You're not my *real* parents." I'd never let them take me. I belonged here, or at least under the ocean near here.

"I've been researching your background." Clayton flipped through a small notebook. "Pearl, have you considered declaring yourself an emancipated minor? I'd be willing to support you in your claim."

"So would I." Tears glistened in Mrs. Fowler's eyes. "If I'd known what these people put you through, I never would've contacted them, never would've asked..." She sobbed.

I understood. She never would've threatened me to perform at the Boardwalk. Chase was raised by a wise woman.

Carlita's expression hardened. Her lips tightened into a mischievous frown. "But you can't become independent. You don't know the whole truth."

A slight smile upturned my lips. A calmness settled in my veins. A streak of pride lifted my chin. "I do know the truth. My truth."

And truth is power.

***

Later that night, after Officer Clayton hustled Carlita and Bill out of town, Mrs. Fowler had returned to her apartment, and Cuda had dived back into the deep, Chase and I sat on the beach staring at the waves.

The quiet of the night should've soothed my nerves but questions stirred in my brain like a tempest. I had to be sure Chase was doing the right thing.

"Will your aunt be upset when she finds out you're going to train to be my Royal Guard and move under Atlas Island with me?" I knew Mrs. Fowler would never tell our secret.

"Not as long as I can visit her." Chase wrapped his arm around my shoulders.

"What about college? Your dream of studying to become a reporter?" I wanted Chase to be happy with his decision. I didn't want him to blame me for things he might've missed above the surface.

"Cuda tells me there are Atlantean schools. And what better way to learn the trade than reporting on a war?"

I angled my chin and arched a brow at Chase. "War?"

"Or the diplomacy required to avoid war." He totally got me.

My heart floated like a helium balloon. Light, shining, and made for happy events. "Thank you."

He kissed my cheek. "You're welcome."

Those were the easy questions to ask. My stomach squirmed. I fidgeted with the sand between my fingers. "Are you upset that I'm only sixteen?"

His arm dropped from around my shoulders and he maneuvered in front of me. "No. You're still the same person."

"Does it bother you that I'm a princess?" With royalty came responsibility. And possibly danger.

He grinned in a playful way. "Does it bother you that I'm *not* royalty?"

I swatted him on the arm. "Of course not. I'm not a snob."

He took my chin in his hands. His face grew serious. "Sixteen or eighteen. Princess or pauper. You're still the same person I fell in love with."

"I love you, too." My chest hitched. My heart swelled. A smile as wide as the Marianas Trench grew on my face. "Are you sure you want to become my personal Royal Guard?"

"I wouldn't have it any other way." He grabbed my shoulders and tackled me onto the sand. "Let me demonstrate."

And then he kissed me, showing just how personal his protection was going to be.

The End

Acknowledgements

A first book has the gestation period of a frilled shark, actually longer. So many people have inspired, critiqued, or cheered me on that if I tried to name them all the acknowledgement section would be longer than the book. In my heart I thank you all.

I do need to thank a few special people. My long time critique partner Addison Fox. Across the miles she's advised, edited, and cheered my successes and failures. My local critique partner Caro LaFever – the ability to meet with another writer face-to-face is invaluable making me feel less alone in this challenging and crazy endeavor. And to the Writer Foxes: Julie Benson, Sandy Blair, Jo Davis, Suzanne Ferrell, Addison Fox, Tracy Garrett, Jane Graves, Lorraine Heath, and Kay Thomas. The most supportive group of writers a girl could find. Thanks for the advice, support, friendship and wine.

Thanks to my parents Marge and Ray who provided the atmosphere to make me the determined person I am today. I will always remember my dad's front porch advice to find what you love and do it. Well, it took me awhile but I finally figured it out!

The switch to writing young adult was inspired by my kids Kyle and Lindsey who asked, "When are you going to write a book we can read?" They helped me find my voice and are my teen inspiration. If they enjoy this book then I am happy.

Thanks to my husband Jim who let me live my dream of becoming a writer. He provided emotional support and is my real life hero. Now that I'm published he has to read the book!

Author Bio

Allie Burton

Allie didn't realize having so many jobs would become great research material for the stories she writes. She has been everything from a fitting room attendant to a bike police officer to a professional mascot escort. She has lived on three continents and in four states and has studied art, fashion design, marine biology, and advertising.

When her kids asked, "when are you going to write a story we can read?" she switched from adult novels to Young Adult and Middle Grade and hasn't looked back.

Allie is a member of the Society of Children's Book Writers & Illustrators, Romance Writers of America including the Young Adult, Dallas Area Romance Writers and Heart of the Rockies chapters. She is also a member of Rocky Mountain Fiction Writers. Currently, she lives in Colorado with her husband and two children.

www.allieburton.com
www.twitter.com/Allie_Burton
www.Facebook.com/AllieBurtonAuthor

More in the Daughters of Atlantis series:

Atlantis Red Tide

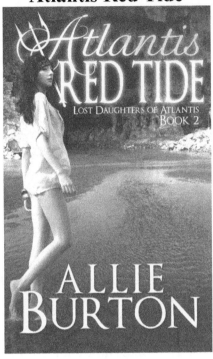

Excerpt:

Chapter One

Prisoner Princess

Escape.
The single word thrummed in my brain.
Escape to show the legend was real. That *I* was real.

Escape to prove my ability to lead. That I wasn't a silly sixteen-year-old girl.

Escape to stop a war.

The thrumming crescendo-ed like a harp seal colony under attack.

Today was the day I declared my independence. Finally, I'd do what I wanted to do. And when I returned in triumph with my two half-sisters, peace would be restored and no one would question my place in society.

Including me.

I slunk around the corner with my back to the coral wall made of filigree carvings. I didn't care about scratching my bare arms and legs on the sharp coral or about the water current tangling my long, brown hair. My esthetistician and stylist would be shocked.

Needing to move while the Royal Guards changed shifts and while I still had the audacity to get out, I pushed my normal response—sit, wait and ponder—to the corner of my mind.

Determination rippled through me, straightening my spine and firming my muscles. I had to be strong. Residents of the palace might think I was a spoiled, catered-to princess, but really I was well-behaved. Did what was expected of me. Did what I was told.

Trying to blend into the background, I hid behind the streamers of seaweed acting like partitions in the palace hallway. I peered into the grand, cavernous foyer. The beauty of the room struck me, so at odds with the ugliness of my emotions.

Star fish decorated the walls in intricate patterns. The crystal and shell chandelier swayed with the flowing water sparking colors of light across the room. A throne room to be admired.

But not in the current conditions. Too much uncertainty. Too much intrigue. Too much doubt.

Like the doubt trickling through my veins.

Despite the risk of being caught, I swam through another seaweed partition. I had to pull this off, get away, finally act on my plan to bring my half-sisters home and stop the war.

For if I wasn't a princess how could I stay in this amazing palace? And if I truly was a princess of Atlantis how could I stay here doing nothing while my people, Loyal and Separatists, fought each other?

My confusion tangled like seaweed.

Was I the true leader of the Atlanteans or a phony figurehead?

"Princess Cordelia?"

Gasping, I swallowed a throat-ful of seawater.

"Ahhh!" I screeched at the guard's deep tone. Calming my expression and trying to look innocent, I straightened and turned to face him. "How dare you scare me like that?"

The guard with four gold stripes on his royal blue swim trunks bowed, but just slightly. "My apologies."

A second guard held a pointy spear. "May I escort you somewhere?"

Which was just a polite way to ask where I was going. I tilted my chin to a haughtier angle. "No, thank you."

"My orders are to escort you, for your own safety." The first guard swam toward me and gripped my arm a little too tight.

A princess never shows fear. I couldn't give away that I was up to something. I forced my most superior princess tone over the fear swamping my belly. "Am I not safe within *my* palace walls?"

Next, I'll be ordered to stay in my bedroom. I'd truly be like a goldfish in a bowl.

"The Royal Guard's duty is to protect you."

Curling my hands into fists, I controlled my biting response. "Who gave your orders, Captain?"

The second guard grabbed hold of my other arm. "Regent Mollusk."

The man who'd raised me, taken care of me, and now ignored me. His lack of compassion had become more apparent in the last few months. As if I was a pet he'd inherited that he had to keep track of, feed, and misinform.

Caught in between the guards like a tuna on two hooks, they turned me around and moved toward the seaweed partition. My legs flayed out in front of me as the guards steered me through the seaweed. I wanted to fight but I needed to act as if I was in control. Plus, struggling wouldn't look very princess-like.

I'd finally gathered my courage to take control of my life, to do what I thought right, and I'd failed. Dismally.

The failure wormed its way through my veins and into my gut. I was a washout. My shoulders sagged with the weight of my flounder. If Mollusk found out, I'd never have any freedom.

"Unhand me." My lips trembled, but I kept my tone firm.

Act strong. Act royal.

"Just because you're a…princess doesn't mean you're in charge." The captain's lip curled in a sneer. I recognized the man as one of Mollusk's favorites.

"I should be in charge." My insides twisted. Self-doubt and pretense braided tight, shooting cramps of uncertainty from my mid-section to my brain. I doubted my authenticity, just like my people. "You can't treat me like this."

"It's for your own good, Princess."

"For the good of Atlantis Captain, I need to find-"

He shifted and slapped me across the right cheek.

My head snapped back. My lips mewed in surprise. And my heart stung like my skin. I raised my hand to touch my cheek, but my arms were still held down.

My head felt woozy. Dizzy from shock. No one had ever hit me before.

"That is a treasonable offense." My voice quavered. I squeezed my eyelids together trying to stop the burning sensation of tears. A guard hitting a supposed-princess. My world was cracking like the fault lines deep in the ocean floor.

"You will do what you are told." The scolding in the captain's voice made me feel like a small misbehaved child, made me feel less than a princess. He glared at me. "A war is about to commence and we need you safe and in the palace."

"I can help stop the war." I struggled against the two guards, while trying to appear dignified—two guards who were supposed to be under my command.

When had the guards stopped treating me like a princess? Heat flamed on my face and burned down my spine like a human fire. They'd never really listened to me but never before had they treated me like a criminal.

If I could make them understand the importance of my mission. "If we produce proof—"

"Be a good princess and get that ridiculousness out of your head. The Separatists will never listen."

The guards dragged me between them, through the

grand foyer and toward the Regent's offices. When we arrived, they deposited me in front of Mollusk's desk like unwanted rubbish.

I used to think of Mollusk as comfortable and grandfatherly. Now, he seemed more like a beached whale. He showed no interest in me, barely looking up.

"What can I help you with, Princess Coral?" His heavy bulk sat behind his ornate desk. He played with the ever-present mangrove root sitting on top.

"Princess Coral, my tush." I murmured under my breath, not wanting him to hear my slight defiance. He had no right to call me by my nickname when he treated me like unwanted algae growing at his side. "If I am a princess, then why do I feel like a prisoner?"

Mollusk let out a deep sigh that made tiny air bubbles spout out of his thin lips. "The Atlantean Separatists are about to start a war."

Every idiot in the palace knew about the war brewing. Yet, it seemed I was the only one who wanted to stop the battle.

I crossed my arms and tried to project fierceness. "Just because the other two princesses haven't reappeared is a stupid reason for a war."

I'd been raised since birth to believe I was a princess whisked away as a baby by a loyal regent for my own protection. My half-sisters had their own regents and separate destinations. They had never returned.

"I agree, but the Separatists have simple minds." Mollusk swished all Separatists with a broad splash as if none of them were very bright.

Usually he spoke to me like that making me feel squashed and lonely.

Organizing my arguments in my head, I leaned

forward and placed my palms on the intricately-carved wooden desk scavenged from an ancient shipwreck. "If we find my half-sisters, we could prove the legend is true and avoid war."

Mollusk shook his head back and forth slowly like I was a dim-witted student and not the leader of our people. "If only it was that simple."

I wanted to burst out in a scream for him to listen to me. For anyone to listen to me. But yelling wouldn't be appropriate for a princess and keeping up appearances, especially now with my own insecurities about my legitimacy, was of the utmost importance.

Instead I straightened my shoulders, and used my most serene voice. "I'm not a child. I'm sixteen and it's time for me to lead my people."

His superior-than-thou laughter echoed, roiling my stomach. "No one with half the brain of a bass fish would listen to an over-protected baby seal who never ruled anything in her life."

"Because you wouldn't let me."

His laughter stopped. His gaze shifted around the large office. He licked his fatty lips. "I wasn't going to tell you this, but the Separatists have made a threat against you." His dire words sent a chill down my spine.

I'd never expected the Separatists to hate me. To harm me.

A hard clot of fear stuck in my throat. Swallowing, I forced the fear down to my belly where it landed with a thud. I continued pushing.

"The legend foretold of the three lost princesses of Atlantis coming together and combining their special powers to save and lead our people." The sharpened edge of my voice didn't hide my frustration. All of our efforts should be directed toward finding my half-sisters.

"We've wasted many hours searching for Pelagia and Marisabel." His belittling tone stomped my drive to find my half-sisters on my own.

If Royal Guards with all their resources couldn't find my half-sisters, how could I?

"But—"

"The legend also foretold of a destructive Seer." Mollusk's lips firmed into a hard line.

"What has she to do with me?"

"Nothing." He answered quickly. Too quickly. "Then tell me where do you think the other two princesses are hiding?"

Like a thermal vent, I wanted to blow, but I couldn't. Instead my spew came in words. "I don't know but we can't give up. We are chartered by Poseidon. I am King Atlas's daughter and Poseidon's granddaughter." The words didn't sound strong and powerful, but weak and hollow.

Mollusk stood and leaned forward. His bushy eyebrows furrowed toward the center of his face. "*And* what is your special power to prove the Poseidon connection?"

Pain sliced across my midsection. I stumbled back. My shoulders bowed and my body folded slightly at the waist. The verbal attack had been deliberate.

I tightened my stomach muscles trying to force away the pain. The pain intensified. I opened my mouth to respond. Nothing came out. Because I had no defense. I'd shown no proclivity to any extraordinary power.

"Exactly." His voice seethed with satisfaction.

Only Mollusk knew that I'd shown no special skill. Like all Atlanteans I had super strength and speed, but nothing out of the ordinary. Nothing to prove my heritage.

He'd thought it best we keep that secret between us. The information would only fan the anger of the Atlantean people. Right now, the people believed at least one princess had returned.

"But I must have a special power. You know I'm the princess and rightful heir. You're my regent. You took me away during the Catalyst and protected me until our return to the new Atlantis."

Mollusk played with the sheaves on his desk effectively hiding his expression. "Things were confusing during the Catalyst. The constant earthquakes, the falling buildings, the people rushing from danger trying to protect their families. Many babies were put in pods for protection." His hands flayed up and down like he was angling to catch a fish. "I'm sure I got the right pod though."

His tone didn't sound so certain.

My limbs trembled like the cataclysmic quake he spoke of. My insides liquefied, gelling together and then ripping apart. My mind scrambled.

His doubts would explain his treatment. My special power bestowed by Poseidon should've already developed.

And if I had no special power, how could I be a real Atlantean princess?

***

Plop. Scratch. Whoosh.

Quiet, but different sounds stirred me from sleep. I listened with my eyelids closed. The buzz of the electric eels lighting the palace hummed in the distance. Nothing unusual, but something felt off.

Stiffening my limbs, I opened my eyes to complete darkness. Too dark, especially when I heard the comforting buzz of the eels. So, only dark in my room?

A hard wave of water sluiced across my skin as if something moved beside me. Before I could react, a hand covered my mouth. Too late to scream. But the scream built inside over-inflating my lungs. I felt like my chest was going to burst. Explode with shock and fear.

I punched and kicked, my foot hitting something hard, solid, muscular.

Familiar.

"Oof." The guy—because with a chest like that it definitely was a guy—grunted.

A smidgen of satisfaction released the built up air in tiny bubbles.

With his left hand still over my mouth, he used his right hand to wrap something around my arms. The binding scratched like seaweed.

The sharp pokes dug into and under my skin puncturing any satisfaction, any superiority, any sane thought. Terror stabbed like spear points. Mollusk had mentioned the Separatists had threatened me. Was I going to die?

I yanked my arms apart. Instead of loosening or breaking completely the binding grew tighter drawing my wrists together. The terror multiplied like algae growing on my lungs, I suffocated. Simple seaweed shouldn't hold against a super strong Atlantean. This guy should know that basic fact if he was an Atlantean.

But if he wasn't an Atlantean how could he be breathing underwater? My ribcage tightened around my lungs adding to my panic. I'd felt no metal and rubber scuba equipment on this guy.

He wrapped the same stuff around my legs. I struggled, pulled on my legs, but the seaweed or rope or whatever he used grew so tight my limbs tingled.

"Don't struggle or it will completely cut off your circulation," the kidnapper said like he cared.

As if.

Trapped like a salmon in a net. I couldn't hit or kick or scream. But I could bite.

Opening my mouth, as much as I could with his hand over my lips, I got ready to clamp down on his skin with my teeth.

He slipped his hand off in a sure motion and slapped something on my face. Rough around the edges, the suction adhered to my mouth. My breathing staggered, choked in my lungs.

Five finger-like points stuck out from the center attached to my mouth. One point stuck on my chin. Two more pointed across my cheeks. And the other two sandwiched my nose.

A star fish.

He'd attached a star fish to my lips to keep me quiet and used super-strong seaweed to tie up my legs and arms.

Pain radiated from my chest spreading helplessness through my veins like a shot of morphine. I wiggled, but basically I was helpless.

There was no way to fight this guy. Nothing I could do.

Just like my life.

Pampered and spoiled which basically means I'm useless. A phony figurehead. A pawn in a game I never really understood.

My heart raced as if I actually still put up a struggle.

But the helplessness pumping through me changed to a paralyzing fear. I was such a wimp. The blood in my veins chilled. Froze like iced fish remembering Mollusk's warning. I was being kidnapped by the Separatists.

The guy lifted me and threw me over his shoulder. Strong arms wrapped around, holding me like precious cargo. Precious cargo who weighed next to nothing, a traitorous voice whispered in my head.

I refused to be impressed. My bare stomach came in contact with his bare shoulder. Tingles raced down my spine.

Must be from the binding cutting off my circulation.

Kidnappers weren't careful with hostages. Right?

Especially not a Separatist who doesn't believe in the princess legend. Who doesn't believe in me.

My tummy revolted at my thoughts. The meager contents spilled over and threatened to come up my throat.

The empty corridors echoed my helplessness. Where are the guards who are supposed to keep me safe or what I called locked away? There was no one to sound the alarm. No one would realize I was missing until morning.

And by the way the guards had treated me yesterday, I doubt anyone would care.

Melancholy swirled in my tummy, mixing with the fear. I was pathetic. I shouldn't care what the guards thought. And whether I was or wasn't a princess. I was still being kidnapped by a Separatist. I had to do something.

Lifting my head, I squirmed to get a glance at my kidnapper. Longish, black hair fell over his forehead making him appear a bit untamed. Like a rogue or a renegade. A starfish, similar to the one covering my mouth, plastered over his cheeks covering most of his face. A strong chin jutted out with determination. Sensual lips a girl could easily kiss.

Not that I wanted to. He was my kidnapper after all.

The shape of his face looked familiar. His chin reminded me of someone I once knew.

This guy obviously didn't know that Mollusk held the real power. I was just a figurehead who they never listened to, never asked for advice, never let out of the palace.

Anger at the usual over-protectiveness soured inside my stomach, wiping out the sadness. The fear still remained. Where was a Royal Guard when you needed one?

The guy made his way along the edge of the corridor as if he knew where he was going. No hesitation or hint of confusion. He swam at an even pace. He knew his way around the palace.

How?

My mind played guessing games with the possibilities. Rogue Royal Guard? Separatist Spy? Palace servant who didn't like me?

We made it to the grand foyer and then the guy stopped. He turned toward the wall with the starfish design. I lifted my head again and watched him counting with his finger. Seven stars from the left. Three down.

My heart jumped like a salmon swimming upstream, then picked up its pace, thudding in my chest. It couldn't be.

He reached toward the starfish and turned it clockwise.

My body froze, waiting for the click to come.

My kidnapper knew the secret.

Questions darted back and forth in my head like a school of fish. No one knew about the secret tunnels.

A hole opened in the wall. The hole led to a series of tunnels I played in as a kid. Many of the tunnels had been blocked to stop spies or Separatists, but the guards hadn't found all of them. I'd planned to use the tunnels to make my own escape, but hadn't gotten this far yesterday.

Ironic that the Royal Guards had caught me trying to get out, but not an intruder getting in.

The tunnels led out of the palace and to the surface of the Pacific Ocean, underneath Atlas Island, off the coast of southern California.

Hmm. My brain clicked, playing out the different scenarios. Maybe being kidnapped wasn't such a bad thing—if I could get away from the kidnapper I could blend with the islanders and the tourists. Escaping a single guy should be easier than escaping from the palace and the entire Royal Guard.

The guy bent low for both of us to fit in the hole. Then, he touched a small shell and the hole closed like it had never been there. Which is the reason why the guards hadn't found all the tunnels.

My gut clenched, panic searing my insides. Heat flashed across my skin. No one would find us now. But that was good. I was out of the palace.

It wasn't exactly how I planned to escape, but what did it matter? I was free.

Well, almost.

End of Excerpt

Atlantis Rising Tide

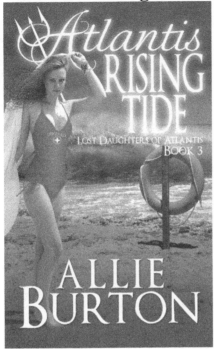

Junior lifeguard Maris Sanders thinks she's a normal high school girl. In reality, she's one of the lost princesses of Atlantis. At sixteen, she's finally discovering her special powers.

Exiled from his community of Atlanteans, Cuda Fisher has taken a special interest in Maris. As he secretly tests her abilities, the two teens grow closer until Cuda realizes being with Maris is risking more than his heart.

An evil scientist is analyzing Maris's skills and putting her in danger. Cuda realizes his father, a leader of the Separatist movement, is behind the scheme and Cuda will do anything to stop him even if it means breaking Maris's heart.

Will Maris accept her real identity, or still hurt by Cuda's betrayal, will she fall prey to the scheme? Will Maris be able to choose between the life she's always known or a new dangerous adventure? And will the choice be hers?

Available June 2013

CPSIA information can be obtained
at www.ICGtesting.com
Printed in the USA
LVHW111529020519
616416LV00001B/69/P